# JOCK ROMEO

SARA NEY

# COPYRIGHT



Editing by Caitlyn Nelson

Editing by Jennifer VanWyk

Proofreading by Julia Griffis

Proofreading by Shauna Casey

Cover Design by Okay Creations

Formatting by Casey Formatting

A touch of love, everyone becomes a poet.

***-Plato***

# PROLOGUE

## LILLY

Go to a house party, they said.

*It'll be fun*, they said.

Wrong.

Seems everyone else on campus had the same idea: hit Jock Row on the first Friday back for drinking and merriment and acting like asses.

*This is not fun*—at least, not in my opinion. There are way too many people here, and I'm starting to feel claustrophobic. Not only that, I have to pee, and the line for the bathroom is insanely long. I'm not a camel—I cannot hold it for days, and I refuse to pee outside in a bush.

There has to be another bathroom somewhere in this massive house. The one beneath the staircase where everyone is lined up is probably just a powder room with a single toilet. My eyes roam the perimeter, scanning for random doors that could lead to relief, but I find none. Nor am I willing to push my way through the dense crowd to the packed kitchen in hopes of finding one—this party is body to body to body, and the closer it gets to midnight, the more people seem to congregate.

*This has to be a code violation.*

There is a staircase leading to a second story, and I assume it's probably off limits up there. Private bedrooms and all that. So that's the direction I go, shouldering my way through the throng until I reach the wooden stairs, eyes focused on the dark hall at the top. There's a door and it's closed, a white piece of paper taped up with bold black Sharpie letters scrawled across it: DO NOT ENTER.

I decide to enter.

After all, I'm a girl with a goal.

It may be a short-term one involving a toilet, but at least I have my sights set on something other than being drunk, yeah?

I turn the doorknob and push through, stepping up into the second level, making sure to close it behind me. It's not as noisy up here but still not exactly quiet, the sounds of people and music finding their way in.

There is a bathroom straight ahead.

Bingo.

I make a beeline for it, sighing with relief as I lock its door, pushing down my jeans and plopping down onto the cool porcelain.

"Ahh."

I haven't even had that much to drink—room temperature beer holds no appeal for me tonight, but I didn't want to sit at home in the dorm rooms on my first official Friday in college.

I'm a freshman!

In college.

Not only that, I made the university's cheerleading team and have added that to my list of accomplishments this year, too. Wasn't sure I'd make it; I was so damn nervous during my tryouts I almost biffed it during the basket toss, one of the most basic stunts. Cheerleading 101.

A few of my teammates convinced me to come out tonight. I'm a social person in general—you kind of have to be when you're a cheerleader, jumping and dancing in front of thousands upon thousands of screaming, shouting fans at a football game—but every so often all I want to do is snuggle up with a good book on the beanbag chair. I brought it with me to college and it's in my dorm room parked in front of the small television set that rests on a chest of drawers.

Built-in desk.

Metal bunk beds.

My roommate hasn't arrived at school yet, but I know her name is Allison and she is bringing the microwave—and I suppose that's another one of the reasons I came out tonight: I'm too nervous to be in the room when she finally arrives.

Classes start Monday.

Practice began two weeks ago.

The first game is Sunday.

I let out a loud sigh as I pee in the toilet of the baseball house, looking myself over in the mirror directly across from it. My dark blonde hair that's lost its curl because of the humidity outside on the walk over. My big brown eyes, lashes coated in mascara that's sure to smudge by the time we finally leave. The big, gold hoop earrings.

There's a sound outside the bathroom door and I hold still, rigidly frozen on the pot, guilty of being a stowaway on a floor the residents of this house didn't want anyone to come to.

Shit.

What if someone tries the door to get in and finds it's locked?

I frantically wipe and flush, washing my hands before pressing my ear to the door and listening for footsteps.

Or voices.

All I hear is the music and noise from down below, muffled but loud.

With bated breath, I turn the lock then twist the doorknob, inching the door open and peering through the small gap. Shoulder my way through and tiptoe back down the hall toward the stairway, pulling open the door at the top so I can disappear back into the merriment below.

There's someone at the top of the steps, and he's sitting.

I know this because I literally crash into him when I put my foot out to descend, followed by an "Oof!" and a profuse apology.

"Oh my gosh, I didn't see you sitting there." I bend to take him by the shoulders as if the force was strong enough to send him flying.

He did not go flying.

"I am so sorry," I enthuse, stepping around him, down two stairs and turning to face him.

"No—it's not your fault. I'm the one who shouldn't be sitting here."

I tilt my head and look down.

It's not easy to see him clearly in the dimly lit stairwell, but he's a gangly boy with a buzz cut. Red t-shirt. Jeans.

Embarrassed half-grin.

"Then why are you sitting here?"

He shrugs, and I notice his lanky shoulders.

He can't be any older than I am, probably a freshman, too.

"I guess I'm hiding." His hands are clasped over his knees and his phone is out—he was probably playing on it as a diversion, if I had to guess.

"Hiding? From who?"

"Everyone." He laughs, pushing up the glasses rested on the bridge of his nose.

"You're hiding from everyone? Why don't you just leave?" That's what I would do if I hadn't forced myself to come and be social tonight—one last hurrah before the football season kicks off and its curfews and check-ins by the coaching staff and rigorous workouts and nutritional regimens hinder my social time.

Also, I'm asking a complete stranger way too many questions.

"I came with my friends from high school."

"So?"

"So—if I leave, they'll make fun of me."

Some friends. Why are guys such dicks to each other? All that toxic masculinity bullshit infuriates me.

"Well do you mind some company?" This perch is a great spot to stay out of the fray without actually leaving the party, which doesn't appear to be dying down any time soon. Hunting down my teammates to say goodbye and leave on my own holds no appeal, either—safety in numbers and all that. It wouldn't be a smart idea walking through campus by myself in the middle of the night.

"Um, sure."

He does not look sure, but I plop down beside him anyway, scooching him over with a bump of my hips.

"I'm Lilly," I say. "Freshman. How 'bout you?"

"Same."

"What's your name?"

His head dips in embarrassment. "Roman."

"Cool name, bro," I tell him, resting my elbows on my knees and gazing down at the bright lights of the living room below. A song has just started that everyone goes wild for, and the floor shakes as students jump up and down, dancing. "Holy crap, the floor is going to cave in on itself."

"Might, depending on where the floor joists are if the weight's not evenly distributed and how old the house is."

Nerd alert. "Are you an architecture major?"

"No, it's just basic physics."

I think we've established that I've been botching up all things *basic* lately, so I'm no help when it comes to physics. Math. Science.

Not my strong suits.

"What is your major if it's not architecture?"

"Tech."

Oh.

That's boring—everyone is a computer science major. He probably wants to create apps and stuff.

"Tech for what?"

The eyebrows above his glasses quirk up and down. "Automotive or aerospace."

"Like—programming cars and stuff?"

Beside me, he nods. "I haven't decided, but yes, something like that."

Oh.

That makes what I'm about to say sound lame and juvenile.

I sigh. "I'm an English major with a business minor. My parents wouldn't let me major in art, so I had to settle." I have no idea why I'm telling him this; he's a stranger and does not give a crap. "I like to craft."

When Roman looks over at me, the lenses of his glasses catch the light from downstairs and I can't see his eyes against the glare, but I can almost hear what he's thinking: *An English major with a business minor? What the hell are you going to do with that?*

I know this because my father has asked me that question a million times, and I never have an answer for him.

"I'm sure you'll find something you're passionate about. We make our own destiny."

I nod slowly.

*We make our own destiny.*

Those are some pretty profound words for a freshman guy at a kegger.

"Is that what you're doing? Creating your own destiny?" I'm teasing him but I'm also curious—I've never heard a guy say something like that before, and it's intriguing.

"Sure. I mean, every decision we make today impacts what happens tomorrow, don't you agree?"

Um.

Yes?

"Of course I agree."

Roman has his eyes trained on the action at the bottom of the stairs, where a small group of girls are congregating and whispering, their heads pivoting every few seconds to watch whatever—or whomever—is across the room.

Probably some hot dude one of them has a crush on but is too afraid to approach.

Roman is watching the girls intently before clearing his throat and glancing over at me.

"Are you seeing anyone?" I finally ask him. He doesn't strike me as the type to be dating; I'm certain his course load will keep him as occupied as I expect to be during the school year, but you never know—maybe he has a cute little girlfriend hidden away somewhere.

"No." He chuckles.

"Did I say something funny?"

"You honestly think I'm dating someone?"

"Why are you saying it like I *insulted* you—are you too good to date? Is no one smart enough for you?"

It would make perfect sense that he wouldn't want to date

a dullard; guys like him—ambitious ones with their lives planned out—rarely find time for a person who doesn't possess the same drive and determination.

I would know because that's how my dad is.

Roman is silent again, eyes trailing back to the girls at the bottom of the stairs.

I recognize one of them as Kaylee Sheffield; she's a cheerleader, too, but she's a flyer and we don't practice in the same groups so I rarely have the chance to talk to her.

"They're pretty," I say. "Do you want to go talk to them?"

He snorts. "As if any of those girls would give me the time of day."

Ahh.

I get it.

Roman doesn't date because he doesn't have the self-confidence. I've seen plenty of people like that before, not just guys but girls too, doubting and second-guessing themselves because they don't think they're good enough—the same way I'd never feel smart enough to date a guy who wants to work at NASA and program spaceships.

"I don't think you should judge them based on their appearances. Everyone has a type."

His neck swivels. "We're on Jock Row at a baseball party—I'll give you one guess as to what their type is."

Fine, he's got me there, but only on a technicality.

Still.

He's stereotyping them the way he's probably stereotyping me, but guess what?

I'm used to it.

Cheerleaders may not be considered the studious type, and sure, I'm no *brainiac* so some of the stereotypes in my case may be true—but I'm kind and determined and give everyone a chance. I try not to judge, and I try to give people the benefit of the doubt.

I fiddle with the bracelet on my left wrist, the one I braided a few nights ago in front of the television, sitting my bum on the floor while I watched a reality matchmaking show. It's made of my favorite colors—green and pink—in an intricate pattern I learned one summer at camp.

I rub the soft yarn between my thumb and index finger.

"So, you think if you went down and talked to those girls, you'd get rejected?"

Roman doesn't look at me. "Um, what do you think."

"I think you shouldn't doubt yourself."

He's silent, but in the dim shadows, I can see his lips purse; he wants to respond but isn't going to.

Then, finally—

"What about you? Why aren't you down there flirting and having a good time?"

My head gives a tiny shake. "I don't have the energy—I have to be up early tomorrow, but since everyone was coming out tonight, I also didn't want to sit in the dorms by myself."

Plus, I didn't want to be there when the new roomie arrived.

"Why do you have to be up early tomorrow? It's Saturday."

"Practice."

"Practice for what?"

Oh god, he's going to make me say it.

I sit up straighter, stiffening my spine. "I'm a cheerleader. We practice six days out of the week."

I brace myself.

Wait for whatever sarcastic, biting remark he's going to sling back about airheads or blondes or cheer—but none come.

"You must be good if you made a college team."

I blush.

Golly gee. "I *guess*."

"Why are you being so modest? You should be proud of yourself."

"I am proud of myself."

I am.

I'm proud. Like he said, it's not easy becoming a collegiate cheerleader; I've busted my ass for the past five years, cheering for my high school, cheering on a competitive team, doing camps, workshops, training. And that doesn't include working out to stay fit and strong.

It's been brutal and certainly hasn't been easy.

Not everyone can do it and not everyone does, but I've proven myself over the years.

"You look like a dancer," Roman comments.

I look like a dancer? What do dancers *look* like? Is that a type?

"How can you even tell?" I laugh. "It's dark up here."

"I don't know—I can just tell." He laughs back.

"What dorm are you in?"

"I'm not in the dorms. I still live at home."

"How do you still live at home?"

"I'm local. It only takes me fifteen minutes to get here, so to save money, I'm not living in the dorms."

"Oh." I pause, searching for some more words. "How is that working out for you?"

"Don't know yet since school hasn't started, but I imagine it's going to be like high school, just have to drive farther."

True. Good point.

"Why didn't you go anywhere farther? Did you, like, not have any choices?"

"Yeah, I had plenty of options. I got a few scholarship offers, too, but my aunt lives with my parents and she's kind of old. They sometimes need help with her, so I couldn't go too far. Plus, I need time to figure out what it is I want to do, you know?"

"Oh. I thought you just said you wanted to work for NASA. Or an automobile company."

"But those are two entirely different things and I don't want to waste my time or anyone's money until I know for sure what I want to do, what direction I want to go, you know?"

He says you know a lot, but I say like a lot, so I guess that makes us even.

"How old is this old aunt of yours?"

"I don't know, maybe eighty?"

"Eighty! I thought you were going to say like forty-five or something. That's how old my mom's sister is."

"I should have clarified. My aunt is actually my great aunt —so, my grandmother's sister." He fidgets with his hands. "Grandma died about three years ago, and she and my aunt lived together before she passed. After she died, Aunt Myrtle moved in with us."

That makes much more sense.

"Aunt Myrtle? That's adorable."

Roman laughs. "Zinger of a name, isn't it?"

"Super vintage."

"Quite vintage," he agrees.

"You sound so *formal* when you talk about it," I finally say, because Roman has the vocabulary of an English professor and the posture of one, too. It's so unlike the vocabulary of any of the guys I'm used to—male athletes, primarily football players, who do a lot of grunting and speak in mostly simple sentences. It's not that I'm knocking them or saying they're all like that—all I'm saying is not a single one of them wants to work for NASA.

"Sorry," he apologizes, and I can see he's embarrassed to be called out, though there's no reason he should be.

Being smart is cool.

And sexy.

Sure, Roman is a tad nerdy, but it's clear he hasn't grown into himself yet. I bet when he's older he'll be really good-looking once he fills out.

"Don't ever apologize for the way you are." I speak with authority, wishing I could take my own advice, knowing that a solid few times a week are spent feeling inadequate and less than.

Blame it on my sport. Blame it on my coaches.

And yes—I can blame it on my parents.

My mother could have starred in a season of *Stage Moms*, pushing me to practice and excel and practice some more to the point of exhaustion. I'm not sure what she wants from me. I'm hardly going to become a Dallas Cowboys Cheerleader.

I don't have the motivation for it, not that I'd ever tell her that.

I'm here at this state school because I couldn't make the team at a Division One university, and I'm glad for it each and every night I lie down to sleep while hearing Mom's voice echoing in my head: *You don't try hard enough, Lilly—you don't want it enough. I want it more than you do, for God's sake.*

She's not wrong.

She *does* want it more than I do.

Mom has never acknowledged that just because I'm good at something doesn't mean I love it or like it. Far from it. I cheer because I *can*, not because it's a passion of mine.

I'm still searching for what that passion is and hope I find it someday soon. I want to discover what my dreams are and chase them instead of being pushed into something by other people. I often wonder if my coaches could tell when I went through the motions, wonder if that's why a few of them were always so impatient with me.

Guess I'll never know.

"So you live at home so you can help out? Don't you want to, I don't know, have a life?"

I know I sound judgmental and I know I shouldn't assume Roman doesn't have a life, but if he lives at home because he needs to help out, that probably means he doesn't get out much. Who knows, maybe he doesn't even want to.

Maybe he's one of those guys who like solitude.

Maybe he's one of those guys who stays in his basement playing video games.

"I guess I don't really need to have a life? I'm really focused on my grades right now." He hesitates for a few seconds before adding, "Well, I shouldn't say that. What I mean is I'm really focused on studying, so it's not like I can afford any distractions. If you don't count Aunt Myrtle."

His laughter takes up all the space in our little corner of the party, sequestered high up on the stairs, away from all the chaos.

"No offense, but having Aunt Myrtle live with you sounds like a drag." For a brief moment, I wonder what my problem is and why I can't stop these thoughts in my head.

"Have you ever seen *The Golden Girls*?"

"Yeah, who hasn't?"

"Aunt Myrtle is like a cross between Blanche Devereaux and Sophia. So picture that walking into the kitchen every morning—not to mention she loves giving unsolicited advice. I have no idea how my mom can stand it."

"What about your dad? Are your parents still together, or are they divorced?"

"They're still together. My dad works a lot—travels for work and stuff. He's a structural and civil engineer, designs bridges and shit. Really stressful since he's part of the family business."

Dang, his dad is really smart, too. "Like gluing popsicle sticks together and creating a building?"

Roman laughs again, and I straighten under the praise, having amused him.

"What about your mom? What does she do?" Why am I asking him this? It's so rude. What does it matter what his parents do for a living?

*You're being nosey, Lilly—stop it.*

"She stays home—I have a younger brother in third grade, Alex. He's a monster."

"So your mom takes care of Aunt Myrtle and Alex the Monster."

"Right. They're a dynamic duo of chaos." He looks over at me. "What about you? I feel like all I've done is talk about myself."

Only because I've asked him a million questions.

I pull a bottle of water out of my bag, suddenly remembering I have it with me, twisting off the top and taking a chug.

"Well. My dad works a lot too, and my mom is a paralegal but also considers herself my manager. Unofficially."

"Manager of what?"

"Nothing. The dancing career I'm never going to have and do not want."

"Oh."

I glance at him in the dim light. "Have you ever seen an episode of *Stage Moms*?"

"Uh, no."

"Well, it's this show about mothers who are obsessed with their children being famous or at least push them to be at the top of their game—in my case it's dancing and cheering. I could be throwing up and my mother would still make me go to practice sick. And she would sit there watching the entire time, yelling instructions at me the same way my coaches would." I take in a deep breath. "I couldn't wait to graduate and get away."

"How far from home are you?"

"Four hours—far enough that she can't come to every home game and harass me, tell me all the things I do wrong afterward."

"Isn't that what coaches are for?"

My laugh is wry. "Ha. You would think. I honestly have no idea what my mom expects me to do with dancing—I don't want to be on Broadway or in a show, and I'm not good enough to cheer for a professional sports team. I don't have the motivation to do that."

"Why does she want you to be a dancer so bad?"

"I have no idea."

"Was she a dancer?"

"No. My mom was pre-law and wanted to be a lawyer but couldn't get into any of the law schools she chose, so she quit and became a paralegal—which, by the way, required lots of schooling too."

"Maybe she feels like a quitter and she doesn't want you to be a quitter."

"Well you can't be a quitter if it's not something you even want." I pull at the bracelet surrounding my wrist. "I didn't ask to be put into gymnastics and dance class and ballet. And I didn't ask to be put in pageants when I was two years old."

"Whoa—back up. You were in pageants?"

"Do you have to say it like that?"

"Sorry. But I've never met anyone from *Toddlers and Tiaras*."

"Ha ha, very funny." But I do pull out my phone and start scrolling through my photo gallery. "Hold on, I think I have a picture in here somewhere of me winning the Little Miss Coco Cabana pageant."

I scroll and scroll and scroll down through the weeks and months and years to find pictures of myself I uprooted and then uploaded as a lark. Headshots of myself as a very little girl usually bring me some kind of amusement. Sometimes they even serve as a reminder that my mom has been pushing me to do things I don't want for my entire life.

I find a photo of myself, blonde hair poofed up in the front and twisted into a professional knot in the back. For these particular headshots, my mother actually put a hairpiece on me so my hair appeared fuller. I mean, come on—what three-year-old has this kind of style? It looks absolutely ridiculous.

I'm spray-tanned, wearing makeup and teeny-tiny little dentures called a flipper.

Apparently my own teeth weren't good enough for my mother.

I take my phone and hold it toward Roman so he can see. In the light from the phone's glare, I get a good view of his surprised face. His raised eyebrows and mouth in the shape of an O.

"Dang."

I take my finger and swipe to the next photograph. I'm dressed in western wear, hands on my hips, in the center of a stage. My pale blonde hair is braided and sticking out from beneath a hot pink cowboy hat. Matching fringe vest and skirt. Matching hot pink boots covered in sparkly rhinestones that I remember my mother painstakingly gluing on individually.

She spent *hours* on that costume. Was so upset when I didn't place in the western wear category.

"You don't look like you're having very much fun," Roman says after a few moments studying the picture.

"Really? You don't think so? Most people think I look like I'm having a blast."

"No, I can see it in your eyes, and you're clenching your teeth."

"That's my toothy grin, see?" I flash him my best toothy grin.

"Nah, that's a fake smile. Anyone with half a brain can see that."

He's not wrong—it was a fake smile, the same smile I've been perfecting ever since. Maybe someday I'll feel joy in my soul, but for now I'm just playing along.

"Do your parents ever push you into anything?" I wonder out loud.

"Not really," he says. "I've always known I wanted to be some kind of scientist." Roman picks at the knee of his jeans, at the rip perfectly placed there. "My dad came home with a bottle rocket once after being in Florida, and I've been hooked ever since. I've spent every moment trying to figure out how particles and atoms create...stuff."

"Stuff?"

"I'm just trying to simplify it so you don't get bored."

"I don't think scientists or science is boring at all—you don't have to dumb it down for me." I wonder if I sound defensive at the same time I wonder if he thinks I'm just an airheaded blonde with nothing going on inside my head but fluff.

He wouldn't be the first, and he certainly won't be the last.

"What kinds of things are your friends from high school into besides partying without you, ha ha." It's time to change the subject before I get all defensive. I take my phone, close out the photo gallery, and slide it back into my bag.

Roman shrugs. "I don't know. In all honesty, we don't actually hang out that much. Just so happens I'm the only one who doesn't live in the dorms, and my parents basically forced me to come tonight because they don't want me to become a hermit."

"How did your parents even know?"

"My mom is friends with Jeremy's mom, and Jeremy must have told her what they were doing tonight, so his mom told my mom and asked if I wanted to come, and my mom automatically said yes."

"Kind of like how my mom used to say yes to babysitting jobs without asking me," I tell him. "I wasn't available often, but when I was, it used to drive me nuts. The last thing I wanted to do in my free time was babysit, especially without committing to it myself."

"I mean I guess it's better than sitting at home with Alex and Aunt Myrtle."

Aunt Myrtle.

The name makes me giggle.

"Do you know what your situation reminds me of right now? There is a movie my mom used to love, and in one scene, this kid is dragged to the high school by his parents and they're trying to force him to go to the dance but he doesn't want to. They shove him through the gymnasium doors and hold them closed while he bangs on the other side shouting, 'I want to stay home with you, I want to stay home with you.'"

Sort of makes Roman laugh. "That hits a little too close to home to be all that funny," he says, but I can tell he's saying it with good humor. "No, the truth is I don't actually get out much, so it's probably a good thing that everybody forced me to come tonight, even though Jeremy and his buddies couldn't have given a shit.

"Maybe someday I'll have a secret mad scientist lab I can lock myself in," he continues. "But for now, I have to get out into the real world and show my face every once in a while."

"I think I show my face too often." I chuckle. "Every weekend during football season I'm jumping up and down on the side of the field, shaking my pom-poms for thousands of people, and let me tell you right now—it gets old."

"Then why do you do it?"

"Probably because it's the only thing I know? And I'm good at it even though I don't absolutely love it." I shrug, looking down at my feet even though they're shrouded in the light. "I just keep waiting for something to jump out at me and change all that." I sigh. "I wish I could craft and glue things all day long. That would make me a very happy girl."

"Why didn't you just major in art?" Roman wants to know.

"My mother would have a heart attack."

"Your mom doesn't even have to know," he tells me, as if that's not something I've already thought of. Eventually she would find out, and she would have a stroke. "Are your parents paying for school?"

I nod solemnly. "Most of it. It's not like I can go and get a job with how much practice I have during the week—I would make a horrible employee, having to take days off all the time."

"Have you ever had a job?"

Other than the occasional babysitting gig? "No, I never had the time. You?"

"Yes, I actually used to work for my family. My grandfather owns—well, he died, but it's still in the family—an industrial factory, and I spend my summers in an assembly line plating paperclips and other office supplies." Roman picks at the threads of his jeans. "The pay is shit, but I have to do it."

"That sounds, um..."

"Boring. That sounds boring—you can say it." He laughs. "Trust me, I could do it with my eyes closed—that's how long I've been at it, and I only get half-hour breaks. Once, I had someone try to break into my car while it was parked outside because the factory is in the city and Grandpa gave zero fucks about security."

"At least you're making money."

He grunts. "Barely. Like I said, he never paid me shit. And now my uncle owns it and he's worse. This was my last summer, and I hope I'm not around next year."

"Where will you be?"

"Traveling." He gets quiet for a few seconds. "I've been applying for grants and scholarships—fingers crossed."

Roman crosses his fingers and holds them out the way my girlfriends and I sometimes will when we need good luck, and I cross mine for him, too.

"Well, I hope it all goes well for you." I sigh, peering into the abyss that is the party down on the lower level. The music is still blasting and people keep coming through the front door, arriving into the late hours. "I'm sure I'll still be here in a few years, doing the same ol' same ol'."

"The good news is, we'll be done in four years."

"That's true." Then I can get an apartment far from my mother and her controlling ways. "Well..." I breathe out. Toy with the bracelet around my wrist and slowly slide it off. "We should probably get back to the party."

"Probably." He stands.

I stand. "It was nice meeting you."

"Yeah, you too." His hands get stuffed into the pockets of his jeans, and I realize then how tall Roman actually is. It feels like he's towering over me, even though I'm standing on the step above him.

Six two? Six three?

Hard to say, but I find myself craning my neck to get a look at his face, the lenses from his glasses catching the light.

"Do you suppose I'll see you around?"

His shoulders shrug. “I’m not a fan of parties, and as it is, I still have to drive home.”

Oh.

Duh—no wonder he hasn’t been drinking. He has to drive. Fifteen minutes I think he said it was? Yuck.

“This was fun though. Thank you for keeping me company.”

“I wasn’t keeping you company, you were keeping me company.”

That makes me smile.

“Here.” Impulsively I hold the bracelet out to him. “This is for good luck this year.”

He hesitates in the dim light before his hand reaches out to take it from me. Slides it onto his own wrist.

He won’t know until he steps into the light that it’s hot pink and lime green, but it’s the thought that counts anyway, isn’t it?

“Thanks.”

“Does it fit?”

Roman smiles. “It fits.”

“Well.” I take a few steps down. “Guess I’ll see you around.”

“Good luck on Monday,” he tells me.

“Good luck.”

# CHAPTER 1

# ROMAN

## THREE YEARS LATER

I cannot keep living here.

My parents and family are driving me nuts, and I've only been back for two weeks. School starts in three days, and I've barely had time to unpack, let alone get all the things done that my mother has demanded from me, like driving Aunt Myrtle to her physical therapy appointments.

I've been gone only one semester, but it feels like I've been away for an eternity. At the same time, it feels like I've only been gone a day, my family not missing a beat when it comes to needing my help.

Damn I miss the UK.

Last year I was fortunate enough to be the recipient of a lucrative educational scholarship to study abroad, and I took it without hesitating; it paid for my room, boarding, and my meals. I studied with the best of the best—some of the most brilliant minds in the world.

And now I'm being told what to do by an eighty-three-year-old woman with purple hair, pink lipstick, and rhinestone glasses. She's a cross between Dame Edna and Elton John, and she is pursing her lips at me in a judgmental way as I wait too long at the stop sign.

"Can't you go any faster?" she asks.

"We're at a stop sign," I tell her. "I'm actually not supposed to be driving at all."

Aunt Myrtle looks out the window to the right. "I don't see any cops around."

The last thing I need is to get pulled over and ticketed before classes start—I have to commute.

"I don't need my driving record gone to shit because you have a lead foot, Aunt Myrt."

"In my day, there was no such thing as getting pulled over for a rolling stop." The old lady can lie with a straight face—we honestly should enter her in a few poker championships.

"That makes absolutely no sense. I'm pretty sure you weren't allowed to just run stop signs whenever you felt like it."

She chuckles beside me, her petite frame overwhelmed by her garish outfit. Actually, it's a caftan and it matches her hair to perfection but also makes her look tiny in the passenger seat of my parents' big Tahoe.

"Are you hungry?" she asks. "I could go for a bite to eat and a martini."

"It's ten in the morning."

My great aunt grunts. "It's five o'clock somewhere."

"Please don't start quoting Jimmy Buffett. You're giving me a headache."

She laughs again. "I was just giving you a hard time. I don't actually do my drinking until at least one o'clock after my nap."

Aunt Myrtle looks out the window and goes silent, watching the scenery go by—I can see the lenses of her glasses reflecting in the window and in the rearview mirror when I glance over, and I wonder for a brief second what she could possibly be thinking about. I wonder what she thinks of the world she's living in now, and how different it is from the one she grew up in.

I feel guilty.

*Maybe I should get the old lady a martini.*

I turned twenty-one last year and am certainly old enough to walk into a bar with her and order her one, although I wouldn't know a single place that's open this time of day.

Oh well, it's the thought that counts.

Guess we'll just have to go home. Besides, Mom is waiting for us there, and she and Aunt Myrtle have their routine. Plus, I still have to unpack and get my shit ready for school.

My bedroom, right next to my brother's, is apparently made of paper-thin walls. It didn't bother me before, but now? Now it bothers me. Why? Well, I'm pretty sure he jerks off when he thinks I'm asleep if the noises coming through the walls are any indication.

I need to move out like yesterday.

"You know what I've been thinking?" Aunt Myrtle speaks at last.

"I can't even begin to imagine what you've been thinking," I say with a laugh. She's good-humored and laughs too.

Of all the members of my family, I am the least like her—she's outgoing and gregarious, and I am neither of those things. Even compared to my parents and my brother, I am introverted and quiet, happy to observe rather than participate.

My great aunt certainly isn't shy about voicing her thoughts, and I'm curious to hear what she's about to say, my hands gripping the wheel as I make a right-hand turn onto our road, drive the five hundred feet to the driveway, and slowly ascend up it.

"I think it's time you left the nest."

Is she implying that I ought to move out of my parents' house?

"I did leave the nest, remember?" I just got back from living in the United Kingdom for several months.

"Eh." She makes a sound in her throat. "You know what I mean, Roman. You need your own space. You can't keep living with that little brother of yours. You're a man now."

"Where do you suggest I go? I haven't lived on campus in three years—I'm not about to go live in the dorms as a senior in college."

"I'm not suggesting you go live in the dorms. Living in the dorms is like riding the school bus—no good comes of it."

"What are you even talking about?" I put the car into park and help her unbuckle her seat belt before exiting the vehicle and going around to the passenger side so I can help her out. There's a little folding step stool beneath her feet, and I remove it from the car and set it on the ground to make this step down easier.

She is a tiny little thing, but she has big opinions.

"All I'm saying is you don't want to sleep on a mattress that's as thin as a piece of toast and that hundreds of people have banged on." She gives her head a shake. "Do you know when the last time they replaced those mattresses was? Probably when I was in college."

Great Aunt Myrtle is one of the few females of her generation who actually attended university. It wasn't common for young women to go to school back in the day, but she and my grandma both went for business and eventually helped my grandfather run his corporation.

Grandma and Aunt Myrtle used to love telling stories about their sorority days, cotillions, and all the young bucks that vied for their attention; two smart and beautiful co-eds living in the fifties were a hot commodity.

"The last thing I want to do is live in the dorms. I'm an old man compared to the people who live there."

I take her frail hand in mine and help her down onto the step stool.

She nods as if to say, *That's true.* "Don't you know anyone who has a place to let?"

"You mean try to find a house to sublease? Aunt Myrtle, it's the beginning of the school year—there's no way anyone has a room to rent. I waited too long."

"You won't know until you try. Don't you know anyone? Not a single soul?"

I do, but no one I want to live with. Jeremy and his buddies live in fraternity houses on Greek row, and those are the only guys I know well enough to potentially live with. Considering fraternities are members only, that's not an option.

Together, Aunt Myrtle and I hobble toward the door, her little shoes squeaking the entire way, and I glance down at them: they're purple and match the long, drapey gown she's donning that happens to be plastered with the image of her dead dog's face—a Bichon Frise named Bitsy that passed away a few years ago from old age.

Aunt Myrtle saw the caftans on a reality TV show and insisted on having one made in two colors. Purple and green, and blush pink.

The stacked bangles on her wrist clink as she grips my arm, watching the sidewalk for cracks.

*She is really something else.*

"I know people," I say defensively. "I just don't know anyone I can move in with." I'll have to give it some thought, some serious thought now that she's voiced my exact mindset out loud. I really should move out.

Besides, studying in this house is virtually impossible with Alex randomly crashing into my room whenever he feels like it —he is such a pain in my ass.

Nor can I sit at the library for hours on end knowing my family has things for me to do at home. I feel like I'm straddling both sides of the line.

Half in, half out—I have to choose.

And if I move out, perhaps that will give me the freedom to have a little less guilt when I'm not here. They're going to have to manage without me; more to the point, my mother will have to find a way to manage Aunt Myrtle without me.

I'm not her keeper.

The old bag is encouraging me to move out, and for the most part, she's got the most wisdom out of all of us, even when Grandma was alive.

"I'll think about it," I tell her as we make our way into the kitchen, the house quiet for a weekend. I wonder where everyone has gone before finding a note on the kitchen counter.

It's a letter scrawled in my mother's handwriting: GONE TO THE GROCERY STORE AND TO HOME DEPOT, WON'T BE GONE PAST 11. TEXT ME IF YOU NEED ANYTHING.

It's cute that Mom still writes handwritten notes. I crumple it up and toss it in the recycling bin.

Taking advantage of a quiet house, I go to my room and begin reorganizing the things I brought back from my studies abroad, remove items from my suitcase that I want to display on a shelf.

*Slow your roll, pal. Maybe you shouldn't get too comfortable here.*

I glance around the bedroom that's seemingly stuck in a time warp of my childhood with scientific studies, accolades, and inspirational posters neatly pinned to the wall.

It's weird. I was only gone for one semester, but looking around this bedroom I was in my entire life seems...I don't know. Confusing? Uncomfortable? I've grown out of it, yet I haven't. I'm still the same science-driven kid but not the same person I was when I left here. I throw my messenger bag on my desk chair and place my hands on my hips.

There's a bracelet encircling my wrist, and I remove it, placing it on a shelf next to my desk, right next to a tall Academic Decathlon trophy. It's one of many I won over the years at competitions during my high school career. My mother still has the cleaning ladies dust them weekly so they don't show a particle of grime.

Did I mention the bracelet I just removed is the same one I got as a freshman from the girl I met in the stairwell of my first college party—think her name was Lilly if I'm remembering correct, though I never once was fortunate enough to bump into her on campus. I know she was a cheerleader for the football team, but I never considered going to a game to see her.

Alright, that's a total lie—I did totally consider going to a game to see her, but I didn't want to be a creep. I'm definitely not the type of guy a girl like that wants hanging around. I would probably give her stalker vibes.

I give the bracelet another cursory glance, its green and pink strands a little reminder of that first night of school. They carried me through my studies in the United Kingdom. Whenever I was having a rough day or night or week, I would wear it and it would give me a little bit of courage, this gift from a beautiful and vibrant girl. It somehow gave me confidence.

Kind of like a shield.

I wonder what she's up to these days—it's been a few years since we ran into each other. I wonder if she's still on the cheerleading squad or if she quit to pursue other passions like she wanted to. Maybe she's still at it, cheering on the sidelines in those cold fall months.

I found it ironic at the time that she would rather craft and do art than athletics, but that's just me stereotyping her based on her looks. There is no doubt in my mind she was stereotyping me, too, most likely pegging me as the giant nerd I am based on the information I gave her about myself.

How I love science and NASA and engineering. I left out the part about atoms and biology and neurons because that's so beyond nerdy even I'm embarrassed by it.

Atoms turn me on, okay?

There, I said it.

I catch a glimpse of myself in the mirror, see the t-shirt I'm wearing with the galaxy emblazoned across the front of my chest, notice that it's getting a little tighter these days. I began working out while studying overseas. The group of American guys—or lads—living in the same dorm were extremely into fitness, and eventually I began working out with them and getting into shape.

I actually have biceps now.

And abs.

Still a complete nerd, but now I'm just one that's physically fit. Kind of an oxymoron, but I've always been into irony. It's not like I'm Arnold Schwarzenegger or Fabio or an Instagram model, but I'm better off than I was before, all puny and weak.

Definitely more confident.

Mom noticed as soon as she picked me up from the airport that I looked broader in the shoulders; it took my father a little longer, mostly because he works all the time and isn't around much. That could be because of Aunt Myrtle lingering about all the time—she likes to give him a hard time, really get his goat. Something of a heckler, she squeezed my upper bicep and chuckled that night at the dinner table like a pervy little creep.

My first night back, they threw a small welcome home party and embarrassed the crap out of me by making a fuss about my appearance.

I never really cared what I look like—still kind of don't—but I'm certainly more conscious of it now that I'm in good shape.

Girls have noticed too. I've never had as many girls hit on me in my life as I have in the past few weeks—then again, I think I must look a little more European? Lankier like the English lads, and that's what the attraction was with girls in Cambridge.

Suddenly my door flies open and Alex barges in, tossing his book bag onto my bed and flopping down as if he owns the place.

"What are you doing with your crap on my bed?" I ask him, hefting a box off the floor and setting it on top of the desk.

"I like doing my homework in here." He makes himself comfortable, crossing his arms behind his head. "I used it as an office when you were gone."

"You used my bedroom as your *office* while I was gone?" I study his face for any signs that he's joking. "You're twelve—what do you need an office for?"

He shrugs. "It's nice to have a change of venue instead of staring at the same wall day in and day out. Kind of like being in prison. And this room has a better view of the backyard."

"It's literally the same view of the backyard," I tell him. Our rooms are side by side at the end of the hallway, Aunt Myrtle taking over the plush guest bedroom that's downstairs, with its huge bathroom and walk-in closets—yes, *plural* walk-in closets.

As in: two.

My parents were part of that McMansion boom a few years back, where everyone thought bigger was better and more space meant the house was more impressive so they built a structure with five bedrooms despite there only being two kids living at home, one of the guest bedrooms so luxurious it's basically a hotel suite.

Now I think they must be thankful for the five rooms with Great Aunt Myrtle living here because she has room to roam and isn't in everybody's way all the time—even though she's in everybody's business.

Ha.

"Well I'm home now so you won't be using my desk. Or my room. And since when do you enter a room without knocking? I could have been naked."

"So? You don't have anything I've never seen before," he declares with authority. "And it's not like you're in here jerking off."

"What the hell do you know about jerking off?" Alex and I have never discussed sex before, and the fact that he's bringing up masturbating as if it's no big deal has my eyes practically bugging out of my skull. Since when did my little brother grow up?

Jesus, I don't even want to think about him wanking it, let alone discuss it with him while he's lying on my bed.

Then again, he is twelve years old and probably has boxes of tissues and paper towels stashed under his bed the same way I did when I first started getting random erections at inconvenient times.

Alex is definitely way cooler than I am, though. There's no doubt he is part of the popular crowd—the one I was never part of while growing up. He plays football and lacrosse and doesn't give a rat's ass about academics, so I'm shocked he would use *any* room to study and do homework in, let alone my room.

Come to think of it, he's probably in here playing video

games on the flat-screen TV I have hanging on the wall across from my bed. It was a gift from my grandmother for my fourteenth birthday, and it's a lot nicer than the one that's in the den downstairs.

Not to brag, but I was always one of Grandma's favorites.

"You know what I would appreciate, Alex? I would love it if you would get out of my bedroom."

"When did you become an asshole?" He makes no attempt to move and give me my privacy, and I can see he's surprised by my attitude. I don't usually kick him out when he makes himself at home in here, probably because he doesn't come in here very often. But now that he's been using my space for his own purposes, I need to set boundaries and reestablish my territory.

I glance at him over my shoulder and pry open the box. "You should probably watch your mouth. Does Mom know you swear like that?"

I catch my little brother rolling his eyes at me. "Dude, I'm twelve, not a baby."

I can *see* that he's not a baby—he looks like a preteen now, having shot up several inches in the short time frame that I was studying in England.

Alex is almost taller than I am and still has growing to do.

"I didn't say you were a baby—I asked if Mom's ever heard you swear like that."

"Yeah right," he scoffs. "She would have a fit, then Aunt Myrt would get involved, and soon everyone would be yelling at me. No thanks."

He's not wrong; since Aunt Myrtle moved in, she's taken a real shine to inserting herself into family drama, including creating drama where none previously existed.

Guess she's bored as hell with nothing else to occupy her time but us.

"It's like living with the Crypt Keeper," Alex continues.

"Hey—don't be mean."

"I'm not being mean! She's a hundred years old. Do you know how not cool it is living with a geriatric?"

I turn and level him with a stare. "Would you say that to her face?"

"No."

"Then you probably shouldn't be saying that in here." I turn back toward my box. "Besides, she's probably listening outside the door with her ear pressed to the wall."

That makes my brother laugh. "Probably."

I turn to face him again. "Are you leaving or not?"

"Not," he says with a laugh that makes me want to throttle him.

"Don't you have anything better to do? And why are you even home, anyway? It's the middle of the day."

"We had a half-day today. Teacher in-service or something like that."

"Who brought you home?"

"Brandon's mom." Brandon is my brother's best friend, has been since they were in kindergarten.

"You should've told me. I was running errands and took Aunt Myrtle to physical therapy—I could have grabbed you on the way home."

"I think Mom forgot, so I just hopped in the car with Brandon."

That sounds kind of like our mom; she is very forgetful and used to do the same thing to me when I was growing up. Every so often, my parents would leave me at church after dropping me off at Sunday school. Don't even ask me how that happens—thank God we have cell phones.

"What's in that box?" my brother wants to know.

"Just stuff from school—textbooks and shit."

"Aren't textbooks mostly digital now?"

"Maybe. But not at Cambridge."

I studied over there on a scholarship I'd been fighting to earn since I was a freshman in high school, busting my ass for good grades and joining every and any club that could be academically beneficial, on top of playing tennis.

Tennis, right? Who even plays that anymore?

"Did you meet any girls while you were over there?" my brother asks as he fumbles with the remote control for my TV. I'm sure he intends to stay awhile and watch one of his favorite programs, something he's probably been doing every day since the day I left.

"No, I didn't meet any girls." I fold a t-shirt that's at the top of my box and set it off to the side. "I mean, obviously I met girls, but I assume you mean did I date any."

"You never date any girls. Do you even know how?"

Smartass little shit.

"What do you mean I never date any girls? I've had girlfriends—I dated Britney Bevins for a few months my freshman year."

"Britney doesn't count," Alex informs me with a scoff. "Our parents are friends."

I mean, that's kind of true, plus it wasn't all that romantic of a relationship. Britney is a brainiac like me and was only enrolled at the university until she got her acceptance to an Ivy League college, which came our sophomore year. She packed up her bags and moved to California to attend Stanford and chase that doctoral degree she's been coveting since we were kids.

I hardly hear from her anymore.

Other than that, sadly, I haven't had any other relationships, if you don't count family and friends. I'm talking about romantic relationships, and yeah—sexual relationships too, I guess. I would say it's because I don't do the casual sex thing, but that would be a lie. The truth is I don't actually have the guts to have casual sex even if I wanted to.

Alex watches as I lift a soccer ball out of the cardboard box and toss it to the ground.

"What are you doing with a soccer ball?"

"I got it while I was in England. They're huge into football over there."

I bought this one during one of the playoffs when every other store in town was selling souvenirs for the different teams. It was chaos but fantastic fun and I wanted something to remember it by, so I brought home the red and blue football.

"You packed a soccer ball in your luggage? Why didn't you deflate it?"

He has a good point—deflating it would have made more sense if I hadn't been in such a hurry to pack up my crap at the end of this semester. Packing was the last thing on my mind; I got swept up in my new friends and working out and, of course, studying, and I waited until the last day to pack up my boxes, address them, and mail them back.

Truth be told, I didn't have a ton of stuff—some clothes, academic tools like textbooks and my computer and other office supplies, and...that's really about it. But I did buy some things while I was there, like gifts for my family.

Alex flips on the TV and begins thumbing through the channels, the volume blaringly loud as if he were hard of hearing.

"Turn that down. You're going to wake the entire house."

"It's not even noon. No one is sleeping."

"Aunt Myrtle might be taking a nap. Do you want her coming up here?"

"No. Besides, she wouldn't come up here—she'd shout at us through the intercom. Myrt loves the intercom, but she doesn't know how to work it properly so she repeats herself ten times and blows into it with her old lady breath. It's obnoxious," Alex grumbles.

"Well turn that down anyway, Jesus. And get your feet off my bed." I smack at his legs.

He's still wearing his sneakers, and I don't want his filthy shoes on my comforter.

Where was this kid raised, in a barn? Mom would have a heart attack if she knew he was running around the house with shoes on.

"Don't they leave you a list of chores you're supposed to do when you get home from school?"

They used to do that with me.

"No. I'm busy with sports."

"You don't look that busy with sports to me."

Alex glances over at me as I pull more stuff out of my box. "Practice isn't until later today. Someone will have to drive me back to school if Mom isn't home by then."

"How about Brandon's mom?"

"Brandon doesn't play lacrosse."

"You're a real pain in the ass. Do you realize that?"

He shrugs. "I'm twelve, and it's too far to ride my bike."

I mean, he's not wrong.

I take the empty cardboard box and toss it out my bedroom door into the hallway just in time to see my mother coming up the stairs. Her eyes flit from me to the box then back to me.

"Someone is getting settled in, I see. I hope these boxes make it down to the recycling. Break them down, would you? And stack them neatly next to the garage."

That's obviously what I was going to do with the boxes, but she wouldn't be my mother if she didn't constantly remind me to tidy up my things and take the trash out.

I glance back at my brother, who is ignoring us both now that he's fixated on the anime series on the television screen.

"Hey Mom, can we talk later?"

I can't get something Aunt Myrtle said out of my mind and now I want to discuss it with my parents, but first I want to talk about it with my mom—feel her out a little bit, gauge her reaction.

"I have time now if you want to talk." She steps into the bedroom and goes to sit next to my brother on the bed. It dips beneath her weight.

"In private?"

Mom raises her eyebrows and looks down at my brother. Notices for the first time that he's wearing sneakers and pushes his legs off my bed. "Hey, get out of here with your shoes on, mister."

Alex grumbles again but bends to untie his shoes, kicks them off, and trudges out to the hallway.

"Close the door behind you," Mom calls.

Alex returns to shut the door a bit harder than necessary.

Mom gives me her full attention, and I take a seat across from her on my desk chair, swiveling it away from the window to face her. This conversation is more difficult to start than I thought it would be, but if I don't have it, it will linger in my mind and fester.

"I didn't realize how much I missed you until you finally got home." Mom looks rather emotional. "I could just squish you right now I missed you so much."

"Please don't." I laugh.

"How was the flight? We haven't actually had a chance to talk alone since you've been back, and I apologize for that. I've been so caught up with this fundraising event for the women's club—we're raising awareness for fostering—that I haven't had time to spend with you. Tell me what's been going on."

This is just going to make what I'm about to say that much worse considering I'm about to drop the bomb on her about potentially moving out and onto campus.

"I thought you'd have a British accent."

She really is funny. "We've spoken every week for four months—you knew I didn't pick up an accent."

Mom picks at some lint on her jeans. "Fine. I was hoping you would. Like Madonna when she lived in London."

"Who?"

She groans and runs a hand down her face. "Don't make me feel old."

I pick up a pencil on my desk and begin tapping it nervously against the wooden top, knee bouncing below it.

"So I've been thinking about my living arrangement the past few days."

This has Mom's attention and she sits up straighter, folding her hands in her lap. She nods.

"And you know I love living here—I've never lived anywhere else—but being on my own the last few months was awesome, and now that I'm back, I think it's probably time for me to find my own place. Or at least find some roommates." I rotate in the chair and look out the window for a moment, down at the neighbor's house and into their backyard where a big, blue swimming pool sits. "It's going to be practically impossible to find someone who still needs a roommate, but I think I should look."

Mom doesn't say much for the next several seconds, but I can practically hear her thinking. "I can understand why you feel the need to..." Her voice trails off. "Spread your wings."

I spin back around. "I mean, Mom—Alex busts in here whenever he pleases and makes himself at home. He's been using this room as a hangout spot and thinks he still can. I have no privacy whatsoever."

I do, but that's not the point—we have a 'No Locked Doors' policy in this house, and I don't see that changing any time soon. Alex doesn't give a shit that I don't want him in this room; he's used to coming in here, and he's going to continue coming in here.

He's spoiled and young and does what he wants.

The point is, there are four other people living here and every one of them is in my business, including my eighty-three-year-old great aunt, who may live downstairs but always seems to be lingering.

Kind of like a ghost.

Almost as if she's here to do my late grandmother's bidding, bossing us around the way Nan did when she'd come by (and she did so often), outlandishly taking over the whole household.

And did I mention Aunt Myrtle is online dating?

Yeah.

"How do you plan on finding an apartment?"

We both know I haven't made a decent number of new friends—not in the three years I've been at school, too wrapped up in my course work for socializing.

"I met someone in England who has a contact here—coincidentally."

Mom doesn't seem convinced. "You went all the way across the ocean and found someone who knows someone who may have a room for you to rent in the same city you need a room to rent?" She furrows her brows. "How is that possible?"

"Give me a second to process what you said," I joke with a smile. "Yeah, crazy right? I met a guy whose brother lives here. Goes to school here and has a house—all I have to do is reach out and cross my fingers. There's no guarantee, but..."

Mom doesn't look pleased. "You're so helpful."

"Mom, I'm twenty-one years old—I can't live here for the

rest of my life just so I can shuttle Aunt Myrtle around and feed Alex when you and Dad aren't around."

It's not fair.

"It's my senior year—how am I supposed to study in this house?" I take a deep breath. "You could hire someone to help with Aunt Myrtle and Alex. A nanny for them both."

Mom buries her face in her hands and laughs. "Oh my god, can you imagine. I don't know who would run a nanny off first, your brother or your auntie."

"One hundred percent it would be Aunt Myrtle and her parade of geriatric boyfriends."

"Please." Mom holds her hands out with more laughter. "Do not remind me. The last guy gave her piña coladas and wine and she wound up puking on the living room rug when he brought her home."

"What?" I shout, shocked and horrified. "Wait—what? Rewind."

"She went out with this younger gentleman who said he was sixty-nine but was actually seventy-eight. He took her to a tiki bar, and it didn't sit well with her."

"What?"

"She's still trying to party like it's 1999, and it came up both ends."

"That's not even funny." Well, it kind of is, but in a weird, *I'm going to hell for laughing* kind of way.

"No one is laughing. It was horrendous. Your father about had a heart attack, and I made him help clean up the mess. Meanwhile, Auntie went to brunch with a gentleman who owns a golf cart dealership while we cleaned the carpets."

"I don't even know what to say to that."

"Nothing. You say nothing. It's been a revolving door of gray-haired single men. Widowed men. Confirmed elderly bachelors. She's having a field day with it all. I don't know how a caregiver could manage, and I can barely manage your brother."

Which is where I come in. "But Mom..."

"I'll have to talk to your dad, but I guess it wouldn't hurt for you to text your friend's brother and see where he's at with his spare room."

I want to fist-pump the air for the small victory but manage to restrain myself until Mom leaves the room.

"And maybe if you live by campus, you'll meet someone."

Meet someone? Like, a girl? "That's not the reason I want to move and be closer to school, Mom."

Girls are distracting, and I have goals.

Mom pats me on the arm. "I know that's not the reason, sweetie. I was just thinking out loud."

That's all anyone in this house does—thinks out loud.

# CHAPTER 2
# LILLY

Kyle cheated.

My boyfriend *cheated*.

Sexting, sending dick pics, late-night phone calls—the whole nine yards.

He was one step away from actual, physical cheating.

But *why*.

Why not break up with me instead? Why sneak around behind my back and lie about being happy? Surely telling the truth would have been easier than the subterfuge.

Let's be real: some guys get off on that shit, and those are not the guys you want in your life.

My roommate Kaylee isn't home at the moment, and I have no desire to be alone with my thoughts. I tap my feet on the linoleum kitchen floor, staring out the window across the street at the university's administration building—at its beautiful rotunda and wide steps leading to the massive doors at the top.

We live directly across the street from campus, conveniently located near—well, everything.

Everything except my friend Eliza's house. Even she doesn't know exactly how many times Kyle and I have gotten into arguments. How many times he's made me cry. How many times I've had doubts about his reliability and faithfulness. The number of times we were 'on a break' in the short four months because he couldn't fully commit.

The number of times I caught him leaving the room to text someone else then immediately put his phone face down.

Red flags.

Red flags.

*Red.*

Flags.

*Kyle doesn't deserve me.*

I know this.

I know he's a bag of shit, but that doesn't make it hurt any less.

I stare out the window, wondering if I only dated him in the first place because he's a popular member of the football team—it's not like he's winning any awards for his humor and personality. Kid can't hold a conversation to save his soul, but he sure is pretty to look at.

Big muscles. Handsome face.

Everyone knows him, not just here but nationwide.

Kyle is going places, most likely to the NFL.

Honestly, our whole relationship was like high school 2.0, and I was foolish enough to get caught up in that fame trap. Hate to admit it, but some might consider me a jock chaser, despite my own popularity and status on the cheer team.

Kyle was not a good fit for me; he made me feel insecure about myself, my intelligence, and my body, and it took his cheating to snap me out of the rose-colored daze.

I bust my ass; I work out and work *hard* to earn and keep my position as a cheerleader for the university, but something about the way he treated me always made me feel...inferior. Always made me feel like I had to work harder to keep *him* than he had to work for me.

I fought harder to date him than I did to stay on the team.

Dating him became a full-time job.

The balance of power shifted the day he had me hooked. Some girls accept that kind of behavior because they want to date an athlete, and I was caught up in it, too.

Well not anymore.

For the time being, I plan on working on myself from the inside out and healing from the emotional gaslighting that was Kyle. Eliza can cheer me up, so I text her to see if she's around —maybe even has a full fridge?

I'm starving.

**Me:** *Are you busy?*

It takes Eliza a few minutes to reply, and I wonder what she could be doing today; she has a new boyfriend and lives in his house in a more residential part of town, not far from campus but not up against it, either.

**Eliza:** *I'm making linner. Why, do you need something?*

**Me:** *What's linner?*

**Eliza:** *Lunch and dinner.*

**Eliza:** *But seriously, is everything alright?*

Can she actually tell from the tone of my text that everything is not alright? Wow. She's good.

**Me:** *I need to talk—can I come over?*

**Eliza:** *Sure. Of course! We're here, just hanging out. New roommate moving in, but his stuff is mostly in the house. Come on over.*

**Me:** *New roommate?*

**Eliza:** *Yeah—Jack and I sublet my room and I'm sleeping with him, LOL.*

**Me:** *Oooo you're a couple now?! You should have told me!*

**Eliza:** *You're so busy and we've been busy...*

**Me:** *I can't wait to hear all about it and see your place. What's the address? I was thinking I'd leave here in a few minutes.*

I'm no more than ten steps inside my friend's adorable new home when she grabs hold of my arm and looks me in the face.

"What's wrong?"

"How do you know something is wrong?"

Eliza cocks her head and pulls me through the house without showing me the rooms—I've yet to have a proper tour—and into the kitchen.

"I can tell by the look on your face. You're faking it."

Faking it.

Ha.

I've been faking it for four months, orgasms included, but I'm surprised anyone else can tell. I have a mean poker face and can charm the pants off most people—that's what cheerleaders do. Smile!

Smile for the crowd, smile for the camera, even when your team is losing.

I set my purse on the counter next to what appears to be a door to the laundry room then take a seat at the counter without being invited to sit.

Rest my chin in my hands with a sigh, eyes scanning the spread Eliza has out.

Pizza slices on a platter, croissant sandwiches, meat and cheese. Crackers.

What the heck is all this for? Is there a pro football game on I wasn't aware of? It looks like a meal for the Super Bowl, not your basic Saturday.

Maybe she's having actual company over.

*Perhaps I shouldn't have come...*

"I'm sorry to pop over like this, but Kaylee hasn't been home much and today I just didn't want to be alone." I lift my hands in an apologetic shrug.

Eliza takes my hand and squeezes. "Why? What's going on?"

"I...ugh." Uncomfortably grab a napkin and fiddle with the edge. "Kyle and I are done. Like, *done* done."

Gotowe.

Finito.

Hecho.

*Finished.*

"Oh no, Lilly! Why?!"

There is no easy way to say this without making it awkward.

"He cheated."

"Are you sure?" Eliza goes still. "How do you *know*?"

Eliza has always been a proponent of love and working things out; when Kyle and I went through a rough patch not so long ago, she was the one who encouraged me to contact him and make things right. She's the one who gave me the courage to take the first step.

What she didn't know was how many rough patches we've gone through in such a short period of time.

Too many.

Not healthy.

"I found the texts. Guess it's been going on for a while." I steal a slice of pizza that's in the center of the counter, the spread fit for a college king. Or several college kings, and for a brief moment I wonder why the heck there is...

So.

Much.

Food.

The pizza is cold, not that I'm complaining, and I chew it slowly while I think.

"Do you know who she is?"

"Not really. Someone he met at a party I think." Most likely there are several someones—I was too traumatized to seek out the laundry list of young women he's likely got on speed dial, but my gut instincts are telling me there wasn't just one.

Eliza screws up her face, genuinely sad. "I'm sorry."

I'm sorry too—sorry it took me so long to wise up and see Kyle for the person he is: selfish, egotistical, and overindulged.

"I guess what I don't understand is why he didn't just *tell* me he was unhappy. We had that huge fight, remember?" Eliza nods. "Why would he get back together with me if he was cheating? He should have just told me then and left things the way they were and gone on his way."

Eliza falls into the chair beside me with a sigh, and I steal a square of cheese from the plate in front of me. "Sometimes people aren't strong enough to be honest when it matters most."

I nod, chewing. Swallow. "I cannot believe I haven't started crying yet. But for real, I've done so good." I steal more cheese. "Ugly crying is not a good look for me. I tend to avoid it at all costs."

That makes Eliza laugh, and she pats my hand before standing again so she can finish prepping linner. She fusses around the kitchen, opening this cabinet and that, taking things out of the fridge.

"Do you want help with anything?"

My old roommate shakes her head. "No. You stay sitting—you are my guest." Her eyes roam my face. "You need a stiff drink, but all we have is soda, juice, and water. What'll it be?" She wants my order as if she were a bartender at one of our favorite bars downtown.

"Water—pour me another."

"Just water? It's Saturday and it's five o'clock somewhere."

"Ha. Yeah, I'm sure. I went out last night and still feel like shit."

A little liquid numbing might have kept the self-pity at bay for a night but sure didn't do me any favors this morning when I went to practice.

"One water coming right up."

More cheese.

A small piece of summer sausage.

"Okay—what's up with all this food? Are you having a party and I wasn't invited?"

Eliza is filling a glass with ice at the freezer before holding it under the faucet for water. "Jack and I have a new roommate and he's moving in today. I thought it would be nice to have food set out in case there were a bunch of people coming in and out to help him out. Turns out it's just him and a few boxes, so...eat up."

"Don't mind if I do!"

Yum.

Free food tastes so good, especially food I don't have to prepare myself—I'm not the best cook in the world.

"Who's the new roommate?"

Eliza rearranges the sandwiches she's already arranged on a plate. "He is a friend of Ashley, Jack's brother." Pause. "Well, maybe not a friend, but someone he met and clicked with who hasn't been living on campus and now needs a place to rent."

"Oh—like a local?"

"I think he's local, yes. I think his parents are in North Liberty?"

Never heard of it. "Where is that?"

Eliza tilts her head to think. "North Liberty is just south-east of school, I think?" She points at the wall above the stove. "About fifteen or twenty minutes away."

I pick at the cheese again. "Has he ever lived on campus before, or has he always commuted?"

"He's always commuted."

"Shit, for real?" That sounds hideous. "I can't imagine living with my parents after I turned eighteen. Then again, my mother is certifiable."

"I love my parents, but I wouldn't want to live at home, either." She plucks a cherry tomato from the tray and pops it in her mouth, chewing. "That's why I moved this far."

"Exactly. I'm too far to visit on a regular basis but close enough that I still get in-state tuition."

God, I can't imagine seeing my mother every single day.

It would be like...being trapped in hell with no escape.

"How does he study?"

Eliza shrugs. "You'll have to ask him that."

We're silent for a few minutes as we pick at the food in the center of the counter, and I put mayonnaise on a croissant sandwich (and a little bit of mustard) before scarfing the entire thing down.

I'm eating my feelings, and Eliza notices.

"Are you sure you're going to be okay?"

"Eliza—I'll be fine." I smile to prove it. "This isn't my first rodeo—granted, it's the first rodeo where the stallion didn't stop himself from banging other horses...allegedly." I add an eye roll for good measure.

She snorts out a laugh. "That was seriously the worst analogy."

"Sorry, that's the best one I could come up with on such short notice." I lick my fingers. "I'm going to take some time for myself. I'm always in a relationship, and this will be good, being single for a while and focusing on *me* and what I want."

Eliza nods along. "I think that's a great idea."

"I've always had a boyfriend." I hate admitting it, but I usually waste no time going from one to another if I break up with someone or he breaks things off with me. Relationship jumper—isn't that what it's called?

Yeah...that's me.

Embarrassing but true. I *love* being in relationships. The problem is, they're typically with immature, emotionally stunted guys who haven't grown up yet and don't know what they want. Spoiled guys with egos. Popular, good-looking men who women hit on and who people always want to chat up, causing them to seek attention in every which direction.

That's been my type, and it hasn't been working.

Something has to change, and that something is *me*.

Me.

I need to change.

*What do I want?*

I don't know.

I've spent my entire life being told what to do by my parents, my mother, my coaches and teachers—I finally feel like I'm at the point where it's time for me to decide what I want. And it's only taken me twenty-one years to realize it.

"I think it's wonderful that you want to take some time for yourself, Lilly. It's time for a little bit of self-love. And you can start by eating some of these chocolate-dipped strawberries." She pushes the little plate toward me and I nick a berry from it, sinking my teeth into it with a scrumptious moan.

"Darn this is good—where did you get these?"

"I made them this morning. It was really easy, all I did was get some meltable chocolate at the grocery store and voila."

I steal another one. "How come you never cooked or put out food like this when we lived together? Maybe Kaylee wouldn't have asked you to leave. Ha."

"Oh, you're a comedian now? Lilly has jokes?" Eliza rolls her eyes and pulls the plate away from me. "No more for you."

"Oh come on, I'm just kidding! Besides, you know Kaylee would have asked you to leave no matter what—she's such a brat and you didn't deserve the way she treated you. Like I said, I had no idea she was behaving that way or that she'd asked you to move out because you were dating Jack, and if I had...I would have done something. I wouldn't have let her treat you like shit."

"I know she's a brat," she says. "I also know she was just jealous. That's human nature." Eliza shrugs her shoulders inside her gray sweatshirt. "What are you going to do about it, right?"

"Um, call her out on her bullshit—that's what you can do about it." I pause to chew so I'm not speaking with my mouth full. Swallow. "She's not completely horrible these days, but she's not completely pleasant either. We're getting by, but... things just aren't the same. The house isn't the same since you moved out. I miss you."

"You always were my favorite of the two." Eliza laughs.

"Duh, obviously."

"Also, Kyle can suck your dick. You were way too good for him. You know that, right?"

I mean—Kyle was the running back on the football team and a visible guy on campus so I'm sure plenty of people would beg to differ with her assessment, but those people also don't know the *real* Kyle.

Still, I can use a bit of fluffing these days, and I'll take any ego boosting I can get.

"I'm not kidding, Lill. You're too kind-hearted for a guy like that. You're kind and sweet and *good*." Eliza stands and comes around the counter to give me a side hug, squeezing my shoulders and kissing me on the cheek. "I love you, friend. You're one of the best people I know."

Just then—and before I can reply—a guy walks into the kitchen carrying a cardboard box, tall and broad with hair just long enough to pull back into a short ponytail.

Dirty blonde.

Looks kind of like a surfer at the beach, if you don't count the fact that he has no tan.

He pauses—halting when he sees us sitting at the counter with Eliza's arms wrapped around me. I'm sure it looks as if he's interrupting something intimate, an emotional and heartfelt moment between friends.

"Sorry, I..." He stammers, glancing around the room as if searching for a place to flee. Locates the nearest exit. "Jack said I can store some of my things in the garage?"

My friend releases me with another gentle squeeze before rising to her full height. "Oh sure. Here, let me get the door for you—that looks heavy."

I watch as my former roommate goes to the side door and opens it for her new roommate, feeling a little regretful about the way things went down with her moving out. Though we are still friends, I have a lot of remorse about the way I allowed Kaylee to treat her. I know I cannot control how people behave, but I could have intervened.

There's no way of knowing whether or not Eliza would have stayed with us or gone, but she would have at least known I was on her side from the beginning.

The new guy disappears outside, returning a few minutes later with a new box, this one with the word FRAGILE neatly scrawled in black marker across each of its four sides.

I study him and his eyes glance around the room.

He has an oddly familiar vibe.

*Have we met before?*

Hmm...

I try not to stare, and he actively avoids looking at me altogether as Eliza, standing near my chair, watches us both. Brows raised but otherwise not commenting on the weird behavior.

He wants to say something—probably to Eliza—but seems

to feel self-conscious with me here, and I can tell he's on the shy side. Definitely not an extrovert.

I have my days; sometimes I'm outgoing, sometimes I'm not, sometimes I'm both.

He blinks over at me.

Opens his mouth to speak then snaps it shut. Hefts the box again to redistribute the weight.

So awkward...

"You must be the new roommate," I say at last to break the silence Eliza refuses to fill, damn her. "I'm the old one."

"I am."

"Rome, this is Lilly."

"Do I know you? You seem familiar."

The guy fumbles with the box he's carrying, nearly dropping it to the floor and blushing beet red in the process.

I wink at him.

This time he does drop his box, the undeniable sound of glass shattering echoing throughout the kitchen.

We all freeze.

Oh shit, that didn't sound good, not good at all.

"Shit." Rome drops to his knees and begins to pry open the box, his entire body sagging when both flaps are peeled back and he peers inside. He goes slack, shoulders hunched over in defeat.

Eliza goes around to stand behind him, and I join her as the three of us look inside.

"What is that?"

Whatever it was, it was sparkly and is now in a million bits, the base of something and its top broken into sharp chunks of debris.

I move to kneel beside him to get a closer look.

"That looks like it could have been an Emmy Award," I say breathlessly, touching the shards of glass gingerly so I don't get one stabbed into the tip of my finger. "What was it actually?"

"It's—it *was* a Cambridge Stein Scholarship Award," he says quietly at long last, after staring holes into the already broken glass. It still shimmers under the light.

I feel absolutely terrible, though I'm not the one who dropped the box and broke the award.

Still.

It's obviously a very important memento for him, and now it's in shambles.

"What was it for?"

He struggles to gulp in a breath. "I won an award to attend Cambridge University in the UK—I spent last semester there."

Shit.

"That sounds prestigious."

"It was."

"I'm so sorry it's broken," I tell him quietly, placing a hand on his shoulder. "Guess we're both having a bad day."

He doesn't ask what that means or why I'm having a bad day, only shakes his head once. I remove my palm, and he regains the ability to take air into his lungs. "It's just a bit of glass. I have the memories from living there in here." He taps on his forehead. "I don't need this as a reminder."

But still...

"We could glue it together?" Jack—Eliza's roommate and boyfriend—strolls into the kitchen as the new guy dumps the pieces back into his box. "Might look like utter shite, but at least you'd still have it."

"I love mosaics. I can do it for you!" I volunteer enthusiastically, suddenly perking up. "I used to take classes at a pottery shop in high school, and we did artwork with shards. You should let me try to get it back in one piece."

"Really, it's fi—"

But the box is already in my arms and I'm already standing, commandeering his busted award.

"Nope. I'm going to fix this."

I am going to make this right.

After all, this was partially my fault. If he hadn't been staring at me shyly and I hadn't winked at him, perhaps he wouldn't have dropped the box in the first place and his award would still be intact.

Yes.

I'll fix it for him, one way or another.

# CHAPTER 3
# ROMAN

Well that couldn't have been more awkward.

Just kidding—it was worse than all that.

Who drops a box because a pretty girl winks at him? That's something that would happen to a nerd in a movie—except in the movie scenario, the nerd would also have wet his pants and humiliated himself, so at least I didn't do that.

I'm bad, but I'm not that bad, although one thing was glaringly obvious: I have a lot of work to do on myself when it comes to girls and dating and my comfort level with being myself around them. If I was a little more confident, I wouldn't have dropped that box and gone frozen when Lilly looked at me.

*"Do I know you?"* she asked, and I was too stunned to say, "Yes, we met when we were freshmen, we sat for an hour on the stairs at a party and spilled our guts to each other. I can't believe you recognize me."

I've changed a lot in the last three years, and she has too. I could see plainly in her eyes that she's matured—I could also see some hurt, although I obviously don't have a clue what the story is behind the tired expression and the drooping shoulders when she was sitting at the counter.

Lilly was only too eager to jump up and help me without even knowing who I was. We may not have a history, but we did certainly spend a lot of time sitting and talking and sharing private thoughts with each other. I remember her telling me about her mother, and I wonder if that relationship has gotten any better. I remember telling her I still lived at home and recall the look on her face when I said I had never lived anywhere else.

*"What dorm are you in?"*

*"I'm not in the dorms. I still live at home."*

*"How do you still live at home?"* I remember her voice sounded as shocked as the expression on her face. *Live at home? Why the hell would you do that?* it said.

Because I thought my family *needed* me there, and I've only just now realized my being home simply enables my mother to gallivant around and do whatever she damn well pleases while I pick up the slack.

*"I'm local. It only takes me fifteen minutes to get here, so to save money, I'm not living in the dorms."*

*"Oh." She paused, still not convinced living at home as an adult made any sense at all. "How is* that *working out for you?"*

It was working out...until it *wasn't*, and here I am schlepping boxes into a house with two people I've only known a day so I can finally break free and have some independence.

The room I'm renting is actually larger than the one I have at home—my parents didn't make any of the bedrooms big because they didn't want us to hang out in them, rather they wanted us to hang out in the loft above the living room and in the basement with the large entertainment and media room.

Family time is what my parents cherish most, and so, my

bedroom in their very large house is actually quite small, which was their attempt at forcing us out.

Of the rooms, I mean.

Well.

It worked because I have no privacy.

I didn't bring a ton of things to move into this new space, but Mom did let me bring all my bedding and the curtains I had hanging in my room so it will feel like this one is my own. I make short work of folding up and storing the current comforter and sheets in the closet, tucking them out of the way in the top right corner.

Next, I unpack my toiletries and stock up the bathroom cabinet with shaving creams, aftershave lotions, and hair products. Things I never thought I would actually use on a regular basis have become my regular routine. It's not that I'm a metrosexual, but I'm probably close enough.

I run a finger through my shaggy hair, the one thing I let go while I was overseas, the longer locks falling to my shoulders in dirty blonde waves. Next, I run a hand across the stubble covering my cheeks and chin, in no rush to shave any of it off. I feel more masculine this way—my appearance is probably the reason Lilly didn't recognize me.

After I'm done putting things away, I survey the bathroom: burgundy shower curtain that actually matches the quilt on my bed and a coordinating rug on outdated tile floor. They're tiny gray squares straight out of the seventies.

I pull back the shower curtain to put my shampoo, conditioner, and razor on the small ledge. Suction-cup a round mirror beneath the showerhead so I can shave there if I feel like it. Less mess to clean up at the sink.

I take a quick piss then return to the bedroom and unpack a box of school supplies I brought, starting with the many science books I've acquired over the years written by numerous experts in the mathematics field. Just some light reading, you know. It's actually been ages since I've read anything fictional for pleasure, not even to put myself to sleep at night. There are only so many hours in the day, and I like to use them to fuel my brain with knowledge—I'm always on a quest to get ahead and graduate early.

I don't always have a mind for mathematics, but it typically ties into everything and therefore I want to stay sharp.

My mind goes back to Lilly.

I could kick myself for the missed opportunity when she asked if she knew me. She cocked her head and studied my face, and in that instant I could feel the recognition in her gaze—the problem is I'm too much of a pussy to have said anything even though she presented me with the perfect opportunity. I'm always missing out on perfect opportunities unless they're academic, and sometimes I hate myself for it.

I wish I were more ballsy. My younger brother has bigger balls than I do most of the time. But maybe that's just because he's younger and spoiled and hasn't had to work for anything.

My parents weren't always wealthy—I remember them being on food stamps when I was younger because my dad was just starting at my grandfather's business—they never received a dime from the family unless they earned it.

Both of them had to pay for college, working full time while going to school—which I personally can't imagine doing; not with the course load I have now.

Mom doesn't have much of a hand at the office anymore—she stopped working there when my brother was born—before that, they leveraged the only car we had to get a small loan for the tiny house I grew up in, robbing Peter to pay Paul as my dad said.

They didn't start the company but never quit hustling and always worked, sometimes to the detriment of the family.

Which is why I think Mom has such a strong hold on Alex and I now; all of the years not being there because she was in the office.

Granted, she was working alongside my dad—but the truth is neither one of them were there for me.

Not really.

Rarely were they at my soccer games, rarely were they at the Science Fairs or Debates.

They relied on my grandmother to keep an eye on me before my brother came along.

And now they rely on me to keep an eye on Aunt Myrtle, who is very similar to a small child. Not because she's incapable of anything, but because she requires so much attention—she's a shifty little thing, and if you turn around for one second, she gets into trouble. No one enjoys having an old man show up at the doorstep unannounced to take her on a date.

Or one who's been invited to family dinner.

It happens all too often, and it became my job to wrangle her.

Anyway.

Guess that's another reason, more or less, that I haven't dated. No time.

My phone is on my new desk, and it pings.

**Mom:** *Do you have a minute?*

**Me:** *To talk?*

**Mom:** *Yes, on the phone.*

I hate talking on the phone, but oftentimes Mom won't let me get away with just texting.

**Me:** *Yeah, I have a minute—I'm just unpacking.*

Two seconds later, it rings.

"Hey babycakes, how's it going? How's your new house?"

"It's good." I stare into the box sitting on the desk chair. "I'm just now starting to unpack all my stuff—got the bathroom organized and now I'm unpacking all my school supplies."

Mom is quiet for a few seconds before admitting, "I really wish you would've let your dad and me come to help you move in."

"I don't have that much stuff, Mom."

I'm not about to tell her I wasn't going to risk needing their help because along with Mom and Dad come my brother and my great aunt, who always seem to be in tow.

I know it's not their fault, but it's extremely inconvenient. You can't have one without the other these days, and the pair of them get into so much mischief it's like having a set of fraternal twins with a seventy-one-year age gap.

"Are you still coming home this weekend for Sunday dinner?"

My mother started this thing a few years ago where she makes spaghetti every Sunday—along with garlic and cheesy bread—and forces everyone to be home to sit around the big dining room table for a few hours of bonding. First, she'll ask how everyone's day was, and then she'll ask what the best part of their day was even though we typically spend each and every weekend up each other's asses.

Then she'll tell us the plans coming for the following weekend so we can add it to our calendars—like going to the apple farm, or the movies, or a fundraiser organized by one of her neighborhood mom friends.

"I think I can come for Sunday dinner."

I mean, the ride is twenty minutes and wouldn't be a hardship.

I should probably stay home and make nice with my two new roommates considering we haven't spent any time together, but they're both really busy, and the last thing I want to do is insert myself or invite myself to anything they've got going on. I already feel like a giant loser; I don't need to make it worse.

"Why don't you bring your roommates along? Dad and I would love to meet them."

"Or, maybe next time? It might be too soon to introduce them to Aunt Myrtle." I laugh.

Mom laughs too. "Yes, you could be right." She pauses. "Is there anything you want this weekend for dinner instead of spaghetti? I could prepare something else, like steak? Or shrimp? Do you want sushi? Maybe we could do pizza."

She's trying so hard—I feel guilty because it's obvious she's not sure what to do without me being there. My mother's whole purpose is being a mom, and she has to find her way again now that I've left the nest; who knows, I may never live there again.

Kind of a depressing thought, yeah?

"Mom, spaghetti is fine. You know I'll eat whatever you set in front of me."

"You don't sound thrilled." It sounds like *she* is pouting.

"Don't change what you've been doing for the past two years because I'm gone."

"But..." Her voice trails off. "I like having you home."

"Mom, I've never been gone."

"You left and went to Europe."

That's true. "But that was only for a semester, and you and Dad came to visit." Mostly she shopped, did high tea, and played tourist while I was at class, but yeah—it's not as if she didn't see me in the time I was gone.

Plus, she FaceTimed me and called every chance she got.

Mom seriously needs to cut the cord.

She's acting like I flew back over the ocean, never to be seen again, when in actuality it will only take me twenty minutes to drive home when she wants to see me and twenty minutes for them to visit.

I knew I should have applied to NYU...

I'm internally grumbling, letting the silence stretch.

"Roman, are you still there?" Mom taps on the phone as if testing out a microphone. "Hello?"

"I'm here. I was just thinking."

"About what? Tell your mother."

She's always saying that: tell your mother—as if those words are going to make me spill my guts and confess all of my sins.

Sins. Ha!

The list would be embarrassingly short, not that I'm perfect. It's just that I'm...boring.

I'd have to leave my desk chair to commit a sin, and I haven't done that in years, which brings me to my new digs.

*Freedom to make some bad choices.*

"About..." How excited I am to be living on my own! "Your garlic bread."

"Oh stop. It's so easy I can practically make it in my sleep. It's no big deal."

I roll my eyes at her false modesty.

"Have you met anyone yet?"

Met anyone? "What do you mean?"

"You know," Mom hedges. "Girls."

"Mom, I have lived here exactly—" I check the watch circling my left wrist. "Five hours."

"Well how would I know the house isn't filled with people? You didn't let us come help move you in," she points out again. I have a feeling I'll be hearing about this a lot; my mother is not one to let things go.

"I told you—I live with two people, Jack and Eliza. Jack is from Britain—I got his number from his brother Ashley, whom I met a few times while I lived there. Eliza is his girlfriend."

Mom is quiet. "I just don't know how I feel about you living with a couple. It feels weird. It's not that I mind you living with a girl. It's just...I don't want you to feel left out because they're together. And God forbid they have sex in the living room. What if you hear them?"

My face flushes as she goes on talking about sex and thin walls and how when she was in college, her freshman roommate Nicole used to have sex with her boyfriend in the bottom bunk while she lay in the top bunk. I try to remind her this *isn't* the dorms and we're adults and both Jack and Eliza seem very respectful—at least they did when I met them so they could interview me and I them for this roommate position.

"It'll be okay, Mom. I'm not worried they're going to have sex where I eat breakfast."

She needs to stop worrying and stop fabricating excuses for me not to live here—I should have moved out when I started school, but I didn't, and now there is no looking back. There is no Alex busting through this door. There is no rushing around to pick up Aunt Myrtle from an appointment or set an extra space at the table for one of her boyfriends. Or listen to her telling me about her singles over seventy dating app.

Mom makes no comment on my sex-for-breakfast quip and instead brings up Sunday supper once more. "Say you'll come on Sunday."

"I thought I did like three times?"

"Just making sure." Mom laughs.

"I'm not going to ghost you, Mom. I'm only living twenty minutes away—I've been taking classes here for two years." Two and a half if you count the semester last year before studying abroad.

"I know, I know, I just worry."

"Worry about what? That I'm going to run out of gas on my way home? Or that I can't manage on my own? I know how to do laundry and make my own dinner, for crying out loud—you taught me how to do all those things, Mom. You don't have to worry that I'm not going to survive. Were you this worried when I lived in England?" Because she nagged me way less than she's nagging me now.

"Of course I was worried. But I knew you were coming home."

That makes sense—she wasn't as freaked out because she knew I was going to be back in her house and down the hall, but instead I came home, packed up my things, and moved into a new house entirely, and that has her reeling.

"Are you sure you don't want to bring your roommates along with you? They might really enjoy a home-cooked meal."

My mother makes one last semi-desperate attempt to get me to bring my new friends home—probably so she can cross-examine them and do background checks and give them the third degree. God, I can't even imagine what that would be like.

*Who knew she was going to be this overprotective?*

I kind of feel bad for Alex; he's going to be taking the brunt of her missing me. Although, I have a sneaking suspicion that within a few months, she will have completely redecorated my bedroom and turned it into either a guestroom or a hangout lounge for my brother. Or possibly even a craft room for herself—lately she has begun knitting, and that might be a sweet spot for her to have some peace and quiet.

No doubt Alex would stay out of her yarn room.

Ha ha.

"Yeah, I'm sure I don't want to bring my roommates home for dinner." Not just yet. I want to get to know them a little bit first.

"Alright, if you're sure." I hear her thinking through the telephone line. "I can always make enough so there are left-overs you can take home—home." She laughs. "I can't even believe I'm saying that. You have a new home! It makes me want to cry. My little baby is growing up."

Ignore the comment about me being her little baby.

"Leftovers would be nice—I have a feeling Jack would eat anything I put in the fridge. He is one of those guy's guys. Totally looks like a garbage disposal."

"Okay, that's the plan then," Mom says, clapping her hands the way she always does when she's settled on an idea. "I'll go grocery shopping—in the meantime, if you change your mind about inviting them, let me know."

"I will."

But I won't change my mind, and I don't change my mind because it just feels weird to invite two strangers to my house, two strangers I'm living with.

After I end the call with Mom, I finish taking everything out of the boxes and have almost everything put in place. The last thing I remove, I remove from my pocket—the friendship bracelet Lilly gave me those three years back when we were both freshmen. Clueless and a little bit scared.

I've held on to it, obviously, and stuck it in my pocket before leaving my mother and father's house for this one.

It goes on the dresser beneath the window overlooking the backyard, probably never to be worn on my wrist again, at least not if Lilly is going to be hanging around this house.

What are the freaking odds that she would be my new roommate's best friend and old roommate?

*What.*

*Are.*

*The.*

*Odds.*

I didn't even know how to react when I walked into the kitchen and saw her sitting on the seat at the counter, nibbling on pizza and vegetables as if she belonged there. She definitely looked like she feels more comfortable here than I do, but I imagine that will change over time.

Since I can't stay holed up in this bedroom forever, I tidy everything up one last time before making my way downstairs. I'm kind of hoping there is still food in the kitchen because I'm starving and didn't actually eat before because Lilly was here and she makes me nervous as hell.

She made me nervous the night we met, and apparently not much has changed. I like to think I'm not the same bumbling, nervous idiot I was as a first-year college student, but I'm still the same bumbling, nervous idiot. I'm twenty-one years old, for goodness' sake—you would think I would be able to talk to a girl without fumbling. Or dropping a box that wasn't even heavy to begin with.

The only thing inside that box was my award, and it only weighs a few pounds. It was wrapped in bubble wrap, apparently not very well since it broke.

How embarrassing.

Lilly took the trophy with her, and I can't imagine what she's going to do with the damn thing, broken into a million pieces.

Guess time will tell.

I make my way downstairs, listening for the sound of my roommates, and hear the television on in the living room. It sounds like they're watching an action film, and soon enough I discover that the fireplace is going and they moved some of the food into that room.

Awesome.

It's freezing outside and the perfect night to veg.

"What are you guys watching?" I can't quite figure out what movie or show this is.

"It's called Bambulon—they just released the first two seasons yesterday," Jack explains, patting the couch cushion. "Come sit down, mate, put your feet up."

"Thanks."

I walk over to the couch and flop down, relieved I can finally relax, and reach forward to snag a carrot from the vegetable tray. Actually, I take a handful of them and lean back to stuff them in my mouth one at a time, crunching and swallowing for the next few minutes.

No one talks.

I crunch.

And I don't wanna be the asshole who makes noise while they're trying to watch their show, so I stop eating the carrots, too.

Eliza eats a chip.

It's loud and as crunchy as the carrots I just ate.

"Sorry." She giggles.

"Do you like horror movies, Rome?" Jack asks. "Eliza and I find Marvel movies brilliant, but we love scary programs, too."

"We started our Halloween marathon early," she explains. "It's my favorite holiday."

Do I like horror movies? Not particularly, but I'm not about to sit up in my room alone while these two are down here being social. "Sure, I like them well enough. Mostly, um..." I wipe my sweaty palms on my jeans.

Should I tell them I like musicals and dramas?

Er, maybe not—that information can wait until the day Jack finds me geeking out to the *Hamilton* soundtrack.

"Will you decorate the house?" I ask, despite already knowing an answer. She is definitely going to decorate the house, especially if she's already watching scary movies in preparation.

"Um, obviously." She says it with a delightful little laugh. "In fact, we've been sitting here kind of discussing what we want to dress up as for Halloween. There's a big party at the end of the month, and of course we have to pass out candy to trick-or-treaters."

Jack puts his hand on her thigh, and I can see him squeeze it. "Babe, you're discussing what you want to be for Halloween. I'm trying to watch the telly." He shakes his head when our eyes meet.

"Fine, I'll stop talking about it."

They're funny and get along well.

I made a good decision to move in here.

Stretching my legs out in front of me, I prop one up on the coffee table since I'm not wearing any shoes and have socks on. It feels good, and I put my arms behind my head as I lean into the sofa cushions.

"Sorry about that whole thing with your award breaking today," Eliza finally says. "Lilly felt terrible."

"It was not Lilly's fault I dropped the box. In fact, the box only weighed about five pounds."

"What happened?"

Jack pauses the show.

"I'm not sure. One second I was walking through the door, and the next second the box was on the ground. I'm the one who feels like a complete jackass—she shouldn't feel bad. Not at all."

"Well, you're in for a real treat, because she is a great artist. I know you probably wanted to throw the entire box out, but when she has her mind set on something, there's no stopping her."

"Yeah, I probably should have thrown it out or insisted that she not take it—what if she cuts herself?"

Shit, I hadn't actually thought about that part of the equation. What if she is at home partying and crafting and hurts herself on the glass? One hundred percent not worth it, not worth any of the trouble she's going to go through because she feels culpable.

*You dropped the box the second she winked at you, loser.*

"Can you text her for me and tell her to toss it in the trash?"

Eliza grinned at me. "Yeah, no. That's not happening. Once she decides on something, that's it—specifically if she's looking for a project." She probably has something on her mind and needs a distraction, which is why she was so adamant about taking it home. "Let it be. She wanted to do it or she wouldn't have taken it. Trust me."

My new roommate winks at me the same way Lilly did.

I'm unaffected by it.

"How long have you known her?" I ask Eliza.

"We met when I was a freshman so it's only been a few years, but I really love her." Beside her, Jack takes her hand then lifts it to his mouth for a kiss. "Aw babe, I love you too."

They are a bit mushier than I was expecting them to be, but a little PDA can't be considered a bad thing. We need more love in this world, as Aunt Myrtle always says. Every chance she gets, especially when she gets busted dating multiple men at once.

Which happens more often than one would expect.

"Lilly is one of my best friends—she has a heart of gold and wouldn't hurt a fly. That's why I'm so pissed off that Kyle is such a scumbag. I mean, I knew he was a scumbag, but it's not like you can tell your friend that, right?" She turns to face Jack for confirmation. "Right, sweetie?"

He agrees. "I've never met the bloke, but based on how

you've described him, he sounds like a fine arsehole. Probably wouldn't use the word scumbag to describe him though, love —that seems a bit harsh."

"And calling him an arsehole isn't?" Eliza pouts. "Lilly is my friend—of course I'm going to be protective. I should've known something was up with him. He just was way too charming."

She narrows her eyes.

Jack looks down at her, tilting his head. "Did he ever flirt with you?"

"No, but still."

I study both of them.

Eliza truly looks like a nice girl, if you know what I mean. The girl-next-door-with-brunette-hair vibe, all sweet with a sincere smile and honest eyes. She has a few darker freckles on the bridge of her nose that make her look more trusting if a person was stereotyping solely based on looks, so I highly doubt she gets hit on very often—just not the flirty type.

"I worry she's not going to trust anyone after this. You know how it is, once someone has completely abused your trust? She told me she is going on a guy detox, and I just don't want that to affect future relationships."

"You're not going to try to set her up with anyone, are you?" Jack asks her.

"No. I don't have anyone to set her up with, unless...you do?"

"I don't know anybody but the chaps on the rugby team," Jack says. "And none of them well enough I would consider matching her with—so don't start cooking up any schemes."

"I just told you she doesn't wanna date anyone. I'm not going to try to set her up."

"I *heard* what you said." Jack grins. "I just don't think you're going to listen."

Eliza leans back to get a better look at him, glancing between the two of us. “Do you believe this guy? He doesn’t trust me to behave,” she says to me. “It sounds like he doesn’t trust me not to meddle in my best friend’s love life—that’s what I’m hearing.”

“Are you going to meddle in your best friend’s love life?” I find myself joining the conversation.

She scoffs. “Not right now. She needs some time.”

We continue watching the show, occasionally commenting on a scene or getting up and going to the kitchen for more drinks or food, the amiable companionship a nice change from the drama and chaos that usually occurs at my parents’ house on a night where we’re trying to watch TV.

My brother isn’t here to heckle me or try to change the channel, and my great aunt isn’t here to constantly ask me for small favors. Like getting her some more ice for her glass, or turning up the volume, or turning down the volume, or running to get her some fuzzy socks because her feet are cold.

All in all, it’s been a pretty damn good day.

# CHAPTER 4
# LILLY

It's Sunday.

It's Sunday and I've spent my free time this entire weekend—between practice, cheering, and working out—painstakingly gluing this award back into its rightful shape. I had to research online to see what the thing is actually supposed to look like, and I must say, I did a pretty dang good job replicating it considering I had nothing to go on but broken glass.

It wasn't easy making it resemble its former self, but luckily, a bunch of the pieces were intact enough that Roman's name is visible.

Legible.

Sort of?

The rest is hodgepodge.

I'm not sure what his full name actually is because the letters of his last name appear to be missing from the shards and I wasn't sure what his last name was to begin with—I feel like this looks okay?

I hold it up and study it in the light, tilting it this way and that. I went to the hobby store as soon as I left Eliza's house and got some clear glitter—the super fine kind that's more expensive and lustrous—to fill in the gaps with.

The whole thing sparkles like a diamond.

I'd even added a few clear rhinestones to the back to patch up a few holes. It looks like a trophy that would be presented during a lip-syncing competition or as a white elephant gift, but at least he will still have it to display on his shelf.

All in all, I'm quite pleased.

Laying it out on my desk, I roll it in a towel so it's safe when I put it back into its box. Clean up the mess I've made in my bedroom, getting out the vacuum and rolling it back and forth across the carpet beneath the desk.

My roommate sticks her head in the room and watches me until she catches my eye and I turn off the loud vacuum.

"Want to come do my room next?" she teases, although I have a feeling there's a bit of truth to her question—Kaylee would gladly allow me to do the cleaning in the entire house, including her bedroom.

"Yeah right," I tease back. "Should I do your windows too?"

I hate cleaning. There is no way on this earth I'm doing her windows, let alone her carpet. The dust on my shelves is the same dust that has been there since the day we moved in.

"Sure, why not?" She leans against the doorjamb. "What on earth are you doing anyway? You've been in here for hours."

I have been, and now I am starving.

"I was crafting." Finished with the carpet, I wind the cord before hanging it back on the handle of the vacuum. "I was working on something for a friend, and now I have to go take it over to his place."

"Oh a friend? Is this a male friend?"

I did just say *his* place.

And she says it in *that* way, her tone implying there is more to this male than friendship—but she would be wrong, and I suppose I'm not really in the mood for her banter.

"Eliza and Jack have a new roommate, and he broke a glass trophy when he was moving in so I decided I was going to fix it up for him."

"Let me see."

I don't mind letting her look, especially since piecing everything back together was a lot of work—I don't mind showing it off to her.

I'm shocked, however, that Kaylee made no comment when I mentioned Eliza and Jack.

See, the three of them have a history, and not a positive one.

I mentioned a few times that Eliza used to be my roommate; well, Kaylee is the reason she's no longer living in this house. Kaylee is the reason we have an empty room. Some people might blame Jack and Eliza—they began liking each other when Kaylee and Jack were talking.

Never fooled around or anything, had never even gone on an official date. But Kaylee met him first and befriended him first and had a crush on him first—which means she automatically considered him...hers. She found him so no one else could keep him.

The night she found out Eliza had befriended Jack, things went downhill, and shortly thereafter?

Our trio became a duo.

Carefully unfolding the newly repaired trophy, I set it down gently in the center of my desk, aware that my roommate is sometimes critical of things she doesn't understand.

As if on cue, she wrinkles up her nose.

"What on earth is that supposed to be?"

"Judging by your tone, I gather you aren't impressed with my skills." I laugh, wiping a smudge off the center name plate.

"Um, maybe I'd be impressed if I knew what it was."

"It's an award he won for a scholarship—a very prestigious scholarship." Pride laces my tone for a guy I've only just met, and I feel strangely protective.

"It looks fancy. Is it for like, yachting or something?"

Wow.

Not even close.

"No, it's an academic scholarship. He won a semester at Cambridge University in England."

Kaylee is also not impressed by this information.

"Oh, so he's a *nerd*?"

A nerd?

What is she, ten?

"I wouldn't call him a nerd. He won this because he's *smart*."

Smart may be putting it mildly; I have a suspicion Roman is actually brilliant and was downplaying the significance of his award. I did a little bit of digging while I was researching photographs of the award online to get an idea of how to reconstruct it and discovered very few college students in the United States receive the honor.

If no eligible applicants apply, there have been years no one has won it.

Furthermore, it's not easy to gain entrance into Cambridge.

Like, *at all*.

I take offense at Kaylee's criticism and comments about Roman and bristle, straightening my spine.

*What an asshole.*

I say none of these things out loud, because pissing her off has consequences I'm not in the mood to deal with—those or the bad attitude that usually follows. So I zip my lips and study the trophy anew.

It shines like a disco ball, and while I love it and think it turned out great, he'll probably be horrified by the shininess. Then again, perhaps he'll also love it in its new form?

One can hope!

"You made that?" Kaylee's voice is laced with disdain—it sounds as if she's eating a sour lemon.

I shake my head. "I didn't make it. I just told you—it broke and I'm fixing it. He dropped the box it was in and it shattered and I felt absolutely terrible."

"Is this a guy you're interested in? Do you like him? As more than a friend?"

Is she serious? I just discovered my boyfriend of four months was cheating on me and she honestly believes I'm going to put myself back on the dating market so soon afterward? I'm beginning to think she doesn't know me well at all.

"No, he's just a really nice guy."

She considers this, and I know doing something nice for someone for no reason and getting nothing in return is a difficult concept for her to understand. It's not a concept she is used to.

"So you don't want to date anybody?"

I'm failing to understand how, from her perspective, me fixing this jazzy award and turning it from nothing back into something is somehow me wanting this guy to take me on a date.

Not to judge her, but she has led a charmed life; she's a very spoiled person, and I want her out of my room. Taking the towel I had the trophy wrapped up in, I spread it back out on the surface of my desk then gingerly lay the award on top of it and fold it like a burrito.

Or a swaddled baby.

Back in the box it goes, away from her perusal.

I make a show of putting on my sneakers and shrugging into a hoodie, grabbing my car keys off of the hook near my door. "I think I'm going to run this back over to him. The glue is dry enough, and I can't wait for him to see it."

"Whatever floats your boat." She gets one last word in before disappearing down the hallway and retreating to her own bedroom.

I wait for the sound of her door closing before hefting the box and cautiously carrying it through the kitchen and out the side door. I set it on the ground while I unlock my car then place it in the back seat, using the seat belt to strap it in. God forbid I have to hit the brakes on my ride to Roman's place and the damn thing breaks all over again.

Can you even imagine?

That would be my luck.

The house is quiet when I arrive, pulling into the short driveway and parking my car in front of the detached garage. Jack's truck is gone and my ex-roommate doesn't have a car of her own, so I'm not sure if anyone will be home. I have no idea and no way of knowing if the Jeep parked on the curb belongs to Roman or one of the neighbors.

I retrieve the box baby from the back seat. Smooth back the hair escaping from my ponytail before knocking on the front door. Wait a few seconds before pressing the glowing button for the doorbell. No sound comes from inside the house, and there don't appear to be any lights on, at least not on the first floor.

Just as I give up and turn to go back to my car, the front door is pulled open.

It's Roman.

And he looks as if he's about to go somewhere, denim jacket covering a collared shirt he has tucked into dark jeans. His unkempt hair has been combed into a tidy style, and I will admit he kind of looks...cute?

Or perhaps I'm just surprised.

When we met, he looked as if he'd just run ten laps around a race track: exhausted, tired, and messy.

"I'm sorry," I hasten to apologize. "Are you about to go somewhere?"

*It's none of your business, Lilly!*

His eyes flit back and forth between my face and the box I'm holding in my arms, cradling it like the precious cargo it is.

He stuffs his hands in the pockets of his jeans. "Actually, yeah. I'm headed to my parents' place for Sunday dinner."

"Oh my gosh, I'm so sorry!" Technically I haven't done anything wrong and therefore there's no need to actually apologize—I just feel like an idiot for standing here holding a box in the middle of the afternoon, unannounced.

He looks as awkward about it as I feel. "Is that what I think it is?"

"Oh!" I remember the award in my hands, inside the box, inside the towel. "Yes! I'm done putting everything back together." Then, because I feel a babble coming on... "It's like Humpty Dumpty sat on the wall."

Er.

Sort of.

But not really.

"All the king's horses and all the king's men...er..."

*Stop talking, Lilly.*

"Couldn't put Humpty together again?"

"Yes. But as soon as I said it, I realized it doesn't actually make sense." I laugh nervously, holding up the box for him to take.

"I got what you meant." He smiles warmly.

*What a nice guy.*

Stepping out of the doorway, he invites me in with a sweep of his hand. "Wanna come in?"

"You have to leave and I don't want to keep you. Here." I

hold out the box so he can take it—and he does, but he still insists I come inside.

"There's no rush. It's just spaghetti, and it doesn't take me long to get there."

The box is in his arms now instead of mine, and I brush past him, stepping hesitantly up into the foyer.

It feels strange being here without Eliza—as if I'm invading her space or something, crashing the house to see her roommate and not her, though my intentions are pure.

Obviously.

Still, the house is almost eerily quiet, not a single peep. "Is everyone gone?"

Roman nods, closing the door behind me and locking it. I imagine when he leaves he'll go out the side door next to the garage. "Jack took Eliza to see some stand-up comedian who's doing a show downtown. They'll probably be home late. Maybe ten?"

"Oh, he took her to a show?" I sigh wistfully. "I love that for her."

He has nothing to say to that, nothing to say about my tone as a teeny-tiny pang of jealousy shoots through my stomach. Eliza has what I want: a boyfriend who dotes on her and treats her to nights out. I bet she got all dolled up, probably wore a dress and heels.

Er.

Or maybe not, as this is Eliza we're talking about. She's much more comfortable in jeans and a cute shirt or hoodie.

All I'm saying is, my last few boyfriends never did squat for me. I can't even recall going to dinner with Kyle—the nicest thing we did for a date night was the movies and the burger place next to campus, and that place is a bar.

Well. He's in the past, and I'm moving forward.

*I'm going to find me a guy like Jack...*

Honest and fun and considerate. At least, I'm assuming Jack is all those things, which I'm judging solely by the way he looks at Eliza and speaks to her. I've gleaned a lot about him in the short time I've seen them together as a couple. Plus, Eliza is a young woman of conviction, and I know the reason she hasn't dated anyone before Jack is because she would never put up with the same shit I've tolerated.

Her backbone is stronger, but I'm working on mine.

As I follow Roman through the house, he flips on the kitchen light before setting the box on the counter.

"I assume you brought this for me?" He taps the top of it with two fingers.

"Yes, it's your award." I wring my hands. "I've been working on it religiously since taking it back to my place."

He nods. "Let's check it out then."

Roman is smiling as he begins tentatively prying open the top of the box I put packing tape on, sealing the flaps down as though I were sending the item on a cross-country journey.

He is tall enough to peer inside before his hands dig around, reaching to carefully grasp it between two very large hands.

I do my best not to stare.

*You are not looking for a boyfriend, Lilly—you're not even looking for a boy that's a friend. Stop looking at him.*

Lifting it out slowly, this piece of glass wrapped in a towel, he lets out a low whistle. "Moment of truth, eh?"

I worry my bottom lip, fearful now that he'll be disappointed—the award is much different than it looked before it was ruined (based on my research), but I'm optimistic he'll be open-minded about the glitter and rhinestones.

Who doesn't want some sparkle in their life?

Roman lays the award on the counter like a baby—the same way I did—peeling back the layers one by one and unrolling the swaddling. Beneath the glow of the overhead light, the newly constructed masterpiece shimmers and sparkles, and I watch his face carefully, waiting for his reaction.

His eyebrows shoot up.

Mouth opens.

Closes.

Oh god. “Do you hate it?”

Roman finally lifts his gaze—his eyes are blue—as a smile spreads slowly across his mouth.

He rightens the award, resting it vertically on the counter.

“Wow, Lilly. This is...”

Horrible.

Ugly.

Stupid.

“...awesome.”

That perks me up, and I raise my chin. “Really? You don’t hate it?”

Rather than staring at me, he’s staring at the accolade as if seeing it for the first time—which he basically is. It was like a puzzle being pieced back together; all it required was patience and lots of super glue.

“No, I don’t hate it. This is amazing.” His hands hoist it up and his eyes inspect it. “Is this glitter glue or just glue you put glitter on?”

“Um, both,” I admit, face turning red as I put my fingers to my forehead. “My bedroom is an absolute mess. I’m going to have glitter everywhere for months.”

Roman studies my face, gaze going to my hairline. “You have some there. And there.” He points to it but doesn’t touch me.

“I love anything that sparkles,” I confess sheepishly, embarrassed that I am a grown adult who loves to craft. “I usually don't have time for it." This project fueled my soul for the short time it took me to complete it, in a way that cheerleading does not.

I should do it more often; maybe I should even consider taking an art class at the rec center—Lord knows I'd never be able to take one through the university. My mother would kill me. There's no chance in hell she would be willing to pay tuition costs for me to putter.

"You should do it more often—craft, I mean. This—what you've done—is incredible. Why don't you take an art class somewhere?"

Is he a mind reader?

I stare at him again, stupefied. "Get out of my brain." I laugh. "I would, but my parents would never go for it."

He's quiet, thinking to himself, brows furrowing. His head nods slowly. "Sure, I get that."

Self-consciously, I'm aware of the sky darkening outside, the intimate setting, the closeness of our bodies as we stand in this space, surrounded by complete silence.

It's getting late.

"I should go."

"You don't have to rush out."

Nor do I want to.

Leave, that is.

The truth is, I don't *want* to go back to my house—Kaylee is still home and she's in a mood, and even if I hang out in my bedroom, the vibes lingering in the air will be weird.

But Roman is being polite, and I should say my goodbyes and be on my merry way.

"Do you want to come to Sunday dinner with my family? My mom said I could bring my new roommates," Roman blurts out, the invitation coming out of nowhere. "Shit. Sorry, I'm not trying to be creepy."

I tilt my head. "What are you having?" Wait...what am I even talking about? No, no, no—I cannot go to some random dude's parents' house for dinner, some dude I just met. No.

"Spaghetti."

Duh, he said that already. Why does he make me so nervous that I forget myself?

"Spaghetti is my weakness and it's sweet of you to offer, but I really shouldn't."

His shoulders fall, but in a relieved kind of way. "Are you sure? It doesn't seem like you want to be alone."

We just met; how does this person keep reading my thoughts? "I can't ambush your family because I don't want to go home—that would be so weird."

I'm a grown-up; I can handle a salty roommate. Besides, it's not as if Kaylee hasn't been difficult before.

Dozens of times, actually.

"But do you want to be alone tonight?"

He knows I've had a rough go of it lately, and he's being kind.

I shrug. "I wouldn't technically be alone if I went home. My roommate is there. It's just...she's in a funk, which makes the mood at the house..." I search for the words. "*Off.*"

Off.

That's putting it mildly. When Kaylee is in a funk or a snit, she tends to make everyone else miserable. I could tell earlier when she came into my room she was itching to start an argument—about what, I do not know.

"She makes the mood off? What does that mean?"

"It's girl speak for 'The whole house feels weird and I have to tiptoe around because any little thing can set her off.'" She's probably getting her period, though I wouldn't dare say that to her face.

She'd metaphorically scratch my eyes out.

"Why don't you hang out here?"

"I can't just hang out here." Pause. "You don't think that would be weird?"

Roman's wide shoulders rise and fall in a shrug. "I'm sure Eliza and Jack wouldn't mind if you stayed here a while until you wanted to go home."

No, Eliza wouldn't mind—she's as kind and giving as a person could be—but would it be weird if I just hung out with no one here?

The idea has merit: lie low until Kaylee's mood swings back into a congenial direction. I have no studying to do—well, there is always studying to do, but I have nothing with me—and there is a new show streaming I wouldn't mind bingeing.

Kaylee and I had to get rid of a few monthly subscriptions after she kicked Eliza out; we're on a tighter budget until we can find a new roommate, so I haven't caught up on my favorites on an actual television.

"Know what? I think I'll take you up on that offer and stay."

Roman locates a set of car keys on the counter near the side door. "This door has a keypad so it'll lock automatically when you leave, if you leave while we're gone. I...um..." He glances down at his feet. "I'll be gone about two hours. I'm just doing dinner. Feel free to do whatever, and my room is upstairs if you'd rather watch the TV in there."

"I won't read your diary." Ha! "I pinky promise."

I hold out my hand so he can wrap his smallest finger around mine, but instead, he just stares down at my hand.

"Thanks a lot for doing this." Roman puts his hand on the base of the award still sitting in the center of the counter, thumb now brushing against the smooth glass. A lot of it was salvageable except the top part, so it's still distinguishingly an accolade...even though his name was part of the broken section.

"Gosh, I was so happy to. I feel terrible."

His head gives a slow shake. "It wasn't your fault I dropped the box."

"No, but that doesn't mean I can't feel sorry for you. The award was a really big deal, and you should have something to show for it."

Roman taps his head the same way he tapped it the day the box fell on the ground. "Still got those memories though."

He's brought that up twice, which means he's a bit sentimental. I think that's very sweet and cute.

I don't mention to him that as a cheerleader and someone who has competed in pageants almost her entire life, physical trophies are more important than memories—at least in my mother's opinion. She loved nothing more than to set another gold trophy on the shelf in my bedroom; it's almost as if she were the one winning.

Roman fumbles with his keys. "I should get going so I can get back at a decent hour—I still have some reading to do."

It doesn't surprise me that he will come home and study tonight, most likely into the wee hours of the morning. Unlike myself. I, on the other hand, plan to sit my lazy ass on the couch and binge whatever shows I can find that I've been missing.

Eventually, he goes.

I watch out the window as Roman climbs into his burgundy Jeep, turns the headlights on, buckles himself into the driver seat, and slowly pulls away from the curb. I watch until he's no longer in sight, his taillights glowing in the dark and the evening sky covering his departure.

Well. Now I'm definitely all alone, and somehow this alone feels even lonelier than it would if I were home. I'm not familiar with this house and I'm not familiar with two of the people who live here—the only person I know, obviously, is

Eliza...and I'm not sure we're good enough friends for me to be loitering alone in her personal space.

I feel like I'm creeping.

Heading to the fridge, I pull open the door to peer at the deliciousness inside. She has way more food than I do, and I'm delighted to find leftovers on the shelf; along with those I pull out a plate of pizza that's been covered with plastic wrap.

There are only three slices, so I put the entire thing into the microwave and hit the start button, pillaging one cabinet after the next to locate a glass for water. After I'm done warming up the food, I carry my plate and make toward the quaint living room off the kitchen where the television is. I futz around with the remote control, completely unable to figure out how to turn the darn thing on.

How hard can this be?

I hit the power button then hit it again, and the only thing that happens is the little red light on the television going on and off.

Well.

This isn't exactly the relaxing evening away from my own place that I hoped for.

It's dark now, but instead of turning on the light, I pick up myself and the plate—I've managed to inhale all the pieces of pizza in the short amount of time I've been screwing around with the TV—and take the plate to the kitchen, rinsing it off quickly before putting it into the dishwasher next to the sink.

Hmmm.

*Should I go or should I stay?* The latter seems useless if I'm just going to sit in the dark waiting awkwardly for my friends to return.

Roman told me to make myself at home, but that doesn't mean I should actually make myself at home. Part of him was just being polite; the other half...actually that half was probably just being polite, too.

Ultimately, I decide I'm going to have a look around—Eliza didn't give me a full tour when I was here over the weekend, mostly because Roman interrupted us then broke his award and I then exited with his box in tow.

My hand slides along the smooth wooden railing leading up to the second story where the bedrooms are, and I take the steps one by one as if in a horror movie with certain peril (i.e. bludgeoning death) waiting for me at the top of the stairs.

Lucky for me, there is a light switch at the top.

I flip it on.

The first bedroom I peek into is a small one with a desk and a couch in it, the only indication that it's actually a spare bedroom the closet. It's outdated with thick drapes and a gold lamp, a damask wallpaper still stuck to the walls.

I'm over to the next one, which winds up being the primary suite—at least I think it must be because the bed is huge. What's giving me pause is the comforter, a Spider-Man quilt more suited for a young person, not a grown-up.

I know for a fact both Jack and Eliza adore comics and film and Marvel, so this does seem fitting. A giant flat-screen television is on the opposite wall, and I poke around to find the large adjacent bathroom.

There's a big bathtub, a shower, double sinks, and a walk-in closet.

Lucky!

*A bath would be so amazing right now.*

I haven't taken one in ages, and maybe it would relieve some of this tension in my shoulders. I would never actually *do it*, but I totally want to.

Can you imagine if I climbed into the tub, made myself at

home, and then Eliza and Jack came home and I was up here bathing in a sea of bubbles?

They don't even know I'm here. How awkward would that be? Plus, it would probably be a dramatic scene when they discover me, unannounced, lounging in their bathroom naked.

I flip off the light and exit their bedroom, retracing my steps and heading back down the hallway to check out Roman's room. I push his door open farther before entering, a little desk lamp glowing on his bedside table.

He has managed to make it his own in a short amount of time, the shelving lining the walls already filled with awards and accolades, even a few medals draping from them. I walk over to them so I can inspect each and every one, my brows rising with interest as my eyes scan the engravings.

All of them are academic, which I already kind of assumed was the case.

On his bed is a basic comforter, but it looks really nice—expensive, even. At the foot of the bed is a trunk. Everything is neat and orderly, unlike my bedroom at home with its unorganized chaos.

I make my way over to the window so I can peer out into the backyard, down at the child's playset the previous owners of the house left behind. It's old and rusty and one of the chains for the swings has broken, limply falling to the ground in a heap.

I used to have a playset like this one in our backyard growing up—back when I was carefree and worry-free. Back before I started dancing and doing gymnastics, before my mother wouldn't let me play on it anymore for fear that I would get hurt and no longer be able to perform.

She worried I would break my arm and not be able to compete in pageants, and things never got better as I grew older; she only became more controlling—your stereotypical stage mom, wanting her daughter to be famous. I don't know what on earth she thought I would do with my life, but being in the entertainment business or being a professional dancer certainly wasn't, isn't, and never will be my dream come true.

We've already established the fact that I am only on the university's cheerleading team so I can pay my bills.

I release the curtain, letting it fall into place before turning back to Roman's bedroom. My fingers graze the top of his dresser, skimming along the wood the same way they grazed the banister rails. He has a small tray with change in it—a few pennies and some quarters—and a guitar pick. I glance around the room and don't see a guitar case anywhere, and I wonder if he got this from somewhere or if he actually plays.

Next, my eyes take in a few receipts, crumpled up and discarded. A pair of black-framed glasses. A bottle of cough medicine.

And a bracelet.

A bracelet.

It's a braided friendship bracelet, and it looks old and worn and oddly familiar—the same familiarity I felt when I first laid eyes on Roman and wondered if I knew him. The bracelet is made of my favorite colors and I used to make them all the time, painstakingly weaving them in my free time and giving them away to people, stacking them on my wrist one after the other. At one point, I had twenty-three bracelets on my arm.

*I gave him this bracelet.*

I gave Roman this bracelet when we were freshmen, and he kept it all these years.

Taking it from the dresser, I hold it between my fingers and sit myself down at the foot of his bed, working the fabric between my fingertips as if I were playing a tiny violin. The yarn has worn as if he's been doing the same thing over and over these past few years.

Threadbare.

Did he recognize me last weekend when we met, down in the kitchen? Did he already know my name? He didn't introduce himself as Rome that night at the party when we were sitting on the stairs talking, but honestly, the two variations aren't distinctly different at all, so I'm embarrassed I didn't make the connection.

*He must think I am a ditz.*

He must recognize me; I don't look that different than I did three years ago. I mean, sure, my hair is a lot longer than it used to be, and yes, I've had it highlighted and dyed more times than I can count since then. But I am the same person—my face is the same, I am the same height.

Roman, on the other hand...

He's gotten taller, a little bit bulkier, and has ditched the glasses. Not to mention his hair is longer and unkempt.

Making myself comfortable, I kick off my shoes and relax further onto his bed, positioning myself to rest against the wall. Locate the remote control for the TV and hit the power button—it goes on way easier than the living room television did.

I can't concentrate on anything except this bracelet in my hands, and I think about it the entire time I'm lying here propped up on Roman's fluffy pillows.

If he recognized me, why didn't he say anything? Why did he let me think we'd never met? Does he not want to be associated with me because I'm not smart? Is he the type of guy who only associates with intellectuals socially?

I'm not completely oblivious; I know there are people like that in this world—perhaps he is one of them.

No, Roman isn't like that. I don't know him well at all, but... my gut tells me he is a sincere person. He comes off as very humble, with his priorities in order. Most people would've gotten angry or upset that their trophy was all but destroyed, but he took it in stride, not losing his cool. Trying to make Eliza and me feel better when we expressed our remorse.

That is a man with his priorities in order.

*People* over things.

Roman is a good person.

His room? Neat as a pin.

Tidy, like he is, except for his unruly hair.

He had it back tonight, in a kind of man-bun.

I make myself even more comfortable, flipping through the channels, readjusting the pillows beneath my back and head as if nesting. The bracelet is still in my hand, and I make a mental note to put it back before I do something stupid like fall asleep with it in my hand.

It's completely dark now outside; I yawn, tired and still hungry, and also lonely.

I manage to find something to entertain myself, my mind whirling with possibilities. What does it mean that he kept this bracelet instead of throwing it in the trash as most guys would have done? Obviously Roman is sentimental; there are so many things in this bedroom that indicate that fact.

But it does nothing to explain why he would keep a bracelet from a random stranger, albeit a female one.

My eyelids are getting heavy as I sit here staring blankly at the television. I should probably turn on the bedroom light because the glare isn't great for my eyesight and makes it hard to watch the program—I'm just so darn lazy and don't want to climb out of this bed and walk the five feet to the light switch on the wall by the door.

Stomach grumbles a little.

Lids get heavier still...

Outside, the moon rises higher into the night sky above the houses in the distance, casting a little light into the bedroom but not enough to make a difference. I wonder what the man on the moon is up to tonight. Perhaps he's just as lonely as I am. Maybe I should've gone to dinner with Roman; at least then I wouldn't be sitting in this empty house by myself.

I'm sure by now Kaylee is curious about where I've gone, so I check my phone to see if I've missed any text messages from her.

Three.

**Kaylee:** *Wanna get dinner?*

**Kaylee:** *Hello?*

**Kaylee:** *Where are you? I checked your location and don't recognize the address. Everything okay?*

I let out a yawn and tap out a lazy *Came to Liza's for something to eat.*

**Kaylee:** *Oh.*

Just "Oh." Classic Kaylee with an Oh that speaks louder than an actual sentence. It's clearly her subtle way of disapproving without actually intoning her opinion.

Passive aggressive.

**Me:** *You were busy when I left and I didn't want to bug you.*

**Kaylee:** *Sure.*

**Me:** *What'd you end up eating?*

**Kaylee:** *McDonald's.*

McDonald's? That doesn't sound like Kaylee at all—she can't be serious. I love McDonald's more than the next person and eat it all the time, but my roommate does not. In fact, the last time I went for a McFish sandwich and fries during Lent because I crave them something fierce, she guilted me the whole time I was eating it to the point that I got up out of my chair and dumped the remaining part of the sandwich in the trash.

**Me:** *Huh. Are we totally out of food?*

**Kaylee:** *No—I was feeling sorry for myself because my best friend abandoned me without telling me where she was going.*

Best friends?

That's a stretch.

I like Kaylee, but we are in no way best friends, and I'd venture to say I'm closer to Eliza than I've ever been to her... even when I wasn't all that close to Eliza. The period of time I was dating Kyle, I was a bit of a shit friend to everyone. I hate to admit I was one of those girls—the kind who ignores all her friends when she starts dating someone new—but the truth is, I was.

Kyle love-bombed me from the beginning, and I fell for every second of it.

**Me:** *Sorry I didn't send you a message, but I told you shortly before I left that I was returning the award to Jack and Eliza's new roommate, remember?*

**Kaylee:** *Whatever. I went to the gym after you left me all alone at the house.*

**Me:** *So you left for the gym without telling me but you're irritated I left to come here?*

Suddenly, whatever guilt I was feeling dissolves, and I take my phone and set it back on the bedside table, closing my eyes and listening to the television rather than watching it.

So peaceful here.

So comfy...

# CHAPTER 5
# ROMAN

Lilly is sleeping on my bed.

It's taken me a few minutes to find her; when I arrived home just a few moments ago and saw her car still parked outside, I assumed she'd be in the living room watching a movie or something.

No Lilly in the living room.

No Lilly in the kitchen.

My heart began to race as I climbed the stairs to the bedroom level, thundering in my chest with dread and anticipation, unsure of where I'd find her, knowing she had to be in the house.

It's eerily quiet, but when I strain my ears, I hear the faint sound of a television and head toward mine.

Why would she be watching TV in my bedroom?

The pit of my stomach rolls.

Oh god.

What if...

No.

*She's just watching TV—relax. Nothing bad happened.*

The light in the hall is on, but it's not on inside my room, nothing but the changing screens from the television illuminating the space.

The door is open.

I see feet before I see the rest of her, long legs stretched across my bed.

Bare feet.

Bare legs up to the calf before her black leggings cover the rest of her.

A gentle snore accompanies the sounds from the movie on the screen, and when I step inside, I find a slumbering Lilly, rolled toward the opposite wall, hands tucked beneath her chin, sleeping soundly.

She lets out another soft snore.

What is she doing in my bed?

I cross to the other side of it, standing in front of her, looking down at her figure, unsure what action to take. I should wake her up, yeah? Definitely cannot let her sleep—it's weird.

*I don't even know her.*

I stare for a few seconds before shaking my head and glancing away.

*You can't stand here and watch her sleep, idiot. You're being creepy.*

She's the one invading your space.

*Right, but everyone knows watching someone sleep is bizarre.*

Just wake her up. Reach over and give her shoulder a shake.

*At least say her name, for Christ's sake. Do something besides stand here.*

Instead, I stare some more. Even after pep-talking myself out of it, I still don't have a goddamn clue what to do in this situation. I've only been living on my own for a week—is this what it's like? Strange girls crawling into your bed and passing out?

It's Sunday—it's not like she's drunk.

*She was waiting for you.*

I hear the words as if there's someone in the room with me speaking them out loud. Look down at her again, studying her face. Her closed eyes. The way her mouth is slightly open as she snores.

The hands under her chin.

*Don't stare at her, don't stare at her.*

God, why am I so awkward? Why can't I just nudge her or say her name without feeling weird about it? What the heck do I think is going to happen if I wake her up right now? She's going to hate my guts?

I don't want to embarrass her and I know that's what's going to happen and I want to prevent her from feeling awkward. But I also can't just let her sleep, can I? It's not that late. I suppose I could sleep on the couch, but what if she wakes up in the middle of the night and forgets where she is and gets scared?

That happens, right?

It seems legit.

"Lilly." I say her name tentatively, just above a whisper, internally cringing at my hesitation. "Hey, Lilly."

Hey?

Ugh.

I try again, this time louder. "Lilly, I'm back."

She stirs slightly, her legs shifting at the foot of the bed, her feet rubbing together but not much else.

"Lilly, wake up."

"Mmm?" she mumbles, stirring.

Maybe I should turn on the light? That would help.

After I flip the switch, Lilly begins to roll to her back, arm covering her eyes to block out the light, her hand open like a shield against the blaring brightness.

"Why did you do that?" she asks with a tortured groan. "Go away."

"Um." I pause. "This is my room?"

She pauses, body going still, hand slowly lowering from her eyes so she can blink at me, the slow realization of it being, well—me—dawning on her.

"Oh my god, Roman." Lilly tries to sit up. "I am so sorry. Oh my gosh, I..." She glances around. "Did I fall asleep? Was I sleeping?"

"Yeah, you were sleeping." I stuff both hands in the pockets of my pants. "Don't worry about it, it's not a big deal. I just didn't want to wake you up and scare you."

"How long was I out?"

"No idea. I actually just got home."

"Lord." She groans again. "I'm sorry."

"You must have needed the rest."

"I guess." Her hands are braced on her knees, and I notice something between her fingers but don't comment on it. Something that looks familiar?

Something that looks like...

Mine?

The bracelet.

Fuck.

*Don't stare at it, don't stare at it.*

She sees me staring at it and slides it onto her middle three fingers, holding it up and studying it like she's wearing a ring, turning it this way and that as if trying to catch the light in its facets.

Lilly wiggles her fingers.

Raises her brows when my eyes slide from her hand to her face.

I clear my throat, stepping back a foot so I don't crowd her, and also I want to get the hell out of this room as fast as I can lest she wants to talk about—

"Why didn't you tell me you knew me? I thought you looked familiar."

Okay. She definitely wants to talk about it.

Shit.

What the hell do I say?

"I'm not trying to put you on the spot." Her fingers—still holding the bracelet—smooth her hair down. The bedhead. Finger-combing it into some semblance of order; she must have tossed and turned a few times during her nap, and the strands stick up in several directions. "I just came up here because it was a bit lonely downstairs and...found it."

That makes sense, I guess.

"I'm sorry if this is making you feel uncomfortable, but I just saw it—I wasn't snooping or anything, I swear. I came up here and looked at a few things before settling myself on the bed and watching TV. Is that okay?"

"Yeah, of course it's okay." The hands I have stuffed inside my pockets come out so I can wipe them on my thighs, despite the fact that they aren't sweaty. I feel like they should be, though. God this is painful.

"So...why didn't you tell me we'd already met?"

"I...don't know. Eliza and Jack were in the kitchen and I thought it might be weird? I don't know, Lilly. Half the time I have no idea what I'm doing unless it's related to school."

I'm tempted to begin babbling to over-explain myself but stop before any more words come out of my mouth.

"Why did you keep this?"

"I don't know."

She twirls it round and around on her hand. "Most people would have thrown it away."

Yes, they would have, but I'm not most people.

"It doesn't mean anything. It's just..." I clear my throat uncomfortably. "I was a nerdy little freshman and you were nice to me on a night where I felt incredibly awkward at a party I didn't want to be at." I shrug my now broad shoulders. "So I kept it."

Lilly seems to preen at that as if I was giving her a compliment, telling her she's beautiful or smart or witty. All I did was say she was nice to me once upon a time, and she's watching me as if I were a saint.

I might live like a monk sometimes, but I am no saint.

"Most guys are assholes." She plucks at one of the green strands. When she stands up and stretches, I back away, giving her a wide berth, watching when she puts the bracelet back on my dresser.

"You can have it back," I say feebly for lack of anything else.

Lilly turns her head. "Don't you want it?"

Yes. "Doesn't matter. It's yours."

"I gave it to you."

I cannot tell her I'm dying inside and that every single second we spend standing here is killing me slowly, mortification wanting to suck me into the carpet.

"Sorry."

Lilly leaves the bracelet, ending the discussion, and snatches her shoes before walking to the door. "I should go. I can't believe I fell asleep. My roommate was pissed when she thought I left without telling her where I was at."

She bounds back down the stairs.

I trail along behind her.

In the kitchen, Lilly stops short at the sight of leftovers sitting in the center of the island. My mother sent me home with a container of pasta, a container of homemade spaghetti sauce, several small loaves of garlic bread wrapped in aluminum foil, and tiramisu for dessert.

Some of the food is still warm and has already begun smelling up the small kitchen with their aroma, namely garlic of course. Mom used fresh parmesan for the sauce and fresh basil and oregano from her garden out back—the smell is overwhelming and delicious. Lilly tilts her nose up in the air and takes a big whiff.

"What is that smell?" She sniffs again.

"That's spaghetti. My mom makes it all from scratch, including the bread."

"Are you serious?" She pauses, still staring down at the food, tongue practically hanging out of her mouth. "My mom hasn't cooked in years. She usually has it delivered."

"Well my mom cooks like there are 30 people coming to dinner when it's just the five of us."

"Correct me if I'm wrong, but doesn't your grandmother live with you?" Lilly taps her chin in recollection.

"You're thinking of my great aunt, and yeah, she lives with us."

Tonight Aunt Myrtle was alone and didn't have a date with her, much to my mother's relief. It was a really good time with my mother falling all over me and my brother objecting the entire time because he was being ignored. You would think I'd been gone for a decade the way she hovered around my chair, fetching me things, insisting that I not help with dishes or clean up as I normally have to do when I'm there. There were a few times she tried to convince me to move back home, attempting to bribe me when my father wasn't within earshot.

"Did you eat dinner tonight?" I ask her as I begin stacking the containers neatly so they'll fit in the fridge.

"Yes and no."

I laugh. "What does that mean?"

"It means I had leftover pizza, which was total crap." Her eyes haven't left the containers.

I hold them forward as an offering. "Did you want some?"

"I couldn't possibly." Her hands go to her stomach, pressing against her belly like she's feeling it for spare room. "I mean—I am still kind of hungry, but I never worked out today."

Ah.

I get it now.

I've heard rumors about cheerleading and the rigorous restrictions they have, how some coaches and staff are complete dicks, body-shaming and measuring and weighing girls.

"If you're still hungry, you should eat—it's not that late, and you'll probably go home and wind up eating junk food."

"We don't have junk food."

Of course they don't. "You know what I mean." I set the containers back on the counter and wait patiently for her to decide whether she wants me to put them in the fridge or crack them open so she can eat. I nudge the sauce container forward. "It was good."

"I love spaghetti."

"Who doesn't?"

"It was my favorite school lunch growing up."

I laugh. "Mine was the square pieces of pizza. I would fold mine in half and dip it in ranch dressing."

Lilly pulls a face. "Ranch dressing—blech."

I go to the cabinet and grab a plate, begin to build her a meal, noodles first. Her eyes watch my every movement intently, tongue licking along her bottom lip.

"Don't ever do that again," I warn her. "That was so weird."

Her elbows rest on the counter as she takes a seat in a

chair, leaning forward with a grin. “You think everything is weird.”

She’s not wrong. “True. But licking your lips is super weird.”

“I’m hungry! I was showing my enthusiasm.”

“Yeah—maybe don’t do that.” I crack open the sauce after tracking down a ladle, spooning a heap onto the delicious pile of noodles. It’s a meat sauce with chopped up herbs and spices, chunks of tomato—and meatballs. They’re my favorite, so Mom loaded my container.

“Um, more sauce please?” Lilly blushes prettily when she asks, and I duck my head so she can’t see the blush on mine.

Gosh she’s cute.

So pretty.

Bet she could light up a room on a miserable, dreary day.

I put more sauce on her plate and set a piece of cheesy garlic bread on the side.

She eyeballs it. “I better not eat that.”

“Why? Because it’s carbs?”

“No, because when I eat garlic or onions, I stink.” Lilly slaps a hand over her mouth and giggles. “I can’t believe I just said that.”

“Come on—I don’t stink after I eat garlic.” I don’t think...?

“I do.” She claps her hands when I slide the plate toward her across the counter. “You know how some people eat asparagus and their pee smells, and some people eat it and their pee doesn’t? I think it must be the same with garlic and onion.” With that pronouncement, she lifts the bread and takes a healthy bite out of one end.

Moans.

A string of cheese hangs between her mouth and the loaf as she groans, “Oh my god, this is so good.”

I know it’s not polite to stare while someone is eating, but she's doing it in a way I can't help but observe. It's completely impossible not to watch her inhale the pasta noodles and the meat sauce, cutting up the meatballs with her fork like she's in a race against time and hasn't eaten in days.

Or like she's in a spaghetti-eating competition and must beat an opponent.

She has no shame.

Or, she just does not give a shit about my opinion or what I think of her—because I'm not someone she finds attractive? Not someone who is a potential boyfriend? Wouldn't she be more conscious of her behavior if she thought I was cute? She probably remembers what a dork I was when I was a freshman and thinks I'm a dork today. Lilly was up in my bedroom; she saw all my nerdy awards, trophies, and ribbons.

Whatever, I'm never going to be her boyfriend, let alone date her, so what do I care what she thinks of me.

I'm cool being her friend.

Besides, she just broke up with some douchey football player; clearly that's her type.

Plus, she's sworn off men, and I fall into that category, don't I?

I glance away to give her privacy.

"Oh my god." She moans, sucking a long noodle back into her mouth. "This must have tasted so much better coming off the stove."

"It was fantastic."

"I should have gone with you tonight. What are you having next week?" She laughs, wiping the corner of her mouth on a napkin she's plucked from the nearby napkin holder.

"Er, spaghetti usually, unless I ask for something different."

She nods. "Heaven."

As someone whose mother was home most days after

school and cooked up a storm every weekend, I suppose I may take for granted the fact that my mom is such a good cook. I can't remember the last time we didn't have family night on Sunday or the last time she didn't make something home-made; I don't have to ask Lilly to know that certainly wasn't the case in her house growing up.

Lilly continues to eat, eventually finishing the entire meal while I stand there awkwardly. She finally puts down the napkin, resting it on the countertop to signal that she's done eating, and smiles at me.

"You're going to have plenty for yourself, I hope."

"Oh for sure, don't you worry about me. Plus, there's more where that came from." I gesture around at the containers. "This is way more than I can eat myself, and I don't exactly love the idea of having spaghetti from now until next weekend."

"So you have the same thing every single weekend?"

I remove her plate while she sits there, rinse it in the sink, and put it neatly inside the dishwasher for the next load.

"Yeah, it's kind of a thing. I should probably cut the umbilical cord, but it doesn't suck having food prepared, does it?"

"What do you mean, cut the umbilical cord?" she asks as I wipe my hands off on a dishtowel then fold it over the edge of the sink.

"Just that..." Let's see, how do I put this without making myself sound like a gigantic pussy? "Um. My mom is..."

"Controlling?"

"No. She just..." I wave my hand, in search of the right words. "I don't know, she's a stay-at-home mom, and I suppose she's attached to my brother and me. Even though she has Aunt Myrtle there giving her grief and causing trouble, Mom acts like she's lost a limb with me gone." I shrug. "It won't kill me to go home every now and again for dinner, you know?"

Lilly nods. "That sounds nice. I don't know if you remember me describing what my mom is like, but it's almost the exact opposite. If I went home, she'd feed me a carrot and make me practice backflips on the lawn for dessert." She sighs loudly, tapping on the water glass with a fingernail. "Guess we can't all win."

I do remember her describing her mom even though it's been a few years, basically a momager who tries to control every aspect of her daughter's life. I also remember Lilly telling me she came to a school as far as she could possibly get to escape her mother's constant meddling.

I have meddling family members too, but in an entirely different way.

She pushes her chair back from the counter and stands. "Do you need me to do anything? The dishes? I feel bad that you fed me after finding me asleep in your bed."

That's right; I'd almost forgotten about that. About her finding the bracelet and my embarrassment about it.

"No. Gosh, don't worry about it. The dishes are already in the dishwasher and there's nothing to clean up, so we're good." I glance out the side door through the glass at the dark night and check the time. "It's well after nine...you should probably get going."

"Are you trying to imply I need a good night's rest?"

"Maybe. Sleeping is my favorite."

"I thought math and science were your favorite."

"Sleeping is my third favorite."

We both laugh and I walk her to the front door, pulling it open and leaning on the frame.

"Thanks again." She's looking down at her feet, and if I didn't know any better, I'd say she's feeling shy. Feeling as awkward in this moment as I feel because it's almost like we were on a date and aren't sure how to end it.

Which is ridiculous, obviously.

"No worries." I remember myself and the reason she came by in the first place. "Thanks for putting Humpty Dumpty together again."

"Huh?"

Has she forgotten her joke already? "Uh, the award?"

"Oh! Duh." She puts a hand to her forehead and taps it.

After she's gone, I still stand in the doorway watching until her red taillights disappear down the street, her blinker indicating a right-hand turn. Slowly close the door and lock it, returning to the kitchen to continue tidying up so that when my roommates return, my leftover containers aren't still sitting out. I don't doubt for a second that Jack would plow through the remaining spaghetti—and I wouldn't blame him if he did. That shit is delicious.

---

## LILLY

WHAT A STRANGE NIGHT.

I can't say it was the *most* fun I've had since school began, but it came pretty darn close. We didn't do anything—I spent most of the evening by myself, sleeping in Roman's bed, of course. But the talking in the kitchen and eating while he stood by...

Was different.

*Nice.*

Dare I say...pleasant?

No pressure, no hassle, no expectations.

That doesn't happen often when I'm with a guy; then

again, I don't often come in contact with young men who are like Roman.

Polite.

Respectful.

Sure, not all guys my age are idiots. Plenty of the athletes on the football team have their shit together—they have to. But there is an arrogance that comes along with being a football player on a team whose games are televised every week with millions of people watching from around the world.

It creates guys who sometimes expect to be the center of attention. Guys who assume the dominant role in the relationship. Guys who think they can do no wrong.

At least—that was Kyle.

It was all about him, all the time, and many of his teammates were the same way. The trouble is, I'm surrounded by them. The cheerleaders train in the same facility, go to the same physical trainers, see the same doctors, eat in the same cafeteria as all the other athletes.

It makes sense that I would date someone in that circle.

Well.

*How is that working out for me?*

It isn't awfully late when I return home, but my roommate is not home—I don't know where she could possibly be on a Sunday night given that we have an early morning, but I'm sure there is a guy involved. There is always a guy involved. If I thought I was bad when it comes to going from one relationship to the next, Kaylee is even worse.

I am wrapped in a bathrobe when I climb into bed, terry cloth turban coiled around my wet hair, having gotten out of the shower just a little bit ago. Freezing cold, I just want to snuggle for a little while before putting my pajamas on.

Yawning, I pull the fuzzy blanket up higher over my torso so it covers my chest, hunkering down.

Just a few minutes and I'll get dressed.

I stare up at the ceiling, blinking.

Is it odd that I find Roman attractive? He's not at all my type, but maybe he could be.

*What are you talking about, Lilly? You've sworn off men. You're on a cleanse. You're on a journey to be alone.*

I never said I was going to marry the guy, but I can wonder what it would be like to date him. Jeez, get off my back.

*Great. Now you're talking to yourself.*

So? Who said talking to yourself isn't healthy? It's good to work through problems, no matter how you have to do it.

*Journaling would be easier, moron.*

Yes, true—but Kaylee can find a journal, and we don't actually trust her, DO we?

*Not even a little.*

I slap a hand over my mouth.

I've never admitted that to anyone, never even admitted it to myself: I do not trust my roommate. Not after that stunt she pulled with Eliza, kicking her out without telling me then giving me half the blame.

Ruthless.

She would toss me over in a heartbeat.

Friends? Ha!

With friends like her, who needs enemies?

And so, dear mental diary, I keep things to myself and won't share them with her or with anyone—except maybe Eliza. I can definitely trust her to keep my secrets.

If I had any.

Lies. I have one: *I'm developing a crush on the nerdy guy.*

I roll to the side and look at the wall where I have motivational quotes taped up where I can see them. I love being inspired as soon as I wake up in the morning and when I lay my head down for bed at night.

***Be enough for yourself first. The rest of the world can wait.***

It certainly can.

As I move to the side, my robe slides open, the belt loose at my waist. It's a pink satin robe an aunt—my dad's sister—gave me for my eighteenth birthday, and I never leave home without it. I feel sexy in it, mature.

Roman's bedroom smelled like freshly washed sheets, so good I closed my eyes, imagining what kind of cologne he wears. I wasn't brave enough to sniff him, though, to see if he was wearing it tonight, but I bet he was.

He wore a polo to dinner, for Pete's sake.

On a Sunday.

How formal are his parents?

Mine aren't formal, but they were strict, and I would guess —judging by the fastidious way Roman studies—his are strict, too. At least when it comes to school work.

My mother, on the other hand? She couldn't have cared less what my grades were as long as they were good enough to:

1. Keep me on the cheer team.
2. Get me into a decent college where I could be on the cheer team.

Maybe in the spring, when I'm done competing, I should leverage the positions and try to get a job at a dance studio teaching little kids. That would be fun, wouldn't it? Perhaps I'd learn to love it again seeing it through the eyes of younger children.

That thought warms me the way this silk robe doesn't, and I pull the blankets tighter against me.

*You don't have a crush on Roman, you're just lonely.*

*I am not lonely.*

*Yes you are—Kyle sucked balls, and you miss the potential he had to be a good boyfriend.*

Too damn bad I can't be in a relationship with potential. Ha!

*Exactly.*

Yanking the covers up over my head, I scowl, wishing I'd at least flipped the light off before climbing into bed. Also wish I didn't have to climb out of bed to put my pajamas on, because if I sleep in this robe, I'll freeze. And if I don't take this turban off my head and blow-dry my hair, it'll look so ridiculously shitty in the morning it will be impossible to do without wetting it again.

My bedhead game is strong, and no that is not me bragging.

I have to blow-dry my hair any time I take a shower or get it wet, because *yikesss...*

Yawning, I feel my eyelids get heavy.

I really do need to climb out of bed...

Yawn again, mind drifting sleepily.

*You don't have a crush on Roman, you don't.*

He's the last thing I think about as I fall asleep.

# CHAPTER 6
# LILLY

I don't usually partake in the food in the student union, but today, for some reason, I'm too lazy to hoof it all the way to the athletic building. The meals are completely different there, way more diverse and definitely more delicious.

Shrimp. A salad bar spread fit for a king.

Pasta. Soup. Fresh vegetables and proteins.

Grabbing a pre-packaged Froot Loop marshmallow bar and a banana, I weave through the small crowd to find an empty table, seating myself so I face the large, panoramic view of the quad. I can see everything outside from this spot, watching aimlessly as I peel back the layer of my midday snack.

I hate bananas.

Don't know why I'm bothering other than it's quick and easy.

Chewing, my eyes never leave the yard, students from various backgrounds going about their business—some speed walking, some strolling, a few joggers. One dude on a vintage ten-speed bike. I watch as sorority girls huddle in a group while nearby, three guys in long dusters appear to be acting out a scene from Dungeons and Dragons.

After I'm done with my banana, I tear open the package on the Froot Loop and marshmallow cereal bar, sinking my teeth into its ooey-gooey goodness, chewing thoughtfully as I look out the window. A few people walking by I recognize, but that's nothing new—as a member of the cheerleading squad, I get introduced to a lot of people during the school year.

It's a miracle that I'm being left alone right now, seated in the center of the student union where students typically come to socialize. It's loud and definitely not somewhere you'd want to be if you were trying to study or do homework. The library is much better suited for that, and I haven't set foot in the library in a very, very long time.

I nibble the corner of the cereal bar, marveling at its overly sugary sweetness. I'm thinking to myself, *Self, you should make these one night. How hard could this be?*

Not sure who would eat them in my house; both Kaylee and I tend not to eat a bunch of sugary sweets. Perhaps a houseguest?

*You are swearing off men, remember? You won't be having any houseguests, and they won't be eating your sugary sweetness.*

Ha!

Pervert.

My gaze wanders, settling on the science building in the near distance, its double doors at the top of a set of concrete steps, not many students flowing in and out.

I contemplate what must go on inside that building, having never set foot inside, never having the need to. I tested out of science and didn't need any of those classes to fulfill core curriculum requirements. THANK FREAKING GOODNESS.

The science building is one of the most outdated buildings on campus, although I heard through the grapevine the university has plans to build an entirely new one with a five-million-dollar budget.

Is Roman in there now? Hunched over some beaker and experimental equipment, lighting things on fire? Or would he be in the math building crunching out equations to solve the world's problems? Why am I even thinking about him right now?

It makes no sense.

For the last week I've been consumed with Kyle and the betrayal I felt after finding out he was cheating on me, the feelings so overwhelming I assumed there would be no getting over them.

It's not like I was in love with him, but something about seeing his faithlessness with my own eyes is going to leave a mark on my soul forever. I certainly learned not to put my happiness in someone else's hands—and I learned it the hard way.

It was so cute the way Roman fed me in the kitchen at Eliza's house the other night, fussing over me to make sure I ate. To make sure I had enough to eat before I left the house. It was really nice of him to invite me along to his parents' house in the first place, a stranger he's only just met.

What a kind person.

*I can't believe we met all those years ago and lost touch.*

What did you expect, Lilly? It's not as if you move in the same crowds. The last place Roman wants to be is at a crowded party with a bunch of superficial snobs.

"Hey."

A hand touches my shoulder and I jump a mile high, gasping like a freak. "Oh jeezuz!"

"Sorry, I said your name twice." It's Rome, and he's lumbering on the balls of his feet, shifting his weight between the two, appearing mighty uncomfortable. Regretful.

Probably wishing he hadn't approached me. Ugh.

"I am so sorry, I was thinking and didn't hear you." *Thinking about you.* "Want to sit?"

Stuffing the cereal treat in my mouth and using my teeth to hold it, I immediately begin clearing room for him at my table, removing both my backpack and banana peel.

Awkwardly, I hold the peel between my index finger and thumb, not sure what to do with the slimy thing.

"Here." Roman takes it from me and tosses it into a nearby trash bin before pulling out the seat next to me and joining me.

"Thanks."

I brush a strand of hair behind my ears; I can feel them getting hot and hope they're not beet red.

"Thanks for letting me join you—I don't hang out here often, so it's nice to find a familiar face."

I fiddle with the marshmallow cereal treat in front of me, picking at the clear plastic wrapper half of it is still wrapped in. "I don't hang out here that often, either. I was too lazy to go to the other cafeteria."

"There's another cafeteria?"

"Well, yeah, but it's in the stadium for the athletic department." My tone is apologetic, though it's hardly my fault he's not allowed to eat there. "It's a hike, one I wasn't in the mood to make even though I have practice there later."

"Ahh." He nods in understanding. "That's cool."

"Are you hungry at all?" I hold out my tasty treat as an offering. "Want some?"

Roman studies the cereal bar, shaking his head. Raises his eyes and scans the perimeter. "I should probably eat something substantial. I have a physics class in a half hour that has a lab directly afterward."

Physics and a lab?

Blech.

"A burger sounds good, eh?"

It does. I didn't want to wait in the line before, but I see it's not as long now. Two people stand at the grill, patiently waiting.

Roman catches me watching. I'm positive there's no drool coming from the side of my mouth, but to be sure, I swipe a finger there.

"Want anything?" He's rising, pulling his student ID card from the pocket of his jeans. "My treat."

"You can't keep feeding me—I'm like a stray cat." But... "Um, a burger if you don't mind? With, um—pickles? And mayo?"

"Anything else?"

"Tomato."

Roman laughs. "One burger with pickles, tomato, and mayo. Anything else?"

"Nope, that's good." My stomach growls even though I just fed it. "I'll hold down the fort."

I trail my gaze after him when he walks off, studying his backside. The jeans fit perfectly, not too baggy, not too long, not too tight. Bright blue hoodie. Red sneakers. Hair twisted up in a knot, pulled back off his face.

He doesn't look like a science geek today; he looks like he could be on a team. He's fit, that much is obvious, and not just from my observations today—I couldn't help noticing the other night when I was in his kitchen, eating his leftovers, doing my best not to notice how fit he is.

A girl can look, can't she?

I watch him order, gesturing and smiling.

His smile is...

Wide and friendly, and the girl at the counter dips her head, embarrassed as she punches his order into the computer, biting down on her bottom lip, sneaking a glance or two.

Yeah, he's pretty darn cute.

I mean—if a person was looking and interested. Which I'm not.

Because I'm on a break.

I feel a certain kind of way watching Roman interact with the girl at the counter. I know he's just ordering us something to snack on, but seeing the other girl get flustered in his presence makes me...proud or something? He's totally oblivious to her, but I know he's shy around girls—I know this because when I winked at him the night he dropped the box, he dropped it because I was flirting and it flustered him. A guy who does that is not overly confident when it comes to the opposite sex.

His phone rings on the table, and I see that it's his mother.

MOM it says across the screen, a selfie of Rome and an older woman lighting up the screen. She's a little shorter than he is, and he's standing with his arm around her in a side hug, looking like the Roman I met three years ago with the nerdy glasses, short hair, and an awkward pose.

His mother is beautiful, with a bright vibrant smile and blonde hair.

The call disconnects and his screen goes black.

It only takes a few minutes for him to return, and when he does, he sets our burgers down along with a few napkins, a few packets of ketchup, and two knives.

"Thank you, Roman." It was gracious of him to pay; he needn't have.

"You're welcome."

Is he blushing? Looks like it.

Unwrapping his burger, he cuts it in half and politely picks up one side, gingerly taking a bite. I watch him chew before doing the same.

His phone rings again.

Rome glances down at it and raises his brows; he doesn't answer the call from his mother.

This is the second time she's called—I wonder if I should say something. What if there's an emergency? Surely he sees the call from before.

It's killing me not to point it out. Just in case. "That's the second time your mom has called. I'm not trying to be nosey, but it rang while you were getting us lunch—I just don't want you to miss it in case there's an emergency."

I'm a worrier, sue me.

Roman finishes chewing and swallowing before responding. "Yeah. She calls a lot." He takes a napkin and wipes his mouth. "I love her to death, but she hovers. She's having a hard time with me being gone."

Well not answering her phone calls probably makes her anxiety worse...*not that it's any of my business.*

We eat in companionable silence, my burger moist and delicious and exactly what I needed, especially with all this tart mayonnaise and ketchup smothered on it. I haven't had anything this greasy in a long time, and I close my eyes during the next bite.

*Mmm.*

My bliss is interrupted by ringing, and I crack an eyelid to spy Roman shaking his head down at his phone.

I can't stand it anymore. "You really should answer that. Now I'm worried something might be wrong. This is the third time she's tried calling."

"She's not calling me—she's FaceTiming me." Roman chews and swallows.

FaceTiming him? That's next level. "I think you should answer it."

He hesitates for a few seconds, and I give him a nod.

"Go on, answer it."

He grumbles, mumbling under his breath about "*helicopter parents and nothing is wrong she's just clingy*" before picking up the phone, gripping it in his large hand, thumb pressing down on the accept button. He holds it up at face level and pastes on a labored smile. "Hey, Mom. Is everything okay?"

"Hey sweetie, I was just thinking about you!" A woman's cheerful voice carries across our small table, her happy greeting at odds with her son's stiff posture. "How's my baby?"

Roman's eyes dart in my direction, and I hide my grin in the collar of my hooded sweatshirt, pretending not to be eavesdropping. I mean—it's impossible not to. He has his phone out in the union held up for everyone around him to see.

"Mom, I have class today," he mutters miserably. "You called three times, so I was worried there was an emergency. Is everything okay?"

"Of course everything is okay. Why wouldn't it be?"

Oh Lord.

"For starters, we have a geriatric aunt living with us. Also, I have a pre-adolescent brother who is a handful, and you just called me three times in the middle of the day. Why wouldn't I think something might be wrong?"

"Can't a mother just call because she misses her son?" I can hear the pout in her voice.

"You could've just texted instead and I would've called you back when I had a chance."

"But look, we're talking now," she says cheerily. "What are you up to, honey? Are you in the cafeteria?"

"No, I'm in the student union having lunch."

"When is your next class?"

"In a half hour, but I don't have much time to finish eating."

"What are you eating, dear?"

"Burger."

I continue eating mine, shoulders bent, head down, fixating on my own snack and not what's happening across from me...

...but man is it difficult.

"Are you with anyone?" I hear his mother ask.

"Anyone where?"

"Are you eating lunch with anyone?" his mom clarifies.

"The room is pretty packed." Roman's eyes dart across the table and meet mine.

I smirk and shove hamburger in my mouth.

"Roman Henry," his mother chastises, displeased that he's being cheeky.

"No ma'am, I'm not sitting here alone."

Ma'am. So formal and polite.

"Oh, did I interrupt something? Who's your friend?"

Roman didn't tell her he was with a friend. All he said was that he wasn't alone—and when he looks up at me, I can tell he's embarrassed to be talking about it in front of me. His mom is kind of talking to him like he's a baby or someone who has no friends, which I know not to be true.

"My friend," he says slowly, meeting my eyes above the table.

"Yes honey, but who are you with? One of your friends from school?"

"Just a friend, Mom, not one from high school."

"I want to meet him," she continues stubbornly.

Roman's face gets red as he clears his throat. "It's not a he, it's a she." He takes his phone and twists his wrist so he's pointing the camera in my direction. "There, are you satisfied?"

"Wait, turn the phone back!" She's shouting. "Who was that? Was that a girl?"

"Mom, she can hear you—lower your voice."

"But who is that, sweetie? Turn the phone around so I can see her again. She looked pretty—is she your girlfriend?"

"I'm not dating every girl I'm friends with."

"But you're so handsome—who wouldn't want to date my baby boy?"

*Oh man, this poor guy.* I feel really bad for him right now; she will not let the subject go.

"It's okay," I tell him. "I'll say hi."

He doesn't look convinced or reassured that his mother is going to let this rest once I say hello.

Standing, I cross to his side of the table, resting my hands gently on his shoulders as I lean forward, getting ample screen time.

Give his mother a little wave and a pleasant, friendly smile.

Her eyes widen and her intake of breath is audible. It has my own face turning hot, wondering if this was a mistake. He knows his mother better than I do—what if she makes more of this than it is? (Which is nothing.)

"Hi Mrs..."

I glance down at Roman, waiting for him to supply his last name, our faces mere inches apart.

"Whitaker," his mom answers for him.

"Hi, Mrs. Whitaker. My name is Lilly. Roman gave me some of your spaghetti the other night, and it was wonderful—some of the best spaghetti I've ever had. And I consider myself a connoisseur." I laugh good-naturedly.

I'm a people person; I may be shit when it comes to picking out men worthy of my time and affection, but I'm hella great with parents.

And old people.

Also: small children and pets.

Mrs. Whitaker's eyes flit back and forth from me to Roman and Roman to me, and it's clear she is stunned and not sure what to say. It takes her a few seconds to gather her wits, and she sits up a little bit straighter in her chair. It looks as though she must be in the kitchen or in a dining room, seated at a table the same way we are seated at a table, though one is certainly more formal.

"You've tried my spaghetti?" She looks at Roman again. "You should have come to dinner on Sunday night. Roman, why didn't you invite her to dinner on Sunday night?"

His body sags beneath my palms. "I did, Mom."

"I would've loved to come for dinner, Mrs. Whitaker, but I was in a bit of a slump and wanted some alone time." I'm still smiling over his shoulder, the clean, freshly showered smell of him filling my nostrils, and *mmm*...it's a bit distracting, honestly. "It was really nice of your son to bring me leftovers though. His new roommates are some of my best friends—that's how we met."

I'm assuming that's something she was about to ask, how the two of us met, so I fill in the blanks for him.

Guys are so different from girls; while Roman just sits there staring at his mother, I already know she wants actual details about our relationship.

She's a woman and I'm a woman—details are my jam.

"Where are you from, Lilly?"

"Plainfield, just four hours from here. Give or take, depending on who's driving."

His mother nods, grinning from ear to ear. "And you met Rome through friends?"

"Yes, his new roommate Eliza used to be my roommate."

"And now you and Rome are having lunch together?"

Oh boy. "Yes, ma'am. We happened to bump into each other while I was sitting here. He bought me a burger." I lift the burger from its paper wrapper and hold it up for the camera. Beside me, Roman groans.

Mrs. Whitaker looks thrilled. "He bought you a burger? That was so sweet."

It really was.

"He's very thoughtful."

Roman's mother slowly bobs her head up and down at my words, and I know she's trying to decipher them. Very thoughtful—*friend zone* thoughtful or *romantic interest* thoughtful?

Put that out of your mind, ma'am. We are not going to be dating simply because your son bought me lunch in the student union.

Mrs. Whitaker seems exactly like the type of mother who is dying to have grandkids even though her son is still in college and barely of legal drinking age. She's also probably the type of mother who brings up wanting grandchildren all the time, and I don't doubt for a second that seeing me on her son's phone screen is filling her with all kinds of hope.

She's probably already planning our wedding even though she's just heard my name for the first time and Roman and I aren't dating, let alone boyfriend and girlfriend.

"What are you doing on Sunday? We have family dinner at our house and I would love to invite you."

"Mom," Roman chastises with embarrassment in his tone.

"What? I can invite your friends for dinner!"

"No, you can't just invite my friends to dinner."

"Why not?"

"You don't even know if she's got anything going on," he says stiffly. "I don't want her to feel pressured."

They're discussing the matter as if I'm not standing right here listening to the entire conversation. But to ease Roman's obviously troubled mind about it, I paste a smile on my face and gently say, "Thank you for the invitation, Mrs. Whitaker. I'll definitely think about it. I have a lot going on—I'm a cheerleader, so I'll have to check the schedule and see if I'm in town."

Her eyes get wide. "A cheerleader? Oh, how exciting! Don't you just love it?"

It's the same question most people ask, more of a conversation filler than a question they expect an elaborate, detailed answer to.

"Yes," I tell her simply—because it would be too complicated for me to explain I feel forced into it by years of financial investment and time commitment on my family's behalf, because my mother wanted me to be a star.

Basically, she wanted me to be the next JoJo Siwa, and we all know that's not happening. So a simple yes will have to do in this case.

"Well, Lilly, it was wonderful meeting you. You're so pretty!"

"Thank you, Mrs. Whitaker," I say with a blush spreading to my cheeks, briefly wondering if her son feels the same way she does.

"I'll let you kids get back to your lunch. I know you have to get to class soon." She looks to her son, and I back away and take my seat on the other side of the table, still listening. "Call me later, would you?"

No doubt when he does, she's going to grill him with a hundred questions about me.

Once Rome has ended the call, we sit in silence as he gathers himself. I can see he is unsure of what to say simply based on his body language, the hunched shoulders and the self-conscious way he sets his phone on the table then slides it into the center.

It certainly looks as if he's searching for words to fill the silence.

He has absolutely nothing to be embarrassed about; his

mom was acting like a typical mom. As far as I'm concerned, everything about their conversation was perfectly normal.

"She's cute," I say at last. "Much friendlier than my mother would have been."

I pick up my burger and nibble from the end of the now cold, lifeless patty.

"How so?"

I swallow before telling him, "Well, my mom wouldn't have been happy to meet you. She considers all males—romantic interests or friends alike—distractions."

"Distractions from what?"

I shrug, chewing. "From...from...world domination."

Roman tosses his head back and laughs, a hearty, pleasant sound that has me smiling around my bun at him, burger in my mouth and all.

"Your mom wants you to take over the world, huh?"

"Yup. One football game at a time."

"How's *that* going for you?"

"Terribly." I take another bite before continuing. "I'm the absolute worst at it." Plus, she would positively freak if she saw me eating a hamburger straight after eating a marshmallow-drenched cereal bar.

Not that my body is any of her damn business, but she has hovered over me most of my life and watched every calorie I've put inside of it, casting judgment.

Well. Those days are over.

This semester? I'll finally be done with cheer, and I can finally live life on my terms.

Get a job. An apartment. Eat whatever I want.

Be with whomever I want.

"I would wager to say I'd be better at world domination than you."

My brows go up. "How so?"

"Duh, science."

That catches me off guard. "Who are you now, Gru from *Despicable Me*? Are you going to have a secret lab in your basement?"

"Secret lab, man cave—same thing, right?"

The idea of a house with a basement and a man with a cave appeals to me. A happy home with kids whose parents don't ride their asses and let them be kids.

I sigh into my burger bun.

"That was heavy," Roman observes.

"What was?"

"That sigh. What was it for?" He checks his watch at the same time he asks, probably needing to keep an eye on the time with a class looming.

Tick tock.

"Just me thinking about what life could be like as an adult."

"Oh? How's it gonna be as an adult?" He sounds genuinely curious.

"Normal. With lots of movie nights with snacks and loud noises. And definitely a dog."

---

There is sweat dripping down my cleavage, sweat dripping down the center of my back and into my butt crack. We worked hard today at practice, and the air inside the field house was oddly humid. I think it's because of all the athletes using the facility—it's a busy season with lots going on. Football is in full swing, the cheer team is in here practicing, then there is the basketball team, the wrestlers, rowers, track team...

The place is packed.

Not to mention there's a pool nearby, which most likely is

the cause of the humidity. I wonder if they'll do anything about that any time soon because man, today was rough. They definitely need to turn up the air conditioning units.

I decide to take a shower at the gym in the locker room, which is not something I normally do. I love having all of my own shampoo, conditioner, and body wash at my disposal. The stuff they have here just doesn't smell as good, doesn't clean my hair as well—it always feels somewhat matted when I'm done. But today I am just too disgusting to put clean clothes on and go home to wash off.

As I'm rinsing out the conditioner, Kaylee comes into the shower stalls and calls my name over the curtain.

"Yoohoo, Lill, is that you?"

She just saw me at practice; granted, we don't practice in the same space—she's a flyer and has different coaches—but still, things have been strained between us since Kyle and I broke up, and I haven't been able to figure out why.

"Yeah, it's me." I scrub my armpits, getting them good and sudsy. "I'm so gross I didn't want to leave without showering."

"Tell me about it. I have sweat dripping everywhere. Something must be wrong with the air conditioning units—today was ridiculous." Her voice comes from the stall beside me, and I hear the water turn on, shower curtain pulled back, its plastic liner dragging against the tile floor because it's too long. Whoever installed it wasn't focused on accuracy—only getting the job done.

My stomach growls.

Guess that burger earlier didn't fill me up as well as I was hoping it would.

"I'm starving," Kaylee muses out loud as if reading my thoughts. "I ate my last protein bar before we got here."

"We could order something."

"True."

It's quiet for some time as we both work on cleaning ourselves, and while it's void of conversation, I step completely beneath the spray and tip my head back, letting the hot stream of water hit my face. Turn so my back is facing the wall; water washes through my hair, weighing it so it falls halfway down my back in a sheet.

Ugh this feels so good.

Body aches.

Muscles hurt.

Brain tired.

"I can't wait until this season is over," my roommate moans in the stall next to me, shutting her water off, followed by the sound of the towel being yanked off the shower bar. The slap of her rubber flip-flops against the floor.

"Same. I feel like I'm getting too old for this." I laugh to make it sound like I'm joking, but deep down inside, we both know I'm not. It's no secret between Kaylee and me that my mother pushed me into this sport—unlike hers, who couldn't care less if she's on a team.

"Let's just watch movies tonight and order pizza. We've earned it."

"Deal."

I stay in the shower, basking in the steamy goodness for another fifteen minutes, letting myself get drenched. Letting my muscles loosen. Letting my worries wash down the drain.

Dress quickly in joggers and a hoodie.

Slide into broken-in Converse.

Hair wet.

Backpack on.

I come up short when I shove the door to the women's locker room open, an unwelcome but familiar figure against the opposite wall.

Kyle leans there, one long leg bent, heel of one chunky black combat boot planted against the cement cinder block.

He stands up straight when he sees me, full attention.

I glance up the hall and down the hall. Is he here to see me?

I'm confused, we haven't spoken in two weeks, and for good reason; *he's a gaslighting liar and I want nothing to do with him.*

"Hey."

I inwardly groan. What the hell is he doing here? Is he seeing someone on the cheer team? "Were you waiting for me?"

"Yeah." So cool. So casual.

*So cringe.*

"What do you want?" I walk past him and head toward the exit, doing my best to ignore the six-foot-three giant next to me.

He stops short of the heavy, glass doors leading to the parking lot.

"Are you avoiding me, Lilly?"

"Yes!" I snort. "Yes, I'm avoiding you! We broke up, Kyle. You were sending people dick pics and sliding into random girls' DMs, remember?"

His eyes go wide when I use the word dick, probably from shock; he's never heard me use profane words like dick or cock because I always thought I had to watch my language in front of him.

Also, why am I explaining to a grown-ass man why he should leave me the hell alone now that we've broken up?

Grown?

Ha! He still acts like an adolescent boy.

"It was a mistake."

I snort again, stepping out into the cold, fall weather. Wet hair suddenly seems like a terrible idea—instant regret.

"Kyle, I don't care what your reasons were—you showed me time and again the kind of person you were, and I'm never going back to that place. Maybe someday, you'll grow out of the phase where you need your ego fueled by random girls sucking your dick and getting on all fours." I shift the backpack on my shoulder to the other side, drained. "You're gross."

"I'm gross," he deadpans.

"Take your dirty dick somewhere else."

His jaw drops—pretty sure somewhere inside his head, his brain has been knocked loose and is rolling around in there, uselessly.

No offense to Kyle, but...

"Uh..." he cavemans. "Can't we at least be friends?"

"Friends?"

"You know." He wiggles his bushy brows suggestively, and I want to throw up in my mouth a little.

Ew.

Ew, ew, *EWWWW!*

Barf.

He doesn't mean friends, he means... "Friends with benefits? No thanks. I'm not looking to catch any STIs, but thanks." His next girlfriend can worry about that. "You have some fucking nerve."

"Where is all this coming from?" he has the audacity to ask, as if I were the problem here. As if I don't have the right to be bitter.

"You made me wake up and see my worth. And you..." I look at him from top to bottom. "*Don't* deserve me."

With my head held high, I leave him standing inside the open door staring after me.

*Snap.*

# CHAPTER 7
# ROMAN

Should I text her, or should I not text her? *That is the question.*

I pace around my bedroom, walking back and forth from one end of it to another, contemplating whether or not to send Lilly an invitation to have Sunday dinner with my family and me. I told her I would invite her again—and my mother followed up after our FaceTime chat in the student union the other day by continuously asking after Lilly. Constantly berating me to invite that pretty girl to dinner.

It can't hurt to reach out, right?

She said we're friends, and this is what friends do—feed one another food. Introduce them to family.

It's been a long time since I've been friends with a female; I believe the last girlfriend I had was Ariel Sanders back in third grade. She was very interested in biology and frogs and wanted to be a marine biologist at the time; we spent hours upon hours in the pond behind her house with small nets and microscopes.

Lilly said 'next time.'

Tonight is technically next time.

Would I be rude not inviting my roommates along also? My parents haven't met them either—not that Mom is planning on an entire crew at the house. She might lose her shit with two additional guests.

Best to keep it small, I rationalize.

Sticking my head out my bedroom door, I give a listen to see where the sound is coming from. Hear someone in the bedroom and cross my fingers that person is Jack.

"Jack?" My inquiry is hesitant, just loud enough to be heard without straining.

"Yeah?"

Great—it's him. Last thing I want to do is ask Eliza for her best friend's phone number. Don't want her to get the wrong idea...

Jack appears in the doorway holding a shirt but not wearing one.

"Do you happen to have Lilly's phone number? I have something to ask her."

"Sure do, mate." He fishes a phone out of the pocket of his track pants, thumbing through it then rattling off a number. "I'll send you the contact, eh? Easier."

My phone pings a few seconds later. "Thanks."

"No problem." He goes to put on the shirt—a long-sleeved tee—but stops short. "You going to be 'round for supper? Eliza and I are off to the cinema if you want to join. Popcorn, crisps, and the like?"

"Uh—thanks, but I've got plans."

Jack nods. "You settling in alright?"

"Totally. The place is great. Thanks again for letting me move in last minute and for being so cool. Wish I'd have moved out years ago."

"Years?" He doesn't look as if he believes me.

"I tried, man—parents weren't supportive."

He nods at that. "I get it. It's rough when your mum can't let go. Never really lived with mine, so it was different. Still strange, but that's how we do it across the pond, yeah?"

I think he means he must have been in boarding school most of his school years, which makes sense—that's common among wealthier Brits. My mother would rather lose a limb than ship me away to school—look at how long it took her to agree to let me live on my own.

Jack and I stand in the hallway shooting the shit for a few more minutes before his phone goes off—it's Eliza, checking on his status, which instantly puts him on autopilot, shrugging into his shirt and grabbing his jacket from his closet.

I watch as he bounds down the stairs for his movie date.

Glancing down at the new contact in my phone, I return to my bedroom and flop down on the bed. I'm completely dressed for dinner, just have to do this one thing.

**Me:** *Hey Lilly, it's Roman Whitaker. We had lunch in the union? I'm Eliza's roommate. Anyway, I'm just checking in to find out if you're hungry—heading to my parents' for Sunday dinner and my mom has extended another invite. Let me know if you're at all interested.*

I stare and stare at that message, change it around a few times, rewording the last sentence.

*You interested?*

That sounds way more chill and less enthusiastic. Or does it? Maybe it sounds way too chill and not enthusiastic enough? Jeez, I'm way overthinking this. It's just a simple invitation to spaghetti dinner with my parents and dumb brother, not a proposal to visit the Vatican.

Lying on the bed, fully dressed and ready to roll, shoes included, I wait for her to reply.

**Lilly:** *Of course I know who you are, silly. You don't have to explain!*

I sit up on the bed. She knew who I was?

**Me:** *Jack gave me your number, I hope you don't mind.*

**Lilly:** *It's totally fine!*

**Me:** *Anyway, sorry to bug you if you're in the middle of something—wasn't sure if you had practice today or not, but*

I delete that first part. It sounds passive aggressive and a bit insecure—less take charge.

**Me:** *Anyway, I'm leaving soon for my parents' place for dinner—wasn't sure if you had practice today or not, but if you want to join me for Italian, I could swing by and grab you.*

There.

Perfect, eh?

**Lilly:** *You know what, Rome? I could eat.*

I could eat? What does that mean? Does it mean she's excited and would love to come, or does it mean she has nothing better to do so why not? Either way, it sounds like a yes?

**Lilly:** *What time were you planning on leaving?*

**Me:** *Soon-ish? Unless that doesn't work for you; I know this is last minute. I should have texted you sooner.*

**Lilly:** *Gosh, no worries. You actually caught me at a good time, I'm already showered and just got done blow-drying my hair. I could be ready in a jiff...*

**Me:** *Is 15 minutes too soon for you, or do you need more time?*

**Lilly:** *How fancy do your parents get? You had a polo on last weekend.*

**Me:** *Not fancy—right now I'm wearing a hoodie.*

I fly out of bed and rip off my polo, tossing it to the closet floor and at the same time yanking a t-shirt and hoodie off their hangers.

Look at my reflection in the mirror at my pressed khakis

and begin the dance of removing those. Grab a pair of jeans and pull those on.

**Lilly:** *Oh great! In that case, yeah—15 minutes totally works.*

As I'm lacing up my sneakers, the next text to come through is her address.

**Me:** *Awesome. See you in a few. It's only a 20-minute drive.*

**Lilly:** *PERFECT because I am starving!!!*

**Me:** *I'll let my mom know we're arriving ravenous.*

**Lilly:** *LOL ravenous. I love it when you use big words.*

She loves it when I use big words? When do I use big words? Rarely, yet I make a mental note to use more of them. Can't hurt to impress a beautiful girl every now and again, can it?

In a t-shirt, hoodie, and jeans I'm not sure my mother is going to fully approve of, I hustle to the kitchen and fetch two water bottles from the fridge for the ride—one for myself, one for Lilly. Quickly toss last week's leftovers in the trash, dumping the noodles and sauce into the garbage before squirting shit tons of dish soap into each container and swishing it around.

Rinse.

Dry.

Couldn't hurt to return Mom's containers on the off chance there are more leftovers tonight and Lilly and I can snag a few to feed us throughout the week.

I wonder if it'll be spaghetti tonight. After my mother suggested—for the thirtieth time—that I invite my friend Lilly to dinner and I said I would, it's entirely possible that she'll switch up the menu.

Steak perhaps, to impress? Seafood?

Burgers aren't her style for a Sunday, and I doubt she'd serve those to a girl I'm bringing home for the first time. Not fancy enough.

Salad, for sure.

Bread? Absolutely—my dad and Aunt Myrtle love carbs.

Aunt Myrtle.

Shit.

Shit, shit, shit—why didn't I think of her when I was shooting off my invite? *Calm down, bro, she might be on a date.*

Or she might have a date at the house.

I text my mother, heart racing.

**Me:** *Mom, please tell me Aunt Myrtle isn't going to be home tonight.*

**Mom:** *Aunt Myrtle is going to be at dinner tonight. She lives here and she is eighty-three, where else would she be?*

**Me:** *I don't know—on a date?*

**Mom:** *Why are you asking?*

**Me:** *Because Lilly is coming and I have a feeling this is going to be a train wreck.*

**Mom:** *Lilly is coming! How wonderful! Of course this isn't going to be a train wreck, why would you say that? You talk as if we don't know how to conduct ourselves.*

**Me:** *Alex and Aunt Myrtle DO NOT KNOW HOW TO CONDUCT THEMSELVES.*

**Mom:** *I can put your brother in the kitchen with his food.*

Ugh. That will only make him worse. No way will that little shit stand for being stranded in the kitchen by his lonesome while there's a cute girl in the house.

No way.

**Me:** *Ugh, whatever, don't worry about it. It's not like I'm trying to impress her. She's just my friend—I don't need to hide my weird family.*

**Mom:** *ROMAN HENRY, WE ARE NOT WEIRD!*

She has her opinion, I have mine—it's not exactly typical having an eighty-three-year-old woman living in the house who acts as if she's a twenty-year-old single out on the prowl, swiping on anything with a pulse and bringing him to the house. It's not typical that her trusty sidekick is a twelve-year-old or that the two of them together are a sassy sarcastic duo.

But I'm not going to argue with my mother, not when my nerves are in full swing, the knots in my stomach wreaking havoc on a gut that's also growling from hunger.

I'm a mess.

**Me:** *I was kidding, Mom. What's for dinner?*

**Mom:** *Lasagna, and thank heavens I made a big pan of it—plenty to go around.*

Sweet. Another one of my favorites.

I grab my keys off the counter and head toward my car, driving in the direction of the address Lilly supplied me with, slowly making my way down street after street—it's not easy seeing the addresses with this sun setting. Many of the house numbers are hidden by trees or not there at all, not to mention there aren't a lot of mailboxes along the road.

If anyone is watching out their window at the slow speed of my car, they'll definitely think I am a creep.

Eventually, I find Lilly's house.

It's directly across the street from the fancy administration building with a red brick exterior to match. It looks quite posh for off-campus housing, not so dissimilar from the house I'm living in, although it's much smaller.

My mother would describe it as *cute*.

As I'm unbuckling my seat belt so I can go to the door and let her know I've arrived, that same door in question opens and Lilly steps out into the dark, cold afternoon. She gives me a little wave before shutting the door behind her and locking it with a key. Makes her way down the sidewalk, pulling her jacket tighter around her.

"Brr!" she says as she climbs inside. "Who knew it was going to be this cold out tonight! I'm freezing."

She shivers, strapping herself in.

"I love this time of year."

"Same—except for the cold part." She laughs. "I love fall and winter, but mostly because of the decorations and pumpkin spice and delicious food."

"You always have food on the brain."

"I'm hungry!" She laughs again. "Don't judge me—I burn a lot of calories from working out and practice. It's a hazard of the beast."

Speaking of food... "We're having lasagna tonight, so I'm glad you brought your appetite."

"Lasagna?" She moans. "Oh my god, I hope it's extra cheesy—lasagna is my favorite."

"I thought spaghetti was your favorite."

"It is! But so is lasagna...and ravioli...and burgers, and lobster and shrimp and sushi..."

"You just described everything."

"It's a curse to be non-discriminating." She glances over at me. "Thanks for picking me up."

"No problem. It'll be fun tonight having someone else for my mom to dote over—all the attention will be on you, and I'll actually be able to eat."

"Ha ha, not funny. Will she mind if I have noodles falling out of my mouth?"

Yeah, she would mind, but she would never correct a guest for chewing with their mouth open. She would simply purse her own lips and turn her head in a different direction.

Ha!

"Also, you know I mentioned my aunt that lives with us? She'll be home tonight."

Lilly studies me in the dim lighting created by the glowing streetlamps that have begun turning on one at a time.

"What does that mean?"

"Well." I clear my throat. "She's practically a hundred years old, but she...er...acts like she's twenty."

Lilly laughs. "And what does *that* mean?"

"She's into online dating and parties."

Her eyes damn near bulge out of her skull. "What! What? Wait. Explain."

"Which part did you want me to expand upon?"

"I'm not sure—I have a thirst for both, but start with the online dating part."

I grip the wheel, grinning. "Well, let me start by saying her last boyfriend was a catfish. He said he was sixty-nine, but he was actually seventy-eight, which is still five years younger than she is."

"Wait—stop. An old dude tried to pass himself off as younger?"

"Yes, and the thing is, Rich didn't look like he was even remotely in his sixties. Super seventy."

"So what happened?"

"She caught him because on their first date, he invited her to his place, and when he gave her his address, she reverse-searched it and got his full name. Which pulled up his age."

"What did she do?"

"She chewed his ass out, but..." I pause to be dramatic, turning up the ramp to enter the freeway. "Went on the date."

"What happened?" Lilly is hanging on my every word.

"They had piña coladas followed by dinner and wine, and Aunt Myrtle ended up puking on the carpet."

"Stop!" Lilly shouts, laughing. "No she did not! Then what?"

"Then she passed out."

Lilly gasps. "No!"

"Yes. She woke up and he was gone. He'd gone home."

"And left her there?"

I nod. "Yup."

"Ew, what an asshole."

"I don't think there's an age limit for being a douchebag. So after that, she began trying to make him jealous by dating a surgeon—well, a retired surgeon. Rich didn't take the bait, so they broke up and she met Dan."

"Who is Dan?"

"Dan is eighty-five and takes Viagra."

"How do you know that?"

"She told us about it at dinner one night. My ears were bleeding all the next day."

"I can't even believe this. Even I don't date this much!" Lilly slumps in the passenger seat. "This means dating doesn't get any better as you get older, which totally sucks!"

Tell me about it.

Not that I've tried dating, although... "I feel like it's easier for women than it is for me."

She looks at me. "How so?"

"I don't know...isn't it easy for you to get dates? Guys must ask you out all the time, whereas zero people ask me out, ever."

Lilly's snort is unladylike. "There is a huge difference between someone asking you out on an actual date as a possible love match that has long-term potential versus someone asking you out with the intention of sleeping with you. The problem is it's hard to tell what that intention is until you're sitting with someone across the table."

"What do you mean?"

"I mean, a guy will ask you on a date, but what he actually means is: I'm trying to screw you."

"Why would a guy take you on an actual date if he's only trying to screw you?" That makes no sense to me at all.

"Because it's rude to say 'I want to bang you' to someone's face—he pretends he's asking you out because he actually likes you and might care, when in fact that's not the case at all. Does that make sense? A guy can be on a dating site with no intention of dating you at all."

"Doesn't it get expensive going on all those dates when you just want to have sex with someone?"

"I use the term date loosely. Mostly it's a drink but not food. So is that a date? Maybe, maybe not. Do they want to chug down a beer and then take you back to their place? Almost always." Her fingers pluck absentmindedly at the strap of her purse. "My cousin is our age—he told me once he doesn't do actual dates because it's a waste of money. He will only do coffee or a drink, and sometimes he goes Dutch."

"Dutch? On a first date?"

"Right, because if he goes on three dates in a week—and by dates, I mean 'sex'—that gets super expensive."

"I'm not even sure what to say."

"Yeah—same." She's looking out the window now at the lake we're driving alongside, the glowing lights from the shore homes reflecting in the water as we pass. "This is so pretty."

"We're not far, ten more minutes."

As if on cue, her stomach growls, and she giggles. "You didn't hear that."

Mine growls too. "My growling stomach cancels out your growling stomach."

"Agreed." She pauses. "Man, I hope there's garlic bread even though I'll stink for a few days after I eat it."

"You're still stuck on the thought that garlic makes you stink, huh?"

"Of course I am. Garlic, onions, artichoke, chives—you name it. No amount of deodorant helps, and I have no idea why I'm saying this to you. You're going to think I'm disgusting."

*I think Lilly is a lot of things, but disgusting isn't one of them.*

She probably smells like roses and sunshine most of the time, and nothing can convince me otherwise.

"I don't think you're disgusting," I tell her with a smirk, entering the city limits of the town where I grew up, stopping at a corner near the high school.

"Is that where you went to high school?"

"Yeah."

"How'd you like it?"

"It was fine." We turn right at the next traffic light. "I did a lot of studying so—not very social. Probably not like you."

I'm assuming she was very popular as a cheerleader and all. Lilly is so outgoing compared to my introverted personality. She dances and cheers in front of crowds of thousands of people whereas I spend most of my time in a lab with goggles on.

Typical nerd.

"I don't know about that. I'm one of those introverted extroverts—do you know what I mean? I would rather be home snuggling than out shouting at people, rah, rah, rah, and all that. I've been forced to come out of my shell over the years, though not by choice. Not always."

"That makes sense. Over the past few years, if I have an exhibit or debate or a championship where I have to defend a thesis to earn a scholarship or grant, I've had to force myself to be more outgoing. Occasionally I've even practiced in front of the mirror, speeches and the like."

"I can see you doing that." Her smile is warm as she watches me.

"When I was in Great Britain, I led a study group, and every week I got it going with conversation starters. It was a huge challenge for me because of my shyness—oftentimes I would have to Google questions to ask because I could never come up with any on my own." I chuckle at the memory.

It's not easy being an academic who would rather run tests and experiments than chat with a group of people.

Luckily those people were in the same boat as I was, not caring to socialize. Our commonalities were what made us enthusiastic—others who were passionate about their thesis or graduate studies would light up like a Christmas tree when discussing whatever scientific breakthrough they'd discovered.

Otherwise those groups were awkward as hell.

I clear my throat. "This conversation is way too insightful and deep for a ride to lasagna dinner." My hands grip the wheel tighter.

"That's not true—I love hearing you talk about your experiences. Mine are boring."

"Boring? How can you call cheering in a stadium boring?"

"It's not as exciting as everyone thinks it is. For example, I'm always worried I'm going to be off count—the only asshole on the field screwing up the routine."

"Guess we have that in common then."

The grin Lilly gives me from the passenger seat has my stomach flipping, and thank God we've finally arrived at my house with its two stories and white picket fence and neatly trimmed hedgerow.

With the last of my mother's flowers blooming before going dormant for winter, it's a scene right out of the movie *Father of the Bride*. On the stoop are her mums and other fall flowers—I'm sure they're vibrant and bright during the daylight hours.

"I'm surprised Mom hasn't thrown any Halloween decorations out on the lawn for you."

"Um, that would be amazing."

She loves the holidays and I'm sure she'll be bringing up Thanksgiving very soon too; planning is her forte, and it's never too soon to plan. I swear my mother has the next season up before she has the current one taken down—during Christmas, it looks like the living room has barfed up a tree farm.

I pull up to the overhang on the side of the house, the covered carport with its climbing rose vines and white trellis, parking there so Lilly won't have to walk far.

The door to the house swings open, my younger brother silhouetted by the lights inside, hair sticking up every which way.

The outside light comes on and Alex hollers, "Hurry up, I'm hungry enough to eat a dead rat."

Okay then—great first impression, Alex.

My mother's voice chastises him from somewhere inside. "Alexander Michael!" She sounds horrified. "Get away from that door!"

She appears, shooing him away, oven mitt still on her hand, hair in a ponytail that swings when she grabs hold of the door so it doesn't slam shut.

"Hello! You made it!"

"Hey, Mom."

Lilly is rounding the front of the car almost bashfully. "Hello Mrs. Whitaker, it's good to meet you." She holds out her hand for my mother to shake, but Mom grabs her for a hug.

Squeezes. "We don't shake hands here—we're a hugging family."

Oh brother.

Over Lilly's shoulder, my mother moves her mouth and has stars in her eyes. "*She's so pretty!*"

I'm in trouble.

"I hope you're hungry, there is so much food! Dinner is already on the table."

"Good, because I have some studying to do yet tonight and don't want to get home too late." I'm all business, drawing boundaries so Mom isn't under the impression we'll spend the night or stick around chatting for hours.

We can talk during the meal. It needn't continue afterward as she often tries to corral me into doing.

"You should live a little, sweetie. It won't kill you to take one night off."

She's not wrong; I'm very regimented when it comes to my education. But then again, I wouldn't be where I am today if I slacked off.

"I'll take that into consideration." My tone is stiff, mostly because I'm fucking nervous.

Never have I ever brought a girl home. Well...I mean, I have, but it's been ages.

"He's an old fuddy-duddy," Mom confides to Lilly, whom she has by the arm and is dragging through the house and into the dining room. If she's noticed how informally I'm dressed, she hasn't commented on it.

"Speaking of fuddy-duddies," I drawl as we round the corner from one room into another. Aunt Myrtle holds court at the long dinner table, sparkling like a jewel on her throne. Gray hair coifed into a puffy confection, decorative hair pin stabbed through the side. She's got on what's likely a housecoat—or caftan—long billowy sleeves and buttoned to the neck.

No idea how this woman gets more dates than I do.

She's short, tabletop meeting her mid-chest, shoulders slightly slouched from old age.

Her wrinkled hot pink lips part. "There he is. Finally. Thought I was going to die of old age from waiting, not starvation."

She cackles and high-fives my brother, wrists jingling with glittery bangles.

"Yeah," Alex echoes. "We thought we were going to die from old age."

Jeez.

"Everyone, this is Lilly. Lilly, that's my dad." My dad stands and leans over to shake her hand. "And Great Aunt Myrtle, and my brother Alex."

Lilly waves around the table, sitting in the chair my mother has pulled out for her. "Hello everyone. Thank you so much for the invitation—I love lasagna."

"Well aren't you a cute little thing," tiny Aunt Myrtle begins. "Please tell me you're up to no good with my nephew. We were beginning to worry he'd never have another girlfriend."

"First of all, it hardly matters if I ever have another girlfriend. Or a relationship—that's not—"

My mother cuts me off. "Please, Auntie, we're here to have a nice dinner. It's too soon to be harassing him before we've even had one bite." She picks up the bread from the table and begins passing the basket to the right. "Are you trying to scare her away?"

My great aunt harumphs, giving both Lilly and me the stink eye. "In my day, you would have been married by now with an ankle biter on the way."

"Auntie. Please." Mom clenches her teeth.

"I'm just saying," she says as my brother politely sets a slice of garlic bread on her plate then passes the basket along to Dad. "I had plenty of beaus when I was your age." She slurps water from her glass, arms shaking a little as she adds, "Even let a few dip their wick before tying the knot with my first husband, Ralph—which wasn't done." She winks. "I was sex positive even back in the day."

Dad coughs.

My mother groans.

Beside me, Lilly starts laughing. "That's a phrase I've never heard of—dipping their wick." Her head bows, and she laughs some more. "I'm sure I'll be using that in a sentence later."

Aunt Myrtle nods with approval. "Finally. Someone who appreciates my wisdom."

"I wouldn't call that wisdom," Dad says good-naturedly.

He's usually super chill where my aunt is concerned; I mean, what choice does he have? The petite powerhouse of a woman lives in his guestroom and commands the attention of everyone twenty-four hours a day.

The man has the patience of a saint.

"I hope you like lasagna. There's enough of it for an entire family." Mom heaves the pan and begins cutting thick, ginormous slices of the baked pasta dish.

"This *is* an entire family," my brother sarcastically reminds her.

"Alex, don't talk back to your mother," my father says sternly, shooting him a warning glance across the table, not missing a beat.

For some reason my brother thinks he's above the law when he is seated next to Aunt Myrtle, like the pint-size elderly pixie is going to protect him from getting in trouble when he runs his mouth. Which I guess is true a lot of times? But only when it involves my mother—Dad is a completely different story and doesn't mind grounding the kid when he deserves it, regardless of where the offense happens. Like at the dinner table with a complete stranger.

We each take turns handing our plates to my mother while she serves us lasagna, which is still piping hot from the oven and steaming. It's cheesy and full of meat sauce—pure perfection. Also one of my favorites. Although, like Lilly, I don't discriminate among food.

I will eat just about anything.

"Did Roman tell you he lived in London last semester?"

Mom asks after she's taken her seat again. "He's very smart—practically a genius."

I blush, knowing this isn't true. I'm nowhere near genius level, although I do have a very high IQ and great cumulative grade point average.

"Mom, I don't want to talk about school."

She sets down her fork. "Well you did other things in England while you were there, didn't you? Why don't you tell her about those things? Tell her about playing squash."

The last thing I need is my mother playing matchmaker in front of my entire immediate family. God, this is embarrassing the way she's pimping me out and trying to make me look good in front of Lilly.

"I actually did know he studied in London." Lilly sweetly smiles at me. "I also did know he's very smart—I got to see his trophy." She does a little flustered headshake. "I'm sorry, I mean his award—the award he received when he was granted the scholarship to study abroad? It's so impressive. I think it looks like a Grammy." She giggles.

"I dropped it," I tell my parents. "It broke and Lilly fixed it."

"It broke?" Dad pauses from taking a bite of food. "What do you mean it broke?"

I shrug, setting a bite of lasagna on my tongue. Chew. Swallow. "It was in a box when I moved, and that box fell."

Mom gasps. Covers her mouth with her hands. "Roman, no! Oh no, honey, you worked so hard for that!"

I shrug. "I worked hard for the scholarship, not for the award." Glancing over at Lilly seated next to me, I grin. "Besides, Lilly fixed it up for me."

"She did?" Mom looks between Lilly and me. "How?"

I fish my phone out of the back pocket of my jeans, thumb through my photo gallery, and produce a snap of the now glitterati honor covered in crystals.

Offer it up so Mom can see.

She leans forward for a better look at my phone. Raises her brows. Furrows them.

Her mouth gapes.

I can see she's appalled but is too polite to say anything rude in front of Lilly. "How...nice."

I show Dad.

He isn't as subtle.

"*What* in God's name?"

I take my phone with a laugh and shove it back in my pocket.

"I wanna see," Alex complains loudly with bread in his mouth.

"Too late." I smirk at him, and suddenly we're both acting twelve.

Lilly happily forks up her dinner, chewing, swallowing and explaining. "So I was there when he dropped the box, and we all heard it crash, his roommates and me. I'm best friends with his roomie Eliza—she and I were roommates last year. Anyway, we're all sitting there when Roman walks in the room, and for whatever reason, the box falls out of his hands. I saw that it had FRAGILE written all over it on all four sides, and we could hear the pieces—literally hear the thing break." Chew, chew. Swallow. "It was so sad, I wanted to die."

My mother's brows rise.

"I jumped up and looked inside the box, and ugh, poor Roman." She hangs her head in mock sorrow. "I love crafting and don't get to do it very often, so I figured if I couldn't fix it, I could at least jazz it up, you know?"

My parents stare at her like an alien has taken over the dinner conversation.

"It looks so great."

"It *does* look great," I agree happily. "Different but great."

Lilly laughs. "I used an entire bottle of glitter glue. I mean, they're small bottles, but that just shows you how messed up the thing was."

The thing.

My mother blanches.

Aunt Myrtle hoots like an old hen. "Loretta, you should see your face!"

"I wanna see!" my brother repeats, sounding like a parrot who only knows one phrase.

"Alex, eat your dinner and stop interrupting." This from Dad.

"The award is splendid. I put it right in the center of my bookshelf."

"Splendid," Lilly says, glancing around the table at my family, her pert nose wrinkling all cute-like. "Don't you love it when he uses those kinds of words to describe things?"

Mom gets a faraway look in her eye as if Lilly has just called her oldest son the most handsome guy in all the land.

She needs to stop.

"When did the two of you start dating?"

"Dating, ha!" Aunt Myrtle's hot pink lipstick has migrated to her two front teeth, the rest of it virtually gone from the occasional blotting of the linen napkin against her mouth to remove pasta sauce—makes for an interesting sight. "What you kids do these days isn't dating. You all get handsy with each other before you know the other person's last name."

"Aunt Myrtle, that's not true." Why am I defending my generation? *It's mostly true.* People these days will have sex with someone and not even know their name—let alone last name.

"What's the girl's last name?"

"First of all, Auntie, her name is Lilly—not girl."

The old woman rolls her eyes like a teenager. "What's

Lilly's last name?" She primly takes a bite of lasagna, little lips pursed as she chews and judges me.

How the heck would I know what her last name is? I've only met her—uh...I mentally do a tally of the times Lilly and I have been in the same room together—three times!

"Aunt Myrtle, you're being ridiculous." Mom's chuckle is a forced, nervous one.

"It's Howard," my friend supplies.

"You weren't supposed to say it! He was!" My old aunt raises her arm, bangles jangling, sleeve billowing, her thin drawn-on eyebrow arched. It's crooked and doesn't match the other one, but Aunt Myrtle doesn't give a shit.

She does just fine judging us without two symmetrical brows.

"Lilly Howard," I tell her with a satisfied smile, giving Lilly a little nudge with my elbow where no one can see it. Beneath the table, she pats my thigh before returning her hand to her own lap.

The move does not escape my mother's notice.

My dick—who also noticed the innocuous thigh pat—twitches a little.

"What's your major, Lilly?" Dad wants to know. I know he's making idle conversation and being polite, probably trying to change the topic, too.

"I'm an English major with a business minor." She hesitates, pushing some food around on her plate before adding, "My parents wouldn't let me major in art."

I heard those exact words three years ago when we were incoming freshmen.

"Why not a business major with an English minor?" My brother chimes in, and I want to clock him for asking such a rude question.

"It's not a major I want to study at all, so I didn't think it mattered."

"Of course it matters." Alex is twelve, but he's also a pompous little know-it-all, partly because he's also brilliant, partly because he's a spoiled brat.

"Hi, we're not talking about school, remember?"

"Oh shit, sorry." Dad apologizes for bringing up the subject, and I can see his brain searching for another one.

Lilly doesn't wait for anyone to ask her questions. She moves on with one of her own. "Aunt Myrtle, Roman tells me you date a lot. Which apps are you on?"

Everyone around the table groans, including my brother.

"I'm glad *someone* finally asked the important questions." Aunt Myrtle's sparkly eyes narrow as she sets her fork down on the edge of the plate and refolds the napkin on her lap dramatically. She's about to start a story, and I'm certain it won't disappoint. "Yes, I do date a lot. It's given me..." Dramatic pause. "My youth back."

"You don't say," Mom deadpans.

Auntie ignores her niece. "There isn't a lot to do when you're my age—no one around here will give me back my driver's license." More narrowed stares around the dinner table. "You get pulled over twice for driving too fast and suddenly you're unfit to drive."

"You can barely see over the steering wheel."

"I'm talking about my *golf cart.*" She rolls her eyes. It's then that I notice her lids are covered in a thin hue of blue shadow, lashes brushed with black mascara. "I would date men from the retirement communities, but did you know they're riddled with..." She lowers her voice. "The clap?"

Yes, I did know that. BECAUSE SHE BRINGS IT UP EVERY OPPORTUNITY SHE CAN.

Everyone groans. Again. Something we do often with Aunt Myrtle around and her wild stories.

Lilly giggles softly. "The clap?"

"You kids call it sexually transmitted venereal disease." Lilly laughs again when Aunt Myrtle says, "I myself narrowly escaped the herp last year."

"The herp?"

We all know what Auntie is about to say.

"You know—the herpes." She dabs at her mouth with the napkin. "Similar to the 'rhea, but not as contagious."

The fact that she uses the word 'the' in front of everything has me cracking up.

"The rhea?" Lilly asks it slowly. "Like...*dia*rrhea?"

"No, the gonge-arrhea."

"That's not how it's pronounced," Alex announces. "Even *I* know that."

"Can we please talk about something else?" Mom begs. "Anything else. *Please.*"

My brother vigorously shakes his head. "Rome already asked us to change the subject once—you can't ask to do it again. House rules."

"Those aren't the house rules. Like, at all." Dad laughs, sounding a lot like one of my peers. "Besides, I kind of want to hear her explain *the 'rhea.*"

"Honestly, Josh, could you not?" This from my mother.

"So what you're saying is, dating apps are much safer for you?"

"Absolutely. Do you know how hard it is to get an old geezer to wrap it up?"

Mom gasps. "Oh *god.*"

"I assume she's not talking about presents?" Lilly whispers. "Is she talking about—"

"Condoms? Yup." Unfazed but still kind of embarrassed, I

busy myself by shoveling food into my gullet, swallowing, sneaking a peek at the watch on my wrist for the time.

We've been here thirty-five minutes.

A half hour more seems fair, yeah? Then we can safely get the hell out of here.

I think my blood pressure just shot up a billion points, and I'm a considerably healthy dude.

"So here I am, swiping on Silver Fox Singles—I swipe a few minutes every night." Aunt Myrtle is rambling on. "Do you know how many free steak dinners I've had in the past two months alone? Go ahead, guess."

"Um...five?"

"Ha!" Auntie cackles. "Twenty-six! And I don't have to put out." She pauses. "Well, I do put out—but I don't *have* to."

# CHAPTER 8
# LILLY

"Well. That was..." My sentence trails off as I fasten the seat belt across my body, testing it to make sure it's nice and secure.

"Horrible? Painful? Torture?"

His tone makes me want to laugh, but I have a feeling he wouldn't appreciate my humor at a time like this. I know without glancing over at him that Roman is embarrassed about the way his family acted at dinner, even though I found it perfectly charming and delightful.

They were exactly as I pictured them, down to his great aunt's hot pink lipstick and muumuu. His mother was sweet and welcoming, albeit a bit stuffy, his dad the funniest one of the bunch. Roman's little brother acted exactly like a little brother.

It was a fun night and a nice change from the norm, which is me eating anything I've managed to scrounge up in my dim little kitchen. A home-cooked meal is always appreciated, and Mrs. Whitaker is an amazing cook.

"I was going to say a blast."

"Okay, now I know you're lying."

"I'm not lying. I swear! That was so much more fun than we would've had with my family—my mom doesn't cook at all, and I don't have any brothers or sisters. It's quiet and boring." Not to mention during meals, my mother uses the opportunity to lecture my father and me about all the things we do wrong.

It's quite exhausting.

"Honest to God, I swear I thought they were going to ask us if we were dating," he jokes with his eyes on the road as we make our way through town the way we came.

I shift uncomfortably in my seat. "Um. About that..."

Roman glances over, regarding me in the dimly lit front seat of his car. "You look like you want to say something."

Ugh. *How do I put this...*

"So you're probably not going to like this."

"What? Lilly, just say it."

I squirm, adjusting the seat belt. Though it's not pulling on my chest, it feels like it's choking me. "When I walked through the kitchen after using the bathroom, your mom kind of cornered me."

"Okay?"

"And asked point-blank if we're dating. I mean...I didn't know what to say. She looked so..." My hands do that thing where you wave them around here and there. "Hopeful. And I didn't want to ruin her evening."

"Ruin her evening?" Rome turns his body to look at me. "Wait. What does she think is happening between us? You obviously told her we're just friends."

"Not exactly?"

He glances over.

Glances at the road.

Glances back over at me. “Lilly. Did you tell my mother we’re dating?”

“No?” Did I? Um. “Not exactly—but I also didn’t deny it.” He looks appalled. Absolutely appalled. “What!? I was trying to make her happy! It’s harmless!”

Shit.

He does not look happy.

*At all.*

I mean, what’s he so mad about? It’s not like I committed a crime! All I did was make his mother happy. She looked so...excited.

And I’ve never had a guy’s mother fawn over me that way—I guess you could say I got caught up in the moment.

“Is it so bad that they think you’re seeing me? Are you that embarrassed about it?” My stomach drops as I cross my arms over my chest, affronted. “I know I’m not winning a Nobel Peace Prize for being smart, but I do okay. I made the dean’s list.” Two years ago, and for one semester only.

“You think I’d be embarrassed to be dating you?”

I look out the window at the little farms and houses in the distance. We’re on the highway now, not too far from school but still driving in the middle of nowhere. Not much to see. I turn back toward Roman.

“I don’t know. What other reason would make you so upset? The next time you go, all you have to do is say we’re not dating anymore, right? No big deal.”

They do that on television all the time and in those cute little holiday movies.

“Lilly. You met my mother—you’ve seen what she’s like, and you only spent two hours with her.” His hands grip the wheel, and if it were brighter in here, I bet I’d see white knuckles. "She's going to hound me to know details about our relationship that don't exist—and I'm going to have to tell her you lied just to save my ass because you thought you were helping."

*Well shit, when he puts it that way...*

"I am so sorry, Roman. I hadn't thought of it that way. I thought telling her we were dating would mean she would leave you alone about it and not bug you."

"I want to make the buzzer sound and rest my head on the steering wheel, but that would only make you feel worse."

"Huh?"

"Crap. Did I say that out loud?"

"Yes, you said that out loud."

"Sorry." He grunts, shifting in his seat, which is no easy task given he's strapped into it. "I get it—you were just trying to help. Which isn't going to solve my problem."

"What problem is that, exactly? You have an awesome family, you get stellar grades, you just moved into an amazing house." I tick off his lack of problems on my fingers one by one.

"True. *However*"—he thrusts one finger into the air—"that's not going to keep my mother from breathing down my neck in the worst possible way."

"Is she that bad? She can't be that bad." Can she? I wouldn't know as my mom has no interest in my dating life other than to discourage me from having one. It seems Roman and I have the opposite problem when it comes to our parents. "She fed me."

Roman laughs, eyes on the road. "What are you, like a stray cat that gets fed once and becomes loyal for life?"

Basically. "Ha! No." But I don't mind a free meal now and again...and again.

Meow.

"Well, maybe it wouldn't hurt for her to believe we're dating for a while. Then maybe she would stop trying to set me up with the daughters of the women she volunteers with. She hasn't done it in a while, but she was gearing up to."

"It's not as if she's going to see me again." I pause, considering this statement. "On second thought, I do want free food, so she probably will be seeing me again." I laugh. "It wouldn't be a hardship to gaze into your eyes and smile adoringly."

I blink and flutter my eyes rapidly in his direction while clutching my chest, pantomiming an old cartoon where the girl skunk has heart eyes for the boy skunk.

"Lord, I wouldn't even be able to take you seriously if you were making that face at me across the table."

"But it might be fun!"

"Alright," he says at last. "We'll pretend to be dating so you can come for dinner, but I can't promise that if she drives me crazy about it, I won't just snap and tell her the truth. That would be the end of your meal plan."

"Okay, we have a deal. I'll be the most adoring fake girlfriend you've never not had."

I purse my lips and try my hand at being adoring.

His laugh has me frowning. "What's so funny?"

"I can't even take you seriously when you're making that face."

"What face!?"

"This face." Roman pulls a face, sucking in his cheeks and pursing his lips—he looks like a fish.

"That is not the face I make!" I'm adorable, dammit!

Roman shrugs. "Potato pa-tah-toe."

I slump down in my seat, pouting with a smile. "You're the worst."

With a grin, Roman concentrates on the road; we've arrived back in town and he is trying to find my house without having to ask me for directions. He is doing a great job of it, heading toward the administration building I live across the street from. It's not hard to find—it's a landmark. Still, I'm impressed he already knows and doesn't need reminding.

As we approach, my body goes still at the sight of a big, white pickup truck parked in my driveway. The taillights are glowing, which means the person driving it is still inside the cab of the truck and not inside my house.

Crud.

Roman begins the slow crawl toward it.

"Whose truck is that?"

Oh my god—I don't even want to say whose truck it is.

*Freaking Kyle.*

I swallow nervously. "Um, my ex-boyfriend's. I have no idea what he's doing here—I told him to leave me alone."

Roman drives slower still, hands at ten and two on his steering wheel. "When was the last time you saw him?"

"This past week." My throat contracts when I take a gulp. "He was outside the locker room when I came out of practice, kind of freaked me out."

"Did it scare you?"

"No—just surprised me. You'd think that, considering he was cheating on me and sleeping with other people, he wouldn't care that I broke up with him. You'd assume he didn't actually give a shit, right?"

"But he does?"

I shrug. "Guess so. He's only approached me *once* since we broke up—which are pretty good odds, considering—and he didn't follow me to my car from the locker room. I have no idea why he's trying to win me back."

"You're incredible, that's why." Roman says it with such conviction I can do nothing but stare at him. "Maybe he realizes he had a good thing and now he regrets being an asshole."

A snort leaves my nose. “That’s called taking someone for granted, and I value myself enough to not let a smooth talker turn my head back the other way after I’ve made my decision. I don’t love him.”

I don’t think I ever actually did.

I love the idea of him, but you can’t fall in love with someone’s potential; you fall in love with a person, and we never got to that place in our relationship before he ruined it.

No.

He didn’t ruin it.

He showed his true colors before I wasted too much time, and for that, I should thank him. Thank God I listened to my gut when I saw the signs. Thank God I didn’t fall for his begging.

Gross.

“What do you want to do? Should I keep driving?”

“And then what? We can’t go around the block all night—you said you wanted to get home and study. Plus, I’m tired.”

But I don’t actually want a confrontation—not tonight.

I see him biting on his bottom lip. “Do you want me to talk to him for you?”

I size my new friend up. Even though he’s sitting, Roman isn’t exactly the puny nerd you might envision; he is tall, strapping, and in great shape.

“I won’t ask you to do that.”

“If you don’t want to speak with him now, I am not taking you home.” His long fingers tap on the middle console. “Welp, guess that settles it—you’re coming home with me.” He glances over, the glow from the streetlamps above lighting his eyes. “That is, if you’re comfortable with that.”

I nod. “I would much rather go back to your place than deal with his bullshit for the next thirty minutes, or however long. I’m tired and just want to crawl into bed—you don’t mind if I crawl into bed when I get to your house, do you? I have to be up really early in the morning to work out and condition."

My eyes find the time on his dashboard. It's early enough that technically we could stay up talking until we're ready to try taking me home—but late enough that I could go to bed and easily fall asleep.

"Do you guys have a guest bedroom?"

Roman shifts uncomfortably. "Yeah, but there's no bed in it."

Hmm. "That's fine. Your bed is comfortable, I can crash there—if you don't mind."

I yawn as I wait for his reply.

It comes in the form of a "Yeah, that works."

I smile, content. And not just because of the warm leftover lasagna and garlic bread at my feet. It's knowing I'm going back to Roman's place instead of home to deal with Kyle.

---

"Roman, are you awake?"

I can tell by his breathing that he is, but just in case, I whisper it low into the pitch-black room.

"Psst."

Wow. I am really obnoxious.

Like a child sharing a bedroom with a friend for the first time. Or a young girl at her first sleepover.

After we arrived home tonight—his home, not mine—I made quick work of removing my makeup, borrowing clean leggings and a sweatshirt from Eliza (who still isn't home), and climbing into Roman's comfortably big bed.

Clean sheets. Down comforter. Fuzzy blanket.

Plenty of room for the two of us. We don't even have to touch.

It's like sleeping on a cloud in heaven.

The bed I sleep in at my place is a twin and came with the house, so there isn't a lot of room to roll around, especially if I have company. No one wants to sleep in a twin bed when they're part of a couple, so I got used to not spending much time in it while I was dating Kyle.

Roman's big bed envelops me, and I hunker down, loving how cozy it feels.

"I'm awake," he finally admits into the dark. "I haven't been able to fall asleep."

"Oh. I'm sorry—was I snoring?"

His chuckle is low. "I would never admit it."

I roll to my side, propping my chin up in my hands. "You wouldn't tell me if I was snoring?"

"No."

"Why not?"

"You'd be embarrassed."

True. "But I want to know if I was snoring."

"Do you *actually*?" His quiet question drifts out of the dark.

"Yes." Hmm. "*No.*"

He laughs, low and gravelly. It's a different laugh and a different sound than the one he makes when he's wide awake. He must be more tired than he realizes because the timbre is deeper.

"I didn't wake you up, did I?"

"No," he says. "I was actually lying here staring up at the ceiling I can't see in the dark. Sometimes it's hard for me to fall asleep because I can't shut my brain off. Is that weird?"

"No, that's not weird—sounds totally normal. I think sometimes the only reason I'm able to sleep is because I dance and cheer so hard and we work out in practice so much I'm just so crazy exhausted my body can't stay awake at night. Otherwise I probably wouldn't be able to shut my brain off either."

Especially now, not lately.

"I bet you're exhausted a lot, eh? I haven't worked out since I got back from being abroad—I've totally let that fall to the wayside. I need to get back into the gym."

"I would probably let it slide too if it weren't, like, my job."

"Do you consider it a job?"

I would shrug, but I'm lying on the bed. "Yes, I actually do. I have to perform and cheer in order to earn my scholarship. No performing, no money for school."

"That's exactly what it's like with an academic scholarship. I'm lucky enough that my parents can pay for most of my school because an academic scholarship doesn't cover very much. Not everyone is that lucky."

I roll over on the bed, fluffing the pillow to get more comfortable, turning in his direction. Toward his voice. "I think part of it has a lot to do with the fact that my mother controls me through cheer. She thinks I'm helpless and wouldn't have any other options if it weren't for my scholarships. It's almost as if she doesn't think I'm capable of working a job and going to school at the same time."

I'm babbling and thinking out loud; I can't believe I admitted that last part to him—I've never told anybody that is how my mom views me. As a little bit helpless and totally dependent.

Yawning, I tuck my hands under my chin.

This is my comfy spot; I found the place on the pillow that might actually get me to sleep, temperature is perfect, Roman's presence is a calming, soothing change.

He's giving me my space, hasn't made a single overture—not that I was expecting him to, but with guys you never know. Ordinarily I wouldn't volunteer to spend the night at the house of a guy I've only just met, but Eliza and Jack live here too. There is safety in knowing that.

Besides, Roman is my friend.

He has no designs on me, and I doubt sincerely that he's even attracted to me romantically.

*He doesn't even flirt.*

To be fair, I don't flirt with him either.

To be *honest*, I'm a terrible flirt regardless of who I'm trying to flirt with—really the only thing I have going for me is the color of my hair and the size of my boobs; otherwise I'm hopeless. Guys have to come right out and tell me they're interested before I get the hint.

I have a feeling Roman would be the same way.

We lie there listening to the sound of the other breathing, and I'm tempted to check the time but afraid it's going to be so late I'll start doing *how many more hours of sleep can I still get* math, which will only depress me if it's not a lot.

The fact that I haven't even thought about Kyle once this entire time is not lost on me; he just popped into my brain after I've been lying here for well over an hour. That's good news considering he showed up at my house unannounced, which normally would have had my mind reeling with questions.

I think I'm starting to move on. Yes, it's only been two weeks, but I'm in a really good place already. Thrilling because it normally takes me more time to get over someone and move on.

*Just goes to show you how insignificant someone actually is in your life even after spending four months in it.* What did Kyle bring to the table other than good looks and a hot body? I never actually had fun with him, and the relationship was so stressful.

"It sounds like you're thinking really hard over there."

I turn my head in Roman's direction as his voice comes out of the dark. "You can't hear me thinking, silly."

"Sure I can." He goes quiet again for a few seconds before asking, "So? Am I right?"

"Yes, you're right. I am thinking really hard over here but didn't realize you could hear it." I laugh quietly, snuggling down deeper. This bed is just so comfortable I could sleep here every night.

"We deep thinkers recognize other deep thinkers."

Roman thinks I'm a deep thinker? For some reason that thought warms my stomach and my cheeks. Does that also mean he thinks I'm smart?

"I'm sorry if I'm keeping you up," I tell him somewhat guiltily.

"You're not keeping me up—if I was actually tired, I would pass out and be dead to the world. Nothing you could do would be able to wake me up."

*Nothing?* I think to myself with a smile in the dark.

Not even a blow job?

Or me fondling his balls?

I keep these thoughts to myself, knowing they would horrify him—he's not at all like me in that way. I like sex; it doesn't seem like that is a priority for him at all.

Then again, what would I know? I don't actually really know Roman.

Still, for him to say nothing could keep him awake or wake him from a slumber makes me want to challenge him. He has no idea what he's even saying.

"We should probably try to sleep now, huh?" I don't want to, but it's probably for the best. If I keep babbling on, neither of us is going to get any rest. Soon the sun will be up and we will have to wake and get to class or practice or whatever he has to do this morning. I still have to be driven home so I can change and grab my workout gear.

Bookbag.

Laptop.

"Shoot," I say out loud, breaking my own oath to keep my mouth shut and try to sleep. "Are you okay driving me home in the morning? I'm sorry. I guess I could call an Uber or something." That would make the most sense, wouldn't it? So I don't have to trouble him?

"I can drive you home. I'm going that way anyway. What time do you have to be on campus?"

"Not too early, around eight o'clock would be good."

"I'm an early riser, so eight is a piece of cake. We should get some sleep though so we're not exhausted in the morning. I can run us to Starbucks, too, if you like."

He is too, too sweet.

"Roman?" I say his name in the dark, liking the sound of it on my tongue.

"Yeah?"

"Thanks for bringing me home with you tonight and for feeding me. That was really nice of you to do. You didn't have to invite me."

"I know I didn't have to invite you—I wanted to." He's silent for a few seconds. "Thanks for tolerating my bizarre family."

"Bizarre? They are awesome. I wish my family was half as unique."

"Is that your polite way of saying weird?"

"No, I genuinely think they're amazing. Especially your dad—he really rolls with the punches, doesn't he? I can tell nothing fazes him."

"Not anymore," Roman tells me. "Used to be a little higher strung because of his job, but he's really lightened up in the last few years. My great aunt kind of has a way about her that brings out the best in people. I think my dad is just appreciative of the fact that we're all healthy and alive."

"Did all that change after your grandma died?"

"Yeah, the big change happened after my grandma died. No one actually wants to move their elderly relatives in with them, but my parents have been great because Aunt Myrtle used to live with my grandma, so you can imagine how lonely and sad she was after she passed. She lost her best friend and kind of went off the deep end, dating and sleeping with all these old dudes to fill that void. So it's really good for her, too, being in our house."

"It must have been difficult for you to move out, huh?"

I can feel him nod beside me. "Yes. I felt a huge sense of obligation, but I knew it had to happen eventually, and there's never a good time to make a big change—so I just had to jump in with both feet and do it."

He's brave. I know he had to stand up to his parents in order to move out; you can't make a bold move like that without support—Roman is living in a house now, which requires money for rent and his share of utilities, plus food and furniture.

"Obviously my mother didn't want me moving out—she's become a little too dependent on me the past few years, counting on me to pick up slack as far as caring for my brother and now caring for Aunt Myrtle, who can be such a pain in the ass."

He says this all with a humorous chuckle.

"I imagine you are really helpful. I wouldn't want you to move out either."

"I guess...but they can't keep me young forever. I had to grow up eventually."

So true. "Growing up sucks."

"*Adulting* sucks." Roman laughs.

I roll to my back and speak toward the ceiling. "Hey, who are you calling an adult?"

"Not us."

As I sigh and yawn, my eyes slide closed. "Good night, Roman." I move my hand across the comforter and feel around for his, fingers touching the flesh on his arm.

Wordlessly, he entwines his fingers in mine. "Good night, Lilly."

# CHAPTER 9
# ROMAN

There's something that occasionally blows about being academically inclined, especially on a Friday night when the world is partying. And by the world I mean the small community of college students, the night young but abuzz with excitement that I am not participating in.

For the first time since I moved in with them, Jack and Eliza are actually going to a baseball party on Jock Row.

For the past few hours, they have been getting ready; first eating dinner, then showering, the blow dryer going on several times. Eliza has been in and out of the primary bedroom with different outfits, shouting down over the banister railing to her boyfriend about which blouse she should wear with what jeans.

I listen from my desk, pencil poised above graph paper. I'm working on a design for an engineering class—a concept car that will be used for a final paper. It will take me weeks to design, and I can't afford any more time away from the project—I've already taken off a few days moving my things into this house. So tonight I'm staying in.

They both invited me several times, which was nice, but I just...can't. I mean, I *could*; it's been so long since I've been to a party, but to be honest, my social anxiety may be kicking in, too.

Eliza is laughing from the bedroom, and I hear Jack in the kitchen cracking open what's most likely a soda—he loves Sprite—before he bounds back up the stairs, taking them two at a time.

Sticks his head in my open door. "Sure you don't want to come, Rome?"

I nod, putting a smile on. "Thanks for the invitation, but..." I glance down at my work, at the papers spread over the small desk. "I shouldn't. I'm behind on this work."

He shakes his head. "You're too serious, mate. Have a little fun."

I do have fun—just not the same kind of fun. "I'll think about it. Maybe I'll change my mind."

"You're full of shite." He laughs. "But that's alright, we'll let you off the hook this time."

All of a sudden Jack gets jostled, a new figure appearing in the doorway that is not his girlfriend. It's Lilly. Without an invitation, she enters my room and puts her hands on her hips.

My eyes cannot help but drink in the sight of her, long tan legs in a black skirt, tight red t-shirt. Strappy heels. She's totally irresistible and way out of my league. And unfortunately, she's staring me down.

"Why aren't you dressed? You can't wear that."

What does she mean why am I not dressed? I'm sitting here in track pants and a hoodie, my Friday night uniform for comfort but not style.

Also, what is Lilly even doing here? She just shows up out of nowhere, unannounced, startling the shit out of me and catching me off guard? Is this my life now? Being ambushed by beautiful girls who just want to be friends?

"I'm not dressed because I'm not going out." I tap the pencil against my desktop to illustrate my business. "I have shit to do."

I immediately regret using the word *shit* and hope my statement didn't come out sounding too harsh. I'm trying to be professional and serious so she doesn't stand there and argue with me.

Too bad Lilly is stubborn. Her brows rise and a leg juts out.

"You'd rather do homework than come out with us?"

I try to ignore how smooth her leg looks, averting my eyes and shooting a gaze to Jack, who shrugs as if to say, 'You're on your own, bro.'

"Me staying in has nothing to do with a lack of desire to go out with you guys. It's just—I'm on this deadline."

"Rome, we are all on a deadline, but that shouldn't stop you from going out and having some fun with your friends. You stay in way too often."

She's not telling me anything I'm not already aware of; pretty sure living with my parents until a few weeks ago is the reason I'm like this. And yes, I know I should get out of my comfort zone and let them take me to the party, but I wouldn't know what to do with myself there except stand in the corner and feel awkward.

I shift in my seat.

The hot seat.

*Don't look at her chest, Rome—don't look at her chest.*

They look great in that tight t-shirt.

*Crap, I just looked.*

My eyes just went there, and who would blame me—Lilly is sweet and gorgeous and standing in the middle of my bedroom harassing me about going to a party with her.

With them.

She would never invite me to a party alone—that would almost be like a date, and that's not what we're doing. Of course it's a group thing and she wants me along; we're friends now.

The friend zone.

Ugh.

Where I'm firmly planted among females near and far for all of eternity.

"You're set on staying home?" she asks one more time. "There's no changing your mind?"

She walks over to where I'm sitting and glances over my shoulder, her boobs pressing against my back as she looks at my drawing.

"What is this? A robot?"

"Kind of. It's called a concept car—it's a rendering for my final grade in an engineering class. It's going to take months to design."

Lilly looks suitably impressed. "That's neat. What is this?"

She reaches around me and points, pressing her finger against the graph paper to the back part of the car I'm working on. I do each section first and then combine them at the end with an entirely new CAD—or computer aided drawing for those who don't use the lingo as part of their vocabulary like me.

I can't concentrate on answering; I can only concentrate on her boobs pressed against my back.

The smell of her is musky and romantic, not fruity or too overpowering—like the seasons and just...good. She smells *good*. Freshly showered and coiffed.

"It's..." I swallow. "Uh."

Her face is so close when she turns her head to grin at me. "It's, uh? So technical." She rises to her full height again. "Well.

I suppose if you insist on staying home and acting like a hermit, there isn't anything we can do to convince you. I don't want to be annoying."

"I should stay home." I'm still getting used to the idea of living in a different place—baby steps.

Of course I don't say any of this; I don't want to sound like a complete pussy.

"Okay. We'll be thinking about you."

Will she be thinking about me while she's at the party filled with other dudes? Doubtful, but it's nice that she's being kind, and a part of me does believe she'll give me some thought while she is in a throng of people at whatever jock house they're going to.

"Thanks. Wish me luck and cross your fingers that I am productive." Chances are I'm going to spend the next few hours staring out the window wishing I had gone along but not really having the motivation to put clean pants on or fake a good time.

Lilly puts her hand on my shoulder and gives it a squeeze. "Good luck."

It takes a little longer for Eliza to pick out an outfit, but soon the trio are on their way and I'm listening to the sound of Jack's truck ambling down the street. I wonder how long they'll be gone, if Lilly will return once the party is over, and if she'll be drunk.

Alcohol—yet another thing I don't do a lot of.

I really need to live a little, jeez. What am I doing home on a Friday night when my friends are out having a good time? Goddamn I'm boring; it's no wonder girls aren't interested in me.

All I do is study and study some more.

My head gives a little bang against my desktop out of frustration. This is no one's fault but mine. I'm the one who's a chickenshit with anxiety about going to this party—it wouldn't actually kill me or my deadline to pop in for a bit.

I put my pencil back to my paper and do my best to focus my energy on my assignment; it's not easy, but I manage, fixating on this engine for the next two hours. Before I know it, I'm registering a dark house that is entirely too still, too cold, and too quiet—almost eerily so.

I'm hungry at one point, so I make my way down to the kitchen to scavenge the fridge, unearthing the shepherd's pie Eliza tried her hand at Wednesday night in an attempt to be domestic. She botched some of the crust, but it's edible, and it's not lasagna leftovers—we've been eating that shit for way too long. I'm sick of it.

I'm at the counter when my phone dings.

Lilly's name appears in my notifications, so I set down my fork and pick up my cell.

**Lilly:** *I know you said you didn't want to come out tonight but could you PLEASE come and help me?*

Help her?

I stand at the counter, wiping my mouth on a napkin.

**Me:** *What's wrong??*

**Lilly:** *Kyle is here.*

**Lilly:** *Which itself isn't shocking or a surprise, but he wants to talk to me and I want nothing to do with him.*

**Me:** *Is Jack there with you?*

I'm already flying up the stairs, shucking off these stupid track pants at the same time, eyes scanning my bedroom for an actual pair of jeans.

There are some tossed next to the laundry hamper; I snatch them and pull them on.

**Lilly:** *Jack and Eliza are both here, but he's like, the center of attention, and the last thing I want to do is cause drama.*

**Me:** *Where are you now?*

**Lilly:** *The bathroom—but I can't stay in here forever, people will get pissed.*

**Me:** *Give me ten minutes tops, I'm already on my way.*

Does she want me to...pretend to be her new boyfriend? As if her last one is going to believe the charade? I'm hardly a match for him. One look at me and he's going to laugh us out of the room.

But she's asking for help, and it's not my place to point out the flaw in her plan.

It's freezing outside, but I skip a jacket, not wanting to waste time fetching it out of the mudroom where I hung it on a hook. Hop in my car and navigate toward Jock Row, glad I didn't have to ask the poor girl for directions.

The red shirt is the talisman I need to spot Lilly immediately in the crowd of mundane, mute colors upon arriving at the baseball house. It's packed and lively, music blaring.

My peers are spilling out of the house and onto the wrap-around porch it's so packed inside.

I feel out of place.

Foreign.

Like a fraud for being here.

But then...

There she is.

Blonde hair, red shirt, black skirt. There is a frown on her face when she looks up and finally sees me, her back pressed against the wall near where I assume the bathroom is.

Kyle is gesturing as he speaks to her.

When she catches my eye—watching as I walk toward her through the crowd—she visibly relaxes.

"Hey, I made it." I kiss her on the forehead in greeting, doing my best to appear like a boyfriend, genuine and not the bundle of nerves I am inside. I feel sick to my stomach, somewhat terrified Kyle Gordeski, star of the football team, is going to punch me in the face for touching his ex-girlfriend.

When Lilly slides her arm around my waist, it causes my entire body to shiver.

She goes up on her tiptoes to kiss me on the mouth. “Hey, babe.”

My lips tingle.

“Who the fuck is this?” Kyle asks. I’ve never actually been this close to a football player on the university team before. He’s big, but so am I—and he’s intimidating, but I’m smart. *Who the fuck is this?* What kind of greeting is that?

He sounds like a Neanderthal.

“This is Rome, the guy I’m dating.”

Kyle barely looks at me. “You’re already dating someone new? Jesus, Lill, you’re not even going to let the body get cold?”

Her chin tilts up. “Yes, I’m dating someone new.”

She doesn’t explain herself like I thought she would, offering him no other explanation. After all, he doesn’t deserve one—based on what she’s told me and from what my roommates have told me, he cheated on her the entire time they were together, which wasn’t very long.

“Just like that?”

She gives a definitive nod. “Just like that.”

“So that’s it?”

I don’t want to open my mouth and get involved, and from the sounds of it, I don’t have to. The guy is giving up quicker than I can say Cambridge Stein Scholarship.

“Yes. Why, did you have something you wanted to say?”

Kyle glances back and forth between the pair of us, glances down at her arm around my waist and the way I casually slide mine around hers. She’s so tiny she fits right under my armpit when I pull her close.

I expect more of a confrontation from Kyle; I threw on

actual jeans to race over here tonight. Sweatpants and arguments do not jive well. Better lower my expectations and lock away my wits now that Kyle is standing before me, seemingly backing down from any type of fight.

"How long have you two been together?" he wants to know, still not walking away. "He doesn't look like your usual type."

"What's my usual type?" she asks.

"Popular and cool."

*Popular and cool?* I laugh, tossing my head and hair back. What are we, in middle school?

Who gives a shit about popularity at this age?

This guy.

This guy gives a shit about popularity, and for a brief second, I wonder what kind of chance a guy like me stands with a girl like Lilly who dates idiots like this.

He might be big, but it's obvious that Kyle Gordeski is harmless.

Lilly snorts at him before I have the chance.

"My type is really none of your business," Lilly tells him with her chin up.

"We *just* broke up."

His arguments are godawful, and quite frankly, I'm having secondhand embarrassment on his behalf.

"You cheated on me with so many girls I lost count. So don't be a hypocrite."

He turns bright red, and I doubt it's from the alcohol he's holding in the plastic cup. He looks at me, studying me. I wonder what is going through his mind as he stares at the nerdy dude with his ex-girlfriend—it's certainly no scene from *Revenge of the Nerds*, but maybe that's what I was anticipating.

Kyle is way calmer. I actually give him kudos for not arguing more.

As if on cue, a girl walks up and takes him by the arm, trying to drag him away. She has big hair and big boobs and is wearing a skirt that's shorter than Lilly's. "Come on, Kyle, we're starting a game of beer pong."

He shakes her off with a curse. "Jesus Christ, Kami, I'm in the middle of something."

The girl pouts. "You said..."

"Wow." I hear Lilly clicking her tongue. "This timing couldn't be any more perfect, could it? You better go, Kyle—you have a game of beer pong to play with Kami, and you're killing my buzz. I want to spend time with my boyfriend."

Kyle hesitates, unsure. Not wanting to walk away, giving it one last-ditch effort. "Lilly, I...I'm really sorry."

"I've moved on." Her grip tightens on my waist. Fingers squeeze. "Don't worry about me, I'm great."

Is she though?

If she was great, she wouldn't have texted me to come tonight, would she? I might not know much about women, but I know enough.

Kyle stands there, beer in hand, staring at Lilly, looking a little...ill. Regretful.

A feeling I'd feel if I let a girl like her get away.

Er.

If I cheated on a girl like that.

What sort of fucking moron does a thing like that? Cheats on a girl like Lilly? She's...

A keeper.

The kind of girl you take home to your mother.

The kind of girl who doesn't think your strange great aunt is bizarre, who thinks your dad is funny and your brother is endearing.

That's the kind of girl Kyle cheated on.

"Bye, Kyle." Lilly's tone implies 'Buzz off and get the hell out of here' without actually saying the words 'Piss off.'

He relents, chewing on his bottom lip as he gives her one last look.

One last look as she goes up on her tiptoes, pressing her mouth against mine, wrapping her arms around my torso.

She kisses me, hands burrowing beneath the hem of my thick hoodie, fingers skimming above the waist of my jeans.

I flinch, body shuddering.

It tickles but it doesn't, the contact of her palms on my skin. Unexpected and bewildering.

I've kissed girls before, *obviously I have*, if Britney and girls from science camp count—I remember it being sloppy and uncoordinated with lots of fumbling.

Oh, and braces.

Lilly's mouth is not sloppy and it's not uncoordinated and we don't have braces. Not anymore.

I open my mouth and her tongue meets mine, tentatively at first.

*Holy shit, I'm making out at a house party.*

In public.

Another first for me this year.

Lilly's lips are soft and her tongue is exploratory, hesitant to push itself inside my mouth. Nothing about this moment feels very *friend-zone-like* to me, but I'm not going to shoot myself in the foot by pulling away and telling her so.

My hands go around Lilly's waist; I pull her close, lifting her into me, hands sliding down her backside of their own accord then squeezing her ass.

Her hand slides up my chest and to my face, cupping my cheek as she kisses me, head tilted so our noses don't bump.

"Lilly," I whisper as I back up—step away slightly.

"Hmm?"

"Are you...drunk?"

She pulls back, dazed, lips puffy and no longer as glossy as they were when she left the house.

She's scowling.

"No I'm not drunk—why would you ask me that?"

Because you wouldn't ordinarily kiss me. Because you pressed your boobs against my chest. Because we are not dating and we're at a drinking party and might I remind you that you kissed me?

I say none of these things; she sounds insulted by my question and looks hurt.

Shit.

"I just..." I spread my hands wide, palms up now that she's completely stepped away from me, leaving my body to continue to hum and buzz.

I shrug feebly.

"I didn't kiss you because I'm *drunk*, Roman." She lifts her cup—her full cup—and presents it to me, wiggling it back and forth. The liquid inside sloshes around. "I have a drink, but I've barely been drinking. Once I saw Kyle lurking from across the room, I lost my enthusiasm for being here. I wanted to leave but didn't want to bother Eliza."

That makes sense.

"Then why did you kiss me?"

"Because...I don't know."

Because Kyle is over there watching? I hate to let my insecurities get the best of me, but this is where my mind goes straight to. I've seen it in the movies enough times to know she was trying to get him off her back by playacting any actual feelings for me, any actual attraction. That's fine. I'm here for that.

I'm her friend.

"Ahh."

Was the kiss fake even though it felt real?

I won't know unless I ask, and asking is out of the question.

I don't have the balls for that—not right now.

"What do you want to do? Stay or go?"

"Leave. I want to go."

"Home?"

"No, I want to snuggle up in your bed and watch movies...is that okay?"

I gulp.

"Of course that's okay." Because that's what friends are there for—soothing and support. She's troubled by her ex-boyfriend's presence, and it's my job to make her feel better.

# CHAPTER 10
# LILLY

H*is lips felt like my mouth belonged there.*

I touch a hand to them, the tingling sensation long gone but not forgotten. Swipe the warm, wet washcloth across my cheeks to wipe away the foundation on my face, rinsing my skin in Eliza's sink.

I've pillaged her closet *again*. This new hobby of mine—taking clothes from her wardrobe to wear to bed with Roman—is becoming a habit, one I know she doesn't mind.

That's what friends do.

I would do the same.

I continue with my routine, washing my face and using Eliza's skin care routine—all of her lotions and potions—watching myself in the mirror the whole time. I wonder what Roman sees when he looks at me, if he just sees the blonde hair and the big boobs or if he sees more.

That kiss tonight meant something to me, and I'm too afraid to mention it to him or ask if it meant anything to him. He did me a huge favor by showing up tonight and whisking me away when I didn't want to stay at the party. It was comforting having him at my side; the conversation with Kyle didn't last long, and that was because I wasn't alone. He saw that I was coupled.

Kyle might be a cheating asshole, but he doesn't like confrontation, and I am confident he's going to leave me alone after tonight and won't try to win me back.

I keep telling myself I want to be alone and unattached, however the shockwave that went through my body when I was kissing Roman says otherwise.

What was that? Clearly, I have been kissed before. Honestly, I've been kissed a lot—there was a time when I was younger when I thought physical contact meant someone loved me, so I dated a lot of guys and my lips are no stranger to that attention.

The difference being I've never been friends with someone first before kissing them, nor have I ever kissed a guy without their permission.

Oh Lord, what if he didn't like it?

What if he was offended?

What if he feels violated?

All these questions race through my mind as I remove the mascara from my eyelashes, the horror of my thoughts wreaking havoc on my stomach.

Bracing my hands on the counter, I lean forward, breathing heavily. I'm going to have to say something when I go back into that bedroom, aren't I? But what?

How am I going to apologize for taking liberties?

Ugh.

I procrastinate, applying lotion and creams and toners I wouldn't usually use to waste time, embarrassed to go back into the bedroom with Rome. It's also too late to go start a movie in the living room. I know Eliza and Jack will be home in a few short hours; I don't want them to feel obligated to stay downstairs watching the television with me.

In my friend's closet, I scrounged up a pair of cotton sleep shorts and sweatshirt; it's appropriate night attire but somehow has me feeling naked. Over that, a thick robe. The weather is changing and it's cold outside. My former roommate loves it chilly inside the house, so I did take a peek at the thermostat only to find it set at a chilly 66 degrees.

Brr.

*Much better for snuggling, my dear.*

I'm not going to address the fact that I could have gone to my own house but instead I came here—not to wait on Eliza and Jack but home with Roman.

Is it strange that I find comfort with him? That he makes me feel safe?

I don't consider him a stranger any longer; I've spent enough time in his presence alone to know he is a wonderful human being who cares about his family and about me.

Impulsively, I wanted to know what his lips felt like, and I may have ruined the foundation we've laid.

Turning off the bathroom light, I head back down the hallway to Roman's room. I find him flipping through the channels on his television when I walk in, fully dressed in pajamas. My eyes scan the room, noticing a pile of clothes—his jeans and what look like sweatpants and a hoodie—next to the closet door.

"Hey." I feel self-conscious, shuffling into the room farther. There is a light on the bedside table glowing, but the room is dim, turned down for bed.

He glances up at me before his gaze flits back to the TV screen, his thumb pressing down on the remote.

"Hey."

I have no idea what to do with myself; maybe coming here

was a huge mistake. I would have been better off going home—I could have distanced myself from Roman instead of fumbling headfirst into the mistake I made tonight.

Kissing him.

Ugh, the look on his poor face.

He must hate me.

Should I sit or should I stand? Should I sit on the floor, or would that be ridiculous? I've already slept with him in bed, and I've been in the bed twice. He's obviously expecting me to plop down beside him or he wouldn't be on the far end...

*Make a move, Lilly, you're making things weird.*

Before I sit down, I remove the robe and climb onto the bed in my borrowed pajamas, legs getting pelted by the cool air. There is no snuggle blanket anywhere, so I pull back the covers and climb underneath. The sheets are cool yet smooth, crisp white linen.

Bright.

I would bet Roman is the type of guy who washes his laundry on a regular basis, which is more than I can say for the rest of the male population on college campuses. He's more mature than anyone I have met, male and female alike.

"Brr." I shiver, my feet doing a little dance where no one can see them. "So cold."

He smiles but doesn't say anything, and my stomach falls.

I inhale a deep breath, letting it out slowly. "Roman, I just want to...apologize for tonight."

He puts down the remote control and turns to face me, his expression one of seriousness.

"You don't have to apologize for feeling scared, Lilly."

Scared? No. Not at all what I'm referring to.

I try again, wringing my hands under the covers. "I meant... I apologize for, um. Kissing you like that. I'm sorry if it made you feel weird—I shouldn't have ambushed you."

"I understand why you did it—I know it must provide a sense of security to have a new boyfriend to keep the old one away from you."

"You think I wanted you to pretend to be my *boyfriend*?"

The thought gives me pause as I stare at him, blinking rapidly.

The horror! *He thought I wanted him to pretend to be my boyfriend?*

Huh.

It didn't cross my mind at the moment, but now that it has—I would be able to go out to party without having to deal with Kyle sniffing around my skirt if I had a new boyfriend.

"Isn't that the reason you kissed me?"

No. That's not the reason I kissed him, but I'm too embarrassed to admit it; far be it from me to change his mind.

I kissed Roman for a few reasons, but pretending he was my boyfriend? Not one of them.

1. I kissed him because I was curious.
2. I kissed him because I was feeling impulsive.
3. I kissed him because...I felt *happy* having him at my side.

I did not kiss him as part of some ploy.

"Honestly, Roman, I'm just really glad you were there tonight. I was so relieved when you showed up that my entire body relaxed. That whole situation was really messed up."

That's true enough.

It's not a lie, not entirely.

I know it's a copout telling him and giving him the impression I was using him, but somehow, telling him the truth in this moment? I can't get the words out of my mouth.

I've never been great at hard conversations, and this one fits that description.

Call me a wuss if you must.

Making myself more comfortable in bed, I recline on the pillow and pull the covers up while he fusses with the television, finally settling on a popular show about a family that lives in a motel. It's a series I've already seen twice but never get tired of.

Rome sets the remote on his bedside table and flicks off the light, settling in beside me, putting his hands behind his head and lacing his fingers together.

I wonder what's going through his head right now. It's on the tip of my tongue to ask, but I know the last thing guys like to hear is *What are you thinking about right now?* Cliché on a Friday night?

No thanks.

My eyes drift closed, and somewhere in the house I hear the sound of other voices; Eliza and Jack must be home already. Sounds like they're rifling through the fridge for something to eat, laughing and definitely flirting.

Eventually the television turns off—he must have had it on a timer—and now we're lying here the same way we did the other night after returning from his parents' house. This time, though, it's more strange and awkward, this tension created by my own actions at the party.

Why am I letting him believe everything about tonight was fake? Why isn't he saying anything?

*Why am I not saying anything?* This misunderstanding is my fault.

I roll to my side to face him, despite the fact that it's completely dark.

"Roman?"

"Yeah?" I notice for someone so eloquent, he says *yeah* a lot.

"I didn't kiss you because I wanted you to pretend to be my boyfriend. I kissed you because..." My voice trails off. "I kissed you because I felt like it. And I'm sorry."

"But is that what you want?"

"Is what what I want?" Wait. Did that question make sense?

"To have me there when you go out so Kyle leaves you alone?"

"It would be helpful, if I'm being honest."

"Okay," he says after a few beats.

"What do you mean, okay?"

"I mean okay—if you want me there when you go out then I'll be there. You're already doing me a solid with my parents, remember? You can come with me to my parents' house and act like you're my girlfriend, and we all win. Maybe it will drive home the point a little more if anyone sees you and me together going to my parents'."

Is this him proposing a fake relationship? Not just for his mom's sake?

Swallowing, I gather up the courage and ask, "Do you still want me to pretend to be your girlfriend?"

It's a bit odd, I'll admit. What on earth does he need me for —all he has to do is tell his mother he's not dating me anymore. I know she wants Roman to have a girlfriend, and the way she acted at Sunday supper definitely leaned in the direction of her wanting *me* to be his girlfriend. Since I didn't do anything to make her think we *weren't* dating, we decided we would continue the charade for that alone, but still...does he mean for more than just his parents? I have to admit, it gives me a bit of a thrill, but also...

If he continues to say he's dating me, won't that create more interrogations from his family?

"You'll be provided with a hot meal every Sunday, remember?" he continues, sweetening the deal with promises of food.

"All I have to do is flirt with you at dinner?"

"And maybe appear in a few FaceTime chats with my mother."

Piece of cake. "And you'll come to parties with me?"

"Yes."

"There has to be more to it than that. What about physical intimacy? This isn't going to be a friends-with-benefits situation, is it?"

"No! *No*, it wouldn't be friends with benefits. I mean, you helping me out is definitely a benefit, but I don't expect you to make out with me."

It's telling that his mind doesn't immediately go to sex or blow jobs or any other intimate activity—it goes straight to kissing, as if that is the most sexual thing he's ever done.

"You can trust me not to take advantage of you," he promises, as if I had any concerns. He's not the type of guy to do such a thing, so it hadn't even crossed my mind to not trust him.

Well...

...shit.

Maybe I want him to take advantage of me. Maybe Roman is the type of guy I should have been dating all along instead of the athletic, meathead type I've been going after most of my adult life. I've been a product of my environment and the things my mother thinks are important, like popularity, good looks, and being in the spotlight.

In a way, my entire being has been based on lies. I lie to my mother every single time we speak, pretending everything is fantastic when in truth, nothing is. I hate being a cheerleader and I hate being a part of the team—I love dancing, but not when it comes with conditions.

I want to do it for me.

I want to do it when I want.

I don't want to date a football player or an athlete.

I'm sick of only seeking them out; it makes me feel like a gold-digging cleat chaser.

I want to date a nice guy who respects me, who thinks I'm funny and intelligent and isn't concerned with how I look 100% of the time. I want to be able to wear sweatpants and sweatshirts and not do my hair or put on makeup.

I want to be the kind of person Roman would respect.

"Did you ever think of the fact that *I* might take advantage of *you*?" I say it in jest, but his reply takes me aback.

"Yeah, actually, I did think you might be taking advantage of me."

I reach over as far as I can and flick the switch so I can look at his face. He blinks against the light as it blinds him, eyelids rapidly fluttering as his eyes adjust.

"Wait. Are you being serious right now?"

"Yes?"

"For real—are you being serious?" I laugh it off, but he's not smiling anymore. "Stop joking around."

"Does that actually sound like something I would be kidding about? Yes, Lilly, tonight I thought maybe you were using me to get back at your ex-boyfriend or make him jealous."

My mouth opens, floundering. My face flushes—not from embarrassment, but from a little bit of shame? Is that what this emotion is? I'm appalled.

Disappointed.

Confused. "I don't understand how your mind would go *there*."

He pulls a face. “All the elements were there, Lilly. You texting me to come save you, your ex-boyfriend cornering you, the kiss in front of him—you’re telling me that wasn’t part of some plan?”

Save me? “Excuse me? Who around here needs saving?”

“’Kay, that didn’t come out the way I meant it, but you get what I mean. You *did* text me and said to save you. What else am I supposed to think?”

“Um, *no*.” Indignation rises in my throat. “This whole night wasn’t a twisted plan to put my ex-boyfriend in his place, and I wasn’t using you. What kind of girl do you think I am?”

Roman shrugs—*shrugs!*—and I want to knock him off the edge of the bed by socking him with a pillow.

Throwing back the covers, I step onto the floor, rising. “That’s your opinion of me?”

My brain floats back to earlier in the evening when he asked if I was drunk. And sure, there might have been a bit of alcohol involved, but not enough to make me forget myself.

“No, that’s not my opinion of you.” His voice is calm and rational, unlike the turmoil I’m feeling inside my gut. “All I’m saying is, think about how the whole thing looked from my point of view. Are you considering how it might have made me feel?”

“Then what is your opinion of me?”

“I think...” He speaks slowly, clearing his throat before continuing. “You’re a girl who just broke up with her boyfriend. You’ve been hurt by him and didn’t want to deal with him tonight, so you called me.”

How is he sitting there so calmly when I have suddenly become a ball of nerves?

“Kyle and I dated for four months—that’s hardly enough time to be brokenhearted. All I need him to do is leave me alone.”

"Right. And you..." He clears his throat again. "Used me to make that happen."

"I was not using you to get back at him or make him jealous or make him go away. I just wanted you there because it's comfortable." I throw my hands up, discouraged. "How did this conversation go from you asking if I'd play your fake girl-friend to you telling me you thought the whole thing tonight was a lark in an attempt to make my boyfriend jealous?" Oops. "I meant my *ex*-boyfriend."

"I'm not trying to turn this into an argument, Lilly. I'm simply explaining to you what was going through my mind."

I walk out of the room without responding, bypass Eliza and Jack's bedroom—skip saying good night—and trudge barefoot down the stairs and through the kitchen to the side door.

Crappers, it's raining outside and I'm not wearing any—

"Lilly, where are you going?"

"Home."

Which is really too far away to walk to.

Shit, now what?

Where are my shoes? Near the front door.

I walk blindly to the foyer, mindful of Roman trailing along behind me.

"Lilly, be reasonable."

"No. I'm not in the mood." I'm hurt and confused and embarrassed, but that's nothing new.

I step into my dumb shoes; they're impractical wedges and look ridiculous with these pajama shorts and the sweatshirt I've got on. I should probably change, but my clothes are in Eliza's bathroom, on her floor, and the last thing I want to do is go knocking and interrupt. Or explain myself.

The whole thing is so stupid and petty.

"At least let me drive you home."

It's not horribly late—not even bar closing time. "I'm fine."

**Fine: /fahne/ *adverb***

Definition: *well or healthy, not sick or injured. In an excellent manner. Satisfactory; acceptable. Also see: women's definition of* absolutely not *fine.*

"Are you just saying that?"

Duh. Of course I'm just saying that. I don't want him driving me home—and I also don't want to walk home, but here I am being unreasonable, putting my shoes on at the door with no option to return unless I want to come across as being, well—unreasonable.

Which I am.

Dammit!

I should have never started the discussion in the first place, should have let him drift off to sleep, should have lay there in the dark and kept my mouth shut.

As I'm buckling the strap of my second shoe, he places his hand on my shoulder, the warm heat making its way to my heart.

"Lilly. Don't leave." His voice is quiet. "Stay. Let's go back upstairs and talk about this. Neither of us meant anything by it."

He's not wrong, of course. The whole conversation got away from us; I wasn't trying to use him earlier and he knows it, and I do want to go back upstairs where it's warm and I can snuggle in his cozy bed.

Roman is my friend.

I don't want to fight with him, and there is no logical reason to. You're supposed to work things out, right?

"*Lilly.*"

I release the shoe I intended to put on, and it drops to the cold tile floor.

"Okay."

"Okay?"

I nod, bending to unbuckle the other wedge, watching as it slides off next to its match.

"I have to call my coach and check in for curfew tonight anyway—I'm going to do that real quick if you don't mind. Then we can talk."

Coach doesn't answer, so I text her a photo of myself in the empty kitchen with a time stamp before following Roman back up to the second floor and into his bedroom. He holds the door open for me like a gentleman so I can pass through, sitting on the edge of the bed but not climbing into it as I did before. I'm reluctant to get too comfortable. Maybe that's been the problem this entire time—my comfort level with him. I feel like we've been friends forever, but I also feel something else—something he doesn't seem to understand.

Something I don't seem to understand myself.

That's fine.

It isn't as though I haven't been rejected before or had a guy not like me—both have happened, just not recently.

Is he stereotyping me because of my cheering career and the color of my hair? I'm too afraid to ask.

"I think we got off on the wrong foot when we got home," he tells me, sitting in the desk chair across the room, swiveling it so he faces me. I don't know when the wheels fell off the bus.

"I'm probably hypersensitive," I confess.

"What do you mean?"

I give my answer a bit of thought before saying, "It's a new semester and I've had a lot of change, and to be honest, I've never had a guy who was just a friend before. I suppose Jack counts, but not really? I haven't known him long, and he's Eliza's boyfriend...it would have been weird for me to ask for his help tonight. I guess I just...don't know how to behave with a guy friend."

"If it makes you feel any better, I have no idea what I'm doing on a daily basis, let alone with a girl who is also a friend. I should never have gone with the plan that you fake it for me for the sake of my parents. That was foolish and I apologize. I can't imagine how that made you feel when I agreed to it."

Aw, the poor guy. "Rome, you don't have to apologize for thinking out loud—I actually think we would have a lot of fun pretending." Plus, he will get some practice!

The thought of him dating someone else fills me with a little bit of dread. But this is what friends do for each other; they help one another out. Not that I believe he needs it, but he could probably stand to gain a little more self-confidence when it comes to the female persuasion.

"What do you say? Should we put tonight behind us and just do it?"

"Do it?" He looks pale and gulps.

I roll my eyes. "You know, the fake relationship thing."

Rome swivels in his desk chair. "It might be fun."

"It could be—I've never done it." Never had to; haven't ever considered it until he brought it up tonight. "And I'm sorry tonight was such a shit show. I wasn't thinking when I texted you—I was only thinking of myself."

"That's what friends are for. It's not like I was doing anything."

"You were studying." His grades are important to him, apparently much more so than mine are to me, and perhaps if I went to fewer parties and cracked open more textbooks, I wouldn't be in a position where I feel trapped.

It crosses my mind to suggest several rules for this new adventure—guidelines—but it's late and it appears neither of us are thinking clearly.

Roman looks exhausted; I am exhausted.

I'm tired, crabby, and keep overreacting. The best thing for me is a good night's rest. I have to be up at six in the morning to practice—there is a home game tomorrow at noon, so it's going to be nonstop from the moment I pry my eyes open.

His bed is so much more welcoming than mine. I got the best night's sleep last time I was here.

Roman finally removes himself from the desk chair and comes to the bed. He hesitates slightly before climbing beneath the covers.

"I'm glad we worked through this," I say softly.

"All a misunderstanding. Things happen when people are stressed out, and running into an ex is stressful."

"It was."

I'm on my side facing him, lights still on.

Scanning the room, my eyes latch onto the award I repaired for him. Rising, I cross to stand in front of it, fingers carefully tracing along the edge where his name is. Where his name *was*.

Such a shame.

Such a good guy.

I turn when he yawns to find him watching me—of course he is; there's nothing else in here to look at, and I'm the foreign object in the room.

"Roman?" I move back toward the bed.

"What?"

"Can I ask you a personal question?"

"How personal are we talking?"

"On a scale of one to ten? I would say an eight."

He mulls this over before nodding. "Okay."

My blonde hair fans out on his pillow as I stare up at the ceiling, pulling the blankets up to my chin. "Have you ever dated anyone? Or had a girlfriend?"

He looks at me, surprised. "That's it? I thought you would ask me something more invasive, like a sex question or something."

"Sorry to disappoint you."

"Ha, you didn't disappoint me." He pauses. "I sort of dated someone freshman year, briefly. If you think I'm awkward, she was twenty times worse."

"I don't think you're awkward at all." Not in the least; I find his manner to be charming and approachable. He is goofy and adorable and says what's on his mind in a way that is quiet yet forthright.

The little bits of alcohol I consumed tonight warm my belly.

Reaching forward, I lay my hand on Roman's. His palm is lying flat on the bed, a gentle indent on the mattress as he looks over at me.

"Feels that way sometimes. I often worry I spend too much time on schoolwork and not enough time interacting—I think maybe my mom was right about that."

"Why, does she harp on that?"

"Yeah. They want me to be successful, but they also talk about balance." His thumb slowly begins stroking the underside of my palm as he speaks.

"You don't think you have good balance?"

"I stayed in tonight because I was fixated on the engineering project when I could have been out with my friends—I'd call that shitty work-life balance."

True. "The good news is, there is always room for improvement, and you wound up coming out anyway!" Silver lining.

"But I wouldn't have if you hadn't needed me."

Also true. "I did need you." Moreover, "I wanted you there to begin with."

"You did? Why didn't you say so?"

I kind of did, he just didn't pay attention to my begging. I shrug, though I'm in a sleep position. "Because you were set on staying home. It's not my place to peer-pressure you into doing what you clearly don't want to do. Besides, not everyone likes parties, and I just figured you were one of those people. You were miserable that night we met three years ago."

"That's a valid assessment."

Valid assessment.

I giggle at his formality, biting down on my bottom lip.

He's so adorably intelligent.

Our hands are entwined now and I don't know how they got that way, but his fingers are laced with mine, which causes my heart to beat wildly inside my chest. It wasn't beating this wildly when I kissed him, but I can feel every pulse. Every rhythm.

It feels like we are too far apart—on an island—not that I would dare move any closer; I don't want to crowd him or make him uncomfortable or put the moves on him in any way. *I did that already, and look where it got us.*

"I should turn the lights off so we can sleep," he finally murmurs, rolling back toward the door. His long arm stretches as far as it can go and flicks off the switch, leaving us in the dark.

Surprisingly, he relocates my hand and grips it the way he was doing before.

I shiver.

"Are you cold?"

Kind of, but not really. But I'm not about to tell him that. Instead I say, "Yes, just a little bit. I probably should've put on pants and also: not gone outside."

Really, I could use a snuggle.

"If you wanna get closer so you can get warmed up, you can. Body heat is nature's defense."

I need no further invitation.

"You can't argue with science." I laugh as I move closer to

him on the bed, rolling into his open arms, spooning my backside into his front.

*Don't wiggle your ass in his junk, don't wiggle your ass in his junk...*

Easier said than done; I'm a natural flirt. Plus, I like Roman as a human being and as a friend. He's handsome and adorable and who could resist that combination?

"I'm not sure where to put my hands." He laughs softly into my ear after a time, sending more shivers down my spine.

"You can put them around me—I won't bite." It's been ages since I've spooned or been spooned. Rome's arms tentatively move from wherever he was hiding them to my arm, big palm on my bicep.

It's nice.

So nice.

Without trying to be too obvious, I scooch back, pressing my backside closer to his pelvis, our height difference when we're standing creating the perfect partnership while we're horizontal.

We fit just right.

Roman must have showered at some point before coming to my rescue tonight because he smells divine.

Fresh.

Masculine.

I've smelled him post-shower before and add it to my list of favorite things. "Things I Could Smell Forever" or "Smells That Turn Me On."

1. Roman
2. Pumpkin spice anything
3. Old Spice? Ha!
4. Roman
5. Rain

6. Fresh-cut grass
7. Gingerbread
8. Baked cookies
9. Babies and baby powder
10. Roman

The list goes on and on so I'll end it at ten, but mostly, Roman tops the list.

I'm one short breath away from licking my lips, even though this cuddle session is anything but sexual.

*Sigh.*

"Are you getting warmer?"

Of course! But there's no way I'm admitting that—he might go back to his side of the bed, and then where would we be? Back to strictly platonic. Sure, that's what we agreed on, but tell that to my body. It is not on board with that agreement.

"It helps having your arms around me, for sure."

We lie like this for a little while and my heart beats wildly from nerves; I wonder what he's thinking about while we are here snuggling like two people in a relationship. I've certainly never cuddled with a male friend before...am I doing it wrong? Because it feels so absolutely right.

Roman, for his part, doesn't move a muscle—he lies absolutely still, like a corpse in a haunted house.

The perfect gentleman.

*I wonder what it would take to break that polite demeanor.*

I've met his family and seen his parents; I know now that his upbringing was one with rules and etiquette and manners —he knows things I wish would have been taught to Kyle and the other guys I causally went out with who didn't know common courtesy from a hole in their ass.

Reaching up, I take hold of his hand and move it from my arm...to the small of my waist.

I swear he stops breathing; I stop breathing too when his fingers grip my body, pressing themselves into my exposed flesh. When I reached up, my shirt hiked up, too, leaving my belly bare.

I make no moves to pull it back into place.

Roman clears his throat.

I cuddle in deeper, moving in a way that has his hand drifting.

Giving him the signal that it's okay for it to roam.

Rome.

Big hand, big heart.

Big dick, too, because I can feel it hardening against my ass crack; whether intentional or unintentional, Roman is getting hard. He doesn't mention it and he doesn't move another inch, so I'm guessing he is embarrassed or isn't sure what to do about it.

This is an exciting development that I want to take advantage of.

We may be in a fake relationship for the sake of his family and Kyle, but there's nothing fake about his hard-on.

I lie here for another five or ten seconds or twenty—I'm not sure exactly because I'm not counting—before I ease to my back, his hand having no choice but to trail along my stomach. His fingers cover my belly button, his massive palm spanning the entire area.

It's warm and sears my skin like a brand.

I make a tiny moaning sound—call it a nonverbal prompt if you will, intended to spur him on.

It does not.

Roman is either too polite, or too shy, or too uninterested.

*But he kissed you back like he meant it,* I tell myself.

Of course he kissed me back—polite or not, he is still a male with male instincts doing what guys do.

My arm goes up again, this time so my hand can slide its way across his neck, fingers raking through his hair, nails lightly dragging his flesh.

Those male instincts I just mentioned? Yeah—they're in full force now as he moves. Not a lot, but enough, his hand slowly beginning a light back and forth, back and forth across my stomach. If this was an actual trail, a foot path would be forming from wear.

We stay like that for a while, me rubbing the back of his neck, him with his hand on my belly, our faces inches apart.

When I glance up at him—in the small sliver of light shining into the room from the light of the moon—he's watching me too, head slightly bent, studying me the way I'm studying the weight of his hand on my body.

The pressure tells me he's not unaffected. The slight curl of his fingers tells me he's exercising control.

His breathing has changed, too; he's gone from not breathing at all to shorter breaths, the same way I have.

It hitches when I wiggle my hips, rubbing against the stiff tip of his cock, and I bet he's wishing he hadn't agreed to keep me warm or invited me back into his bed to begin with.

We're not dating.

We are not a couple.

Roman does not strike me as the type of guy who does anything casually—he does it with his whole heart and his whole self, putting all his effort into whatever he starts.

Which would make for an amazing orgasm.

*Don't be selfish, Lilly.*

It's not selfish to want to be touched, especially not by someone you like.

Friends kiss.

Friends fuck, too.

Just because I swore off men doesn't mean I have to swear off sex, although the two do go hand in hand nicely. Vibrators obviously do not count, nor does using my own hand. And why should I deprive myself if I've changed my mind? I'm allowed to do that—I wasn't anticipating meeting a guy like Roman when I decided to go on a detox.

He was a pleasant surprise I never would have predicted.

I want him so bad, and not because he's changed position so his big dick is pressed into the side of my hip.

Okay—that's one of the reasons.

But not the only reason.

Okay *fine*—maybe right now that's the only reason, plus I mentioned he smells like a wet dream, yeah?

I inhale a breath when Roman's hand does the one thing I never thought it would do: travel north. Tentatively...so tentatively I may lose my mind, but north it goes in the direction of my breasts, and thank God I didn't put a bra on earlier when I was pouting and wanted to leave.

Damn fool.

Roman's hand stops roaming.

I stop massaging his neck.

Pull him down a bit, touching my lips to his.

A soft, feathery, barely-there kiss to get the message across.

Message received.

Suddenly we're kissing, mouths locked, our entwined tongues doing incredible things to my lower half. *God, I want him so bad.*

I bend my leg, and when I do, Roman's palm grazes up the smooth skin from my knee to my thigh to the trim of my cotton sleep shorts, fingers teasing inside the fabric.

Yes...

More.

*Don't stop teasing me*, I want to tell him so he won't quit. *Don't you dare stop.*

I open my mouth wider so he can kiss me deeper, and he does, his body rolling closer to mine until he's pressed so firmly against me it's damn near a dry hump.

Which I would love, *by the way...*

Side note: I tried to bring dry humping back in a big way last year—kick it old school, if you will—but none of my ex-boyfriends went for it. Something about 'chaffing their balls while wearing jeans' and wanting to be balls deep instead? They hated it no matter how much I tried.

Lame.

Finally, Roman's hand finds my breasts, carefully moving over one of them, the gentlest caress as he explores.

"Is this okay?"

I nod, almost unable to speak. "Yes" comes out as a whisper.

He's so tender with me I actually crane my neck to watch his hand explore, the sweatshirt I had on long gone, t-shirt hiked up past my chest. I can see it well enough when his fingers splay, thumb brushing my nipple.

"You're so beautiful," he says as his head dips, mouth latching on, lips sucking. Kissing where his hand was.

Oh shit, that's going to make me wet...

I'm so easy when it comes to foreplay. The smallest things get me hot and bothered. Turned on.

Words.

A slight stroke.

Watching.

The combination intoxicates me, and I feel powerful even as I lie here like a pillow princess doing none of the work.

I stretch out my body, affording him more access and a better view, one hand now propped behind my head while the other one runs down the back of his shirt—tugging at it slightly so he'll get the hint and tear it off himself.

He does.

Lord I need a light on, because from what I can see in this dimmest of light, Roman has the body of a Roman god—broad shoulders and firm chest with a smattering of hair that's exactly the right amount.

I run a hand across his pecs, shivering with excitement.

He might not be an athlete, but his body is athletic and toned, warm beneath my palm. He's beautiful.

He shivers, too.

I lean up so I can kiss his shoulder. Collarbone. The center of his chest, below his Adam's apple.

His mouth.

"Don't you think it's only fair that you have your shirt off, too?"

"Good point." I like the way he's thinking and quickly shuck my shirt, also peeling off my shorts although no one asked me to.

I'm in nothing but a thong, grateful I had the good sense not to wear what I call my "nighttime underwear," which are high-waisted granny panties that come in packs of six with elastic bands.

*I highly doubt Roman would notice if I was wearing a brown paper bag.*

In fact, if there's one thing I've noticed about guys in general, it's that they do not judge your naked body—all they see is that you are naked. They see boobs. They see vajayjay.

Naked flesh is so seductive men don't see what I perceive as flaws.

He has no idea where to touch me first, his hands roaming the entire length of my body starting with my feet. Graze up my leg (and thank God I shaved yesterday), over my hip, up my stomach, over my boob. Down my arm and up again, brushing the hair off my shoulder before kissing me there.

Kissing, warm breath below my ear. I get wet between my legs all over again.

"You are so sexy," he tells me.

"You are, too."

Our mouths meet again, more heated this time, more tongue, more excitement, more urgency.

I cannot get enough of him; I want to eat him up and swallow him whole. Judging by the way his hands are all over me and his tongue is in my throat, he feels the same way. I pull at his shoulders so he will crawl on top of me and cover me with his body. He obliges without much urging.

He's wearing bottoms, but I can still feel him through the fabric, the thin thong I'm wearing doing little to conceal or barricade my vagina from his swollen dick.

It wants to summon him inside.

As if he was reading my mind earlier, Roman begins an unhurried, steady and rhythmic thrusting motion. We begin mimicking sex, the tip of his dick easing inside my swollen folds.

So. Wet.

So needy.

*More.*

*Thong. Sleep pants.*

Nothing but skin on top, my nipples pressed against his bare chest, the hairs tickling my boobs.

Still, I want more.

I push the hemline of his bottoms until he's lifting his thighs in the air, making it easier to shuck them and kick them off onto the floor beside the bed.

He kisses me everywhere, inching his way down, reaching

the apex of my thighs, taking off my thong then parting my legs with his elbows.

Licks me. *Sucks.*

I squirm, anticipation reeling through my core. Clutch at the bedcovers, teeth biting down on my bottom lip when he parts me with his fingers so he can suck harder in the one spot I want sucked.

Sucks like he's eating or lapping up ice cream.

"Oh god..." I keep my voice down, knowing if I'm any louder, Eliza and Jack may be able to hear me. I would die if they came into the room.

"You taste so fucking good."

Do I?

I've heard it before but have never believed it. How does a pussy taste good? It's not candy and it's not fruit—*what's so great about it?*

I do not raise the debate.

I do not want to come in his mouth, so I pat the bed, urging him to take his mouth off my lower half and crawl up beside me. I want to straddle him, take a bit of control.

Make him feel *oh so good.*

He stays down on me for a few more seconds—minutes—hours—TOO LONG BECAUSE I WANT HIM UNDER ME before relenting; I am good and lathered up when his back hits the mattress and I climb on top of my new friend.

My friend.

What an odd sensation to be friends with the person you're sleeping with—we're connected in ways I've never been to someone. I've never allowed myself to connect to a guy before, and now I want his dick inside me, fingers crossed.

And toes.

I gaze down at him, hair falling in waves around my face, hitting his chest.

"Hi," I whisper, kissing him on the cheek.

Kiss the tip of his nose.

"Hi." He is whispering too, hands now curiously trailing along my spine, up and down, fingers pressing into the vertebra. When he is done with that, those same fingers sweep the hair back from my face. "You're beautiful."

I know that. I've been told so a hundred times beginning when I was a young child, but until this moment, I'm not sure if I've ever...felt it.

Being pretty and cute was my job.

My mother wasn't happy unless there was a bow in my hair and on my dress. She wasn't happy unless I was winning a pageant or a dance competition. She wasn't happy unless I was smiling.

Being pretty is a *chore* that I resent most days.

Hearing it and feeling it are not the same thing, nor do they go hand in hand.

I let him play with my hair, his hard erection meeting my backside as I sit on him *and I swear to God I feel it twitch*, his eyes never leaving my face. He doesn't stop meeting my gaze.

"So are you," I tell him in response to his comment, believing every word of it. His light shines inside and out, and I want more of it.

I lower my mouth and kiss him.

"Guys aren't beautiful," he scoffs against my lips.

"*You* are."

I don't want to argue with him; I know he carries the same insecurities around with him that I do, though they're a different breed of self-consciousness.

We kiss and his hands find their way to my breasts, cupping them as they sway gently. They sway more when I grind on top of Roman, lifting my ass so I can place his cock under me and bask in the hard length of it.

Back and forth...back and forth...

It would be so good if we were naked.

Correction: if *he* was naked.

His breathing is hard, labored.

His hands? All over.

I'm not sure who pushes at the waistband of his boxer briefs first—Roman or me—or who it is that actually shoves them down, but soon they're down around his knees and his dick springs free.

My mouth waters.

My vagina throbs.

My heart pounds.

Our mouths latch on, wet, desperate kisses—the kind you see in the movies—his hand on the back of my head pulling me in closer so he can kiss the hell out of me.

I move over him, dry-fucking the tip of his cock as it flirts with the entrance to my core, getting me hotter and hotter and hotter.

"God, I want you so bad." He groans into my mouth, hand still gripping the back of my scalp; I can feel how bad he wants me—his entire body is tense from the tips of his fingers to the tip of his dick to the position of his legs.

His knees are bent, legs slightly spread—he's doing his best to maintain his sanity the same way I'm trying to maintain mine.

The intention tonight was not to have sex with him.

The intention tonight was not to come home with him.

He didn't even want to go out.

Yet he did.

*For me.*

"I want you, too."

*What to do, what to do...*

Just because we're horny and naked does not mean we

should be having sex right now—I know it and Roman knows it.

My head dips again, mouth falling open—I swear my eyes roll to the back of my skull when the head of his cock accidentally goes inside me the slightest bit, giving new meaning to 'just the tip.'

He hisses.

I begin to sweat, beads of perspiration forming on my forehead in the unsexiest of ways. But it's hot in here—or is it just us?

"Should we just do it?" I muse out loud, not expecting him to say, "Yes."

We kiss again, the only thing we can do now that we've had a good and thorough discussion on the matter.

I move to readjust, ready to have him bury himself.

"Wait—if we're going to do this, I should put something on."

So. Responsible.

I'm on the pill—obviously I am—but don't tell him that, pleased that he's looking out for us both.

Nodding, I watch as he leans over to pull open the bedside table drawer with me still sitting on top of him, rooting around. Produces a box of condoms as my fingers drag up and down his back.

What is he even doing with condoms? I didn't think he was the casual sex kind of guy.

"These aren't mine," he explains. "They were left here by the person who lived in this room before."

Um—that person was Eliza, but okay.

Naughty, naughty, smart, safe girl.

I mentally salute her preparedness and thank her for the sex I'm about to have.

Giving Roman room to tear open the condom wrapper and

roll it onto his hard-on, I slide over but still never take my eyes off the process, mouth watering in anticipation of what's to come. Literally.

I never found dicks appealing until this very second —never.

But Roman's penis is incredible to look at, at least in my eyes: not too big and not too small, not too thick and not too thin. Perfect if there is such a thing, and I do not say this lightly because let's face it, we all know dicks aren't cute.

Like, at all.

He slides the condom on, fumbling through it a bit, hand shaking.

He's having a rough go of it, and I help, on the off chance his clumsy approach kills his boner—I'm way too worked up not to bang him at this point, and him going down on me again will not do.

I want—nay, NEED his dick inside me.

Together we slide it on, nice and snug.

I kiss him again to get the ball rolling once more, get us more turned on, get him worked up. Flop down onto the mattress, onto my back, pulling him along for the ride so he's on top, missionary for the win.

I'm wet, so it's easy for him to slide in, one slow inch at a time, holding his breath the entire way until he's to the hilt.

He feels big, just right.

I squirm beneath him, wanting him to pump—hard.

Instead, he does a steady rocking back and forth that does everything to drive me out of my mind. More, more, more!

I try to spread my legs but pause when he moans, "Oh fuck. *Shit.*"

Shit?

Is that a good thing? I've never heard a guy say that while he was inside me before.

"Oh my god, Lilly." His forehead presses against mine and he stops mid-thrust.

"What's happening?" I whisper.

"I need a second."

A second? A second for what?

Is he...

Going to come?

Already?!

We've only been having sex for like, thirty seconds.

Dammit—I knew I should have sucked his dick when we started fooling around; he would last longer.

I lie still as he hovers above me, and a bead of sweat drops and hits the center of my chest.

*It's okay,* I want to whisper to him. *I get it, you hardly have sex.*

Stroking his back with my nails, I wait him out. He's still terrified to move, afraid he'll blow his load.

"I'm so sorry."

"Sorry?" I breathe out. "For wh—"

And that's when his body wrenches with a spasm, orgasm spilling into the condom.

# CHAPTER 11
# ROMAN

I cannot look at Lilly.

Can't be around her after I humiliated myself, this entire week a practice in circumvention and evasion.

She comes into my house, I go out of it.

I even catch a whiff of her presence or impending arrival, I pack up my shit and scram.

I came in under a minute.

Show me a guy in his twenties who can hold his head up and look a girl square in the eye after he comes inside her after thirty seconds, and I will bow down to him.

Metaphors for pumping and dumping flow through my brain, even as I do my damnedest to concentrate on my engineering project. It's no use.

Pump and dump.

Three-pump chump.

Single-barrel action.

Tossing my mechanical pencil onto the desk, I stare out the window into the backyard. There's an alley at the very end of the property where the garbage cans are stored and get picked up on Mondays, and I watch as a woman lifts the lid on the red recycling canister and tosses in a bag. I decide to make my way to the living room.

*"Roman, it's no big deal..."* Lilly reached for me as I rolled away from her, fingers grazing my backside as I stood and grappled for my underwear. I couldn't look at her then either, humiliation seeping through my body as quickly as the orgasm did. *"Maybe if we had a vibrator or something so I could...you know..."*

I lay in bed next to her that entire night—through the night until the sun came up and she slowly came awake. I pretended to sleep when she sat up and glanced at me over her shoulder, watching me far too long, waiting for me to stir or say something.

I didn't.

I squeezed my eyes shut and did my best to control my breathing, not wanting my chest to constrict, giving myself away.

Waited until she'd risen and gotten herself dressed then tiptoed out of the room, but not before leaning over to my side of the bed and planting a kiss on the side of my neck, lips warm.

So kind and caring.

I lay there like a coward.

How the hell do I fix this?

*It's been four days.*

Four days of avoiding her. Four days of thinking about her. Four days of remembering her body, naked. The sounds she made, the faces she made, the way she smelled.

*I couldn't make her come.*

There is no one I can talk to about this without sounding

like a twat, a British word I keep hearing Jack use to describe his old friends on the rugby team.

Perhaps I should talk to him about it? Get some advice on how to get a woman excited?

Just kidding, he seems like the kind of guy who was born into this world knowing how to have sex with a female and exceling at it from day one.

Unlike myself.

Pump and dump—literally.

Honestly, I came in under a minute—I should be drawn and quartered or publicly called out.

How the hell am I going to see Lilly again without sinking into a hole in the ground?

As if on cue, my roommate walks into the living room carrying a bag of potato chips and a soda, plopping down onto the opposite side of the couch, immediately ripping into the bag.

Pops a chip in his mouth and chews. "What are we watching, mate?"

Nothing. I was watching nothing because I cannot concentrate.

"Erm, nothing really." I toss him the remote and he catches it on the fly, instantly flipping through the channels before clicking open the app and scrolling through those shows.

He settles on an action film about the end of the earth where only one man can save it from destruction.

Jack chomps on a chip, cracks open the pop, and slurps off the top. Eventually, after lots of chewing and slurping, he glances over at me.

"What?" He leans forward, setting the pop can on the coffee table, licking the chip salt off his fingers. "Something on your mind? You look ill."

How can he tell something is wrong just by glancing at me for a few seconds? Do I look that sick?

Because I am; I want to vomit at the thought of Lilly out there, thinking I'm a premature ejaculator when I'm not. I was nervous and excited and it felt so fucking great. Amazing, like nothing I'd ever felt before.

"Nothing is on my mind," I lie.

"Bollocks," Jack argues, putting the chips on the couch beside him and crossing his arms. "You've got something on your mind. What is it?"

Honestly...

I barely know the guy; I'm not going to spill my guts and tell him I spilled my load within one minute when fucking his girlfriend's best friend.

Not happening.

"Does this have anything to do with Lilly?"

I raise my head a bit too fast, his keen eyes sparkling.

Shit. Is this guy psychic?

He nods. "I got it right, didn't I?"

"Uh..."

"Did something happen? She was here yesterday looking for you but seemed troubled."

He resumes digging into the potato chips, bag crinkling in a way that's almost triggering as one of my pet peeves.

Ugh, the sound!

"I wouldn't say something happened, no." On the contrary, something didn't happen—her orgasm.

And by now she must be on to the fact that I'm avoiding her; if she's stopping by to see me and I'm not returning any of her calls or text messages—this is indeed a problem.

One I'm too chickenshit to resolve.

Sex is a big fucking deal, and I blew it.

*Literally.*

I probably came off as a selfish, greedy asshole. Should I have gotten her off after I climaxed? Why did I just roll over and pretend to die?

Why didn't I give her an orgasm—what is my fucking problem?

"Mate?" Jack is staring at me from his place on the sofa. "Did the two of you have a row?"

"Not...exactly."

His hand is buried in the bag as he cocks his head, fishing out some chips then slowly putting them into his mouth, one by one as he thinks.

"Then what could she be cross about?" He crunches loudly. Pauses. "Wait. Bloody hell, did you shag?"

That settles it—Jack has psychic abilities.

I don't know what to tell him; do I admit it or deny it? Either way, I'm screwed. He's going to have questions—and though I definitely need answers and advice, I'm certainly not ready to admit I'm a failure in the sack.

"Erm..."

He smacks his knee like an old codger. "I bloody *knew* it. I told Eliza you were shagging when we came home from the party Friday night, but she didn't believe me. Kept going on about Lilly being on a guy detox and giving up dick for good." Crunch, crunch. "Told her that couldn't possibly be right or you wouldn't have had your door closed."

He's not wrong, but it's still weird he hit the nail on the head.

"Did something happen?"

Now is the time to confess that I was unable to fulfill Lilly sexually. Do guys talk about this shit with each other? Will he think I'm nuts for bringing it up?

"Not per se?"

"But..." He licks his fingers again, seemingly done eating

junk food in favor of listening to me. “There is more to this story—I can feel it.”

I squirm in my spot uncomfortably then unenthusiastically admit, “Yeah, there is more.”

He waits.

And waits. Then, “For bloody sake, do I have to pry the details out of you?”

*YES* BECAUSE I DON’T WANT TO SAY THEM OUT LOUD!

“I thought the pair of you were getting on brilliantly. Did something happen?” he asks again in an urging way, but he also sticks his hand back into the bag, setting off a frenzy of bag sounds.

It’s very distracting.

“Did. Something. Happen?” The way Jack is eyeing me up, there is no need to deny it. He knows. I don’t think he would have heard Lilly and me through the walls—we weren’t loud—but if she’s been coming around and asking about me...it only makes sense that he would suspect something is off between the two of us.

Jack is a smart dude.

Not as smart as I am, but intelligent.

Emotional intelligence.

He possesses much more than I have apparently.

“I wouldn’t say something happened as much as I would say it happened...too soon.”

He stares blankly, chip in hand. “What’s that mean?”

Let’s see, how do I put this?

Jack chomps.

Why is he eating chips at a time like this? It’s making me anxious.

“Does this have anything to do with shagging?”

“Yes?”

“Thought so.” His nod is authoritative, just like he is.

"Couldn't get it up?"

"What? NO! I mean, yes I could get it up."

"Oh." Why does he look disappointed? "Couldn't get her wet?"

Oh she was wet enough alright...

"That wasn't the problem."

He thinks, and I can see his mind working, putting the few clues I've given him together, clicking the pieces into place.

"Don't tell me you..." His voice trails off as if he can't possibly finish. "That you...*you know*." He flicks his gaze and his hand toward the dick lying limply between my legs.

I don't know.

He could be referring to any number of things. "Eh?"

"Are you going to make me say it?"

"Probably—I'm not sure what you're alluding to." Although he's been spot-on until this point, so why wouldn't he guess that I couldn't satisfy Lilly?

"You blew your load too soon?"

I feel my face turn crimson red, the urge to stand up and bolt from the room strong.

"Blink twice if I'm right," my roommate says with a grimace. "Are you still breathing, old chap?"

I force myself to nod. "Barely."

"Don't be embarrassed—happens to the best of us."

I raise my head. "Does it?"

"Well, *no*—not usually. But it does happen, I'm sure of it."

I groan, resting my face in the palm of my hands. "Fuck."

"Hey, no worries, mate—you're in good hands. I give stellar advice, know a thing or two about the ladies." He pauses. "Not because I've been with a slew of them, but because my ex-girlfriend was such a twat and hated sex so much I made it my mission to pleasure her."

"We are *not* having this conversation." I haven't been living here all that long—it's way too soon to be having the humiliation talk about sex and ejaculation.

I don't even talk to the friends I've known since kindergarten about this shit, though maybe if I did, this conversation wouldn't suck so bad. Maybe it would be easier.

The only sex talk I've ever had was my dad coming into my room when I was thirteen and saying, *"Your mother wanted me to come in here and have the sex talk with you."* He ran a hand through his hair, glancing around my room at all the debate, math, and science trophies. *"I don't think we have anything to worry about yet."*

We were both horrified by that little speech, although it was a brief one.

Jack, on the other hand? Seems to be taking this in stride, seeming to relish this new information. In the span of time I've known him, there is one thing I've gleaned: he takes matters head on and likes to talk things out.

Not very British of him, I must say.

"The wheels are in motion, my friend, but the answer is simple: you need to wank off before you have a date. It'll make you last longer."

He sounds confident.

"Wank off?"

"You know—beat the bishop."

That's a term I haven't heard.

He goes on. "Fire off some knuckle children. Jerk the gherkin."

"Stop. I know what you mean."

"Tug of war with the cyclops?" Jack smirks. "That's my favorite one."

I haven't stopped blushing since he started talking. Don't get me wrong, he isn't being crude—he sounds like a normal twenty-something-year-old dude going on about sex. And masturbating.

I'm the odd one here, blushing beet red and wanting to avoid the subject entirely.

"So what did she say afterward?" Jack gets back to the subject, wanting more information.

"I don't know—I washed up and didn't talk to her afterward."

"You didn't talk to her afterward?"

"No."

"Why not?"

"I wasn't sure what to say."

He drags a hand down his face. "Bloody hell. That's not good."

*Hindsight is always twenty-twenty.*

"Did she finish?"

"Um. I don't think so."

"Mate—how do you not know if you made her come?"

I shrug, humiliated. "I was...only thinking about myself, I guess."

"You guess?" His snort makes me feel a million times worse. "Blimey, no wonder she tenses up when we say your name."

"Do you think she hates me?" Even as I say it, I know it's not true—Lilly wouldn't be trying to get ahold of me to talk if she hated me. Or perhaps she does and just wants to chew my ass out, give me a piece of her mind.

"Don't be daft—of course she doesn't *hate* you. She'd stop coming over altogether if she didn't want to run into you." He resumes popping chips in his mouth as if it's the last meal he's ever going to have.

"Good point."

"You have to start trusting your own instincts, Rome—

especially when it comes to women. Don't operate on assumptions. Don't assume she hates you—grow a pair of balls and get back to it."

The thing is, I'm not sure I can.

No matter how I feel about Lilly—how much I care—I don't think I have the guts to look her in the eye and tell her I fucked up. She put the moves on me; she wouldn't have done that if she didn't give a shit, especially considering she has taken a sabbatical from dating.

"I thought you and Lilly were mates. Eliza and I didn't realize the two of you were shagging." Crunch, crunch.

"We are friends, and we're not...shagging."

"Then what do you call the fact that you boned?"

"I just meant it's more than that. I think."

"So you love her?"

That's a good question. Do I?

"I've never been in love before, so how the hell would I know if this was it?"

"I think you just know." At last he's finished stuffing his gullet with junk food, rolling up the bag and tossing it onto the coffee table. "Honestly, I had to google it when I thought I might be in love with Eliza."

"You googled it?"

"Yeah. I google everything."

Interesting. "What did it say?"

Jack produces his cell phone, the bright screen lighting up his face as he begins tapping on the screen. "Alright, found the article." He clears his throat before reading aloud. "You're happy and a bit nervous."

Sounds like me.

"The person is on your mind literally all the time."

What kind of scientific article uses the word *literally*?

He goes on. "For example, you don't just think about

calling or texting them throughout the day. You might wander into a clothing store to buy something for yourself and wind up buying something for your sweetheart, too."

Wander into a clothing store...?

"Wait. What article is this?"

He glances up from his phone. "It's from *Teen Life* magazine."

"Goddammit, Jack, find a more reputable list. That's a magazine for kids."

"Is not!"

"Find a different list."

Jack grumbles but complies, thumbing through his phone after another search. "You always make time for them. You love the way they smell. You look at them while they sleep."

Look at them while they sleep? *What the fuck?*

He keeps reading, nodding along in agreement. "Oh, this is good. Yes."

"What does it say?"

"It says 'You're all like, ex who?'"

"That's what it says? 'You're all like, *ex who*?'" I can't keep the sarcasm out of my voice.

He nods. "Yeah, I'm reading it verbatim."

Lord.

"You're actually entertained by their cute AF childhood pictures." He glances up. "I mean, who wouldn't be entertained by their girlfriend's cute baby pictures. That one is stupid." He scrolls. "You regularly catch yourself doing a deep dive on their social media."

*Who wrote this list, a fifteen-year-old?*

I rise, wanting to go to my room, shut the door, and *think*. "You can stop reading, I've heard enough."

Jack tosses his phone on the couch next to him. "So what are you going to do?"

I shrug. “I don’t know. Avoid her forever?”

He smiles, but it’s rueful. “Not possible, mate. You best figure your shit out before the opportunity passes you by.”

Very wise words.

I only wish I knew how to take the advice.

# CHAPTER 12
# LILLY

My mother didn't bother calling to tell me she and my dad aren't going to be around for Thanksgiving this year.

She texted.

**Mom:** *Wanted to let you know Dad and I are going with the Parkers to Michigan this year. Linda rented a cottage and we're going to ski if there is snow.*

**Me:** *Who is "we?"*

**Mom:** *The grown-ups.*

I don't point out the fact that I am, in fact, a grown-up, too.

It would be pointless—lost on my mother.

**Me:** *Okay...*

**Me:** *What am I supposed to do?*

**Mom:** *Whatever you want! Don't you kids always do that Friendsgiving thing?*

**Me:** *When have I ever not come home for the holidays?*

**Mom:** *Don't be sarcastic—I'm just letting you know. You're an adult now, it's time to start your own traditions.*

Wow.

I feel my face burning, from rage, disappointment, and humiliation. Briefly wonder how my dad feels about this sudden development of a trip without me during the holiday, or if she even discussed it with him. Pointless to ask; she steamrolls over everyone and wouldn't take his opinion into consideration even if he did have one.

My nose tingles, a telltale sign that I'm about to cry.

**Me:** *Okay.*

I toss my phone to the bed and throw myself beside it, staring up at the ceiling, blinking back tears.

It's been a shitty few days—a shitty week, really, and this news makes it all the worse.

First Roman and I aren't talking and now I'll be alone for Thanksgiving?

Great.

Not like it's my favorite holiday—I don't particularly care for turkey. But that's hardly the point, is it? The point is, my parents are going on a vacation with their friends and don't give a crap that I'll be alone.

On top of that, I had sex with Roman and he's still ignoring me, which makes me feel furious and abandoned.

Roman is my friend. Why did I have to go and ruin it by sleeping with him? Things were going great up to that point—if I hadn't called him to come to that party, I wouldn't have gone home with him, and if I hadn't gone home with him, I would have been in my own bed, where I belong.

A blow to a guy's pride when he's not good in bed can scar him for life, or so I've heard.

Fine.

I know exactly why he's avoiding me, but that doesn't make it easier.

I want to wallow in self-pity, allowing myself to feel empty and lonely for a few minutes, accepting the things I cannot change:

1. My mother and her inability to be maternal.
2. The shift in my relationship with Roman.

The house is quiet.

I'm not sure where Kaylee has gone, but I'm certain she's no longer home.

Rolling to the side, I groan. Beat from the workout we had this morning, my muscles are sore and could use a stretch.

A good walk will do the trick.

Yes.

I should get up and move around rather than lie here motionless.

Rising, I remove my sweatpants and swap them for blue leggings and a navy hoodie before lacing up my sneakers. I grab my earbuds, throw my hair into a ponytail, and get my rear moving.

It's not dark out, but it will be soon. I lock the door behind me, eyes scanning the street.

The leaves on the trees have changed colors and begun falling, a sign that the cold weather of winter is approaching. I kick at a few, loving the sound of them crunching beneath my feet, keep kicking them along on my way down the sidewalk.

Somehow I find myself standing in front of Roman's house—er, *Eliza's* house—the lights inside glowing; people are home, probably doing something cute and cozy, like watching movies and eating whatever treats Eliza has put out.

I stuff my hands inside the pockets of my hoodie, debating my course as I continue standing in front like a gawker.

A gust of wind blows, leaves swirling around me.

It's cold so I can't stand out here forever, especially once it gets dark, but I can't exactly go knocking.

I am here to see Eliza.

*Screw Roman—if he's too big of a pussy to talk to me, that's on him. It is not my fault. He was in that bed, too.*

Words I've been repeating to myself on a loop since the last time I was here and he avoided me, leaving out the side door within minutes of my arrival and not returning home all night. I haven't had a single chance to say a word to him, and he hasn't been responding to my texts.

That is not a mature person.

I am better off without that drama in my life.

When will I learn my lesson?

First Kyle, now Roman? No thank you.

Eliza is my friend—I have every right to walk up to the door and hang out with her without feeling guilty or weird or like I'm imposing on Roman's space.

He can go to his damn bedroom if he doesn't like it.

Decision made, I stomp to the door, pressing on the doorbell with more confidence than I feel.

Rub my hands together to warm them as I wait, a shadow appearing in the foyer, porch light flicking on.

"'Allo!" Jack opens the door wide. "Come inside before you catch a chill."

*Catch a chill.*

I step over the threshold. "I love it when you speak British."

"I am British, love."

Laughing, I remove my earbuds and wind them up, storing them in my pocket. "Is Eliza home?"

"Yup, kitchen."

"Awesome." I ruffle my ponytail, shaking out the cold as I enter the bright kitchen at the back of the house, my friend in the throes of loading up a tray of treats. "Hey hey."

I slide onto one of the stools at the counter with a smile.

"Oh hey!" My former roommate sets down some cheese and wipes her hands so she can squeeze me into a hug. "This is a fun surprise—are you here for the football game? I'm throwing together a charcuterie board."

"Sure, I'll stay for the game!" I say it with more enthusiasm than I'm feeling, my gut in turmoil as my eyes stay homed in on the arched doorway leading to the stairs.

What if Roman walks through it? What will I say? How will I act?

I spy his car through the kitchen window, parked near the detached garage where Jack has an at-home gym his brother actually built during his time here.

I shift my gaze, heart racing.

Pluck a carrot off Eliza's tray.

She scowls. "No snacking until the game begins."

"When does the game begin?"

"'Bout half an hour?"

"Ugh!" That long? I'm kind of starving now that I see food, and staying for the game sounds like a blast.

Jack goes in and out of the kitchen, busying himself with taking out the trash as Eliza makes food, carrying small bowls of chips and Goldfish crackers into the living room.

They certainly know how to entertain, and I'm here for it.

And then...

Roman enters the room, just as I knew he would. When he sees me, he halts in his tracks like a romantic comedy cliché. Deer in headlights if I ever did see one.

His eyes flash to Jack to Eliza to me, back to Eliza then back to me.

He clears his throat, palming the cell phone in his hand. "Hey."

"Hi." I lift an arm and give him a feeble little wave. "What's up?"

"Not much." He barely moves.

"Roman, get in here and sit. I'm making snacks," Eliza commands, moving around the room efficiently, continuing to load her wooden board with tasty vittles. "Sit."

She has to tell him twice before he hesitantly pulls out the stool at the end of the counter, two stools now separating us.

Two stools of separation, ha!

His phone rings, and when I look down, I see that it's his mother.

He hesitates again.

"That your mom?" Eliza asks. "Answer it so we can say hello!"

Lord she's bossy tonight; I wonder what's gotten into her.

Roman hits the green button to accept his mother's Face-Time chat.

"Hey, Mom."

"Hey, honey bunches of oats! How is my baby doing today? Getting ready for the game?"

Roman's face turns red at the endearments. "Yeah. Eliza is making food and we're going to watch it." He pauses. "What's up?"

"Well, as you know, Thanksgiving is next week and I'm trying to plan the meal. Dad doesn't really want turkey this year and Aunt Myrtle can't eat yams, so I was going to see if—" His mother stops talking. "Is that Lilly in the background? Turn your phone."

Roman groans but obediently turns the screen in my direction.

"Lilly!" his mom enthuses. "How are you?"

"I'm doing good, Mrs. Whitaker. How are you?"

"So good. I'm planning Thanksgiving—I don't want to keep you if you kids are having a party."

"Not a party—just a few of us gathered at Jack and Eliza's house. She's making food."

Roman pans his phone around the room, and Eliza gives it a wave.

"Oh yummm!" Mrs. Whitaker makes the appropriate noises. "I remember those days, but back then we ate more junk food than you kids do now. So health conscious!"

She's not wrong. I would choose a bottle of water over a bottle of wine or soda any day of the week.

"Alright, well, I just had a few questions for Rome about Thanksgiving—don't want to be a party crasher." I can clearly see a spiral notebook set in front of her on the kitchen counter, and she's holding a pencil in her right hand. "You must be excited to go home for the holiday. What's your favorite item on the menu?"

"Well..." I speak slowly, feelings still fresh in my heart. "My, um, parents are going on vacation this year so I'm not going home. But my favorite thi—"

"Not going home!" Roman's mother's voice has risen ten decibels. "I insist you come here with Roman. And what about his roommates? Jack and Eliza, what are you doing for Thanksgiving?"

Jack doesn't miss a beat, sliding toward the phone on his stockinged feet and hamming for the camera. "I'm from the UK, ma'am, and Eliza lives three hours north of here, so we were planning on going to a restaurant for dinner."

Roman's mom is shaking her head so vigorously I'm surprised her reading glasses haven't fallen off her nose. "Absolutely not. You are coming here—we have plenty of room at the table and a huge living room. You can watch the Turkey

Bowl after dinner or whatever that college football game is called."

Not only do we not have a game on Thanksgiving this year, our team isn't in any bowl games, either, which means I get the week off.

"That would be brilliant!" Jack is nodding and clapping his hands. "I love a home-cooked meal. My mum doesn't cook, and obviously we don't have the holiday in Britain—this will be my first!"

"Your first Thanksgiving in America!" Mrs. Whitaker could not look more thrilled at the news. "And you're going to spend it here! I am honored." She scribbles on her paper. "That settles it then—the four of you are coming for the holiday."

And that is how I wind up seated at the Whitaker family table, next to Roman and across from Great Aunt Myrtle, wearing a soft sweater vest in a deep burgundy color. Gold necklace around my neck, tweed skirt beneath the table.

Jack sits next to Roman, Eliza next to him, the four of us taking up one entire side of the table.

I adjust the napkin across my lap, the aroma from the gravy boat making my mouth water. I love stuffing and mashed potatoes, but I love fresh bread even more, helping myself to another serving—after all, it's Thanksgiving, and I've been working my tail off.

To say the ride here was awkward is an understatement.

Both Eliza and Jack claimed the back seat of Roman's car before I could protest sitting in the front seat with him, though their truck has way more passenger space.

Dammit!

I'll have to be craftier for the ride home...

"Why don't you play any sports?" Alex Whitaker is asking Jack as I steal another dinner roll—my third. "You're huge."

Mrs. Whitaker gasps. "Alex, where are your manners?"

"Yeah," their dad says. "You can't just call someone huge." He winks at his younger son as he spoons green beans onto his plate.

"Sorry. I meant, you look like an athlete. Why don't you play?"

"I played rugby for a bit. Do you know what that is?"

Alex rolls his eyes rudely and gets another scolding—he is the perfect human being to have around. He diverts all attention from me and Roman, whose family corralled us into the formal living room when we first arrived so his mom could take photos of the two of us sitting on her fireplace hearth.

*"You're all dressed up, I don't want to miss an opportunity." She flutters around, messing with the camera on her cell phone before insisting Roman put his hand on my shoulder, positioning him beside me. "You look so good together!" she fusses.*

*"Do not put this picture in the Christmas card," he warns, hand hovering above my waist but not actually making contact with it.*

*Mrs. Whitaker trills her tongue, excited, clicking away. She then invites Jack and Eliza into the photo for a small group picture, Alex wedging himself in beside Jack—his new hero.*

"Yes, I know what rugby is," Alex is saying in a less sarcastic tone, pushing his mashed potatoes around his plate with a fork creating a gravy river. He gets scolded for that, too. "I don't understand the rules though."

"Neither do I, mate." Jack laughs. "It's why I quit."

"You quit?"

"I was getting pummeled. Wasn't at all fun." He's eating and talking at the same time, and with a smile on his face, too, as if remembering rugby fondly.

I heard he was terrible at it, remember Kaylee coming back to the house, embarrassed that the "hot guy" she was "in love with" was so bad at his sport, actually pitied herself about it.

Eliza does not seem to care one bit that Jack isn't a college athlete.

They'd both rather watch action movies and read comic books and spend their free time at this little café they love on the outskirts of campus.

Basically they are couple goals, *if there is such a thing*.

"I went out with a rugby player once," Aunt Myrtle is saying from her side of the table, a small blob of cranberry sauce stuck to the corner of her already bright red lips. "Worst lay of my life."

Mrs. Whitaker groans.

"I'm not kidding. He had a glorious shaft but didn't know where to stick it, if you catch my drift." She blinks twice, but I'm convinced she's trying to wink. "That man shoved it in the wrong hole so many times I started to get a complex." She delivers the line without so much as flinching. "Gives new meaning to the phrase butt hurt."

"Aunt Myrtle!" Mrs. Whitaker's eyes dart from her great aunt to her young son, whose eyes are as round as saucers.

"What wrong hole?" he immediately wants to know, glancing at both his parents. "Her butthole?"

His mother gasps as if he's dropped an F bomb. "Don't say butthole at the dinner table." Roman's mom is the exact shade of the cranberry sauce.

"Butthole isn't a swear word, Mom. Chill," Alex smarts back.

To be fair, he's not wrong. But in this context, Aunt Myrtle is basically implying accidental anal sex, which makes it inappropriate? At least it does in Mrs. Whitaker's eyes.

She is. Freaking. Out.

So very entertaining, I must say.

Way more fun than staying home and watching subscription TV, which is what I would have been doing had I not chosen to drop in on Eliza and Jack unannounced last week.

It was fate.

And Roman smells amazing—better than the food—as he leans forward and kicks up his cologne. He's shaved, and have I mentioned his haircut?

Gone are the shaggy, long locks. Gone is the man-bun.

Gone is the face scruff.

I thought Roman was handsome before he trimmed his hair and shaved, but now?

He looks like Prince Charming from a movie screen.

A modern-day Romeo.

A Greek god who isn't remotely Greek.

Handsome.

Cute. Hot. Attractive. Gorgeous—pick your adjective; I'm no thesaurus, and I'm no poet. All I know is, when I climbed into that car tonight, I could barely keep my eyes off him. And because Roman is sweet, and charming, and smart—he's all the more beautiful to me.

I fidget in my seat, our knees bumping.

He's tall so our knees have been bumping a lot, and each time has my blood pressure skyrocketing.

To avoid looking over at him again, I gaze out the dining room window, noticing for the first time the winter white trees. The snowflakes are not just falling but falling sideways in a frenzy.

"Wait. Was it supposed to snow?"

Everyone's heads swivel toward the windows.

"Let me check the weather," Mr. Whitaker announces, pulling the phone from his pressed khakis and swiping open what I assume is a weather app of some kind.

"You don't have to check the weather, *Josh*—everyone can

see it's coming down in buckets." She looks at Alex. "You're going to have to shovel."

Alex Whitaker lets out a groan so loud Aunt Myrtle startles in her seat.

"Eight inches!" Mr. Whitaker broadcasts the news. "There's a winter weather advisory in place." He sets his phone on the tabletop and resumes slicing through the meat on his plate. "Bit early, wouldn't you say?"

"Eight inches?" Roman's mom's eyes widen.

"That's what she said." Alex laughs, unable to contain himself.

His mother ignores him. "Eight inches—no one is driving anywhere tonight." She's shaking her head furiously. "Do you know how many accidents there are going to be? First snow of the season?" She wipes her hands on a napkin and stands. "I'm going to go get the guest bedroom ready—Eliza and Jack, you can sleep in there. I'll go make it nice and cozy."

She's practically buzzing with excitement. Her son home for the night?! It's what she's wanted since the day he moved out. The fact that he has friends with him?

Bonus!

"She's momming so hard right now." Roman laughs and we laugh along with him, but deep down inside, my mind is reeling. If Mrs. Whitaker is putting Eliza and Jack in the one guest bedroom, that means she expects me to sleep with...

Roman.

"Roman is the modern-day Romeo," his mother tells me with a sly smile, reading my mind just then—and I half-believe he *is*, despite the way he's frozen me out after we had sex. "I don't mind you two spending the night together."

"Oh no. No, no, no, ma'am—Eliza and I can bunk together if the guys want to stay in Roman's room. I totally understand if you're not okay with it."

I'm a tad over the top, even to my own ears, protesting the sleeping arrangements, mind whirling. Roman must be dying inside—it's not his fault he's shy, and it's not his fault he had no idea what to do after we slept together.

Sex and sleep.

Is that all it was to him? All it meant?

Am I so terrible that he had to avoid me?

Well.

Plot twist: now he has no choice!

I thought we were developing a friendship, but even that couldn't withstand the physical turn our relationship took.

*So much for maturity.*

"Did you just call him Romeo?" Aunt Myrtle cackles. "In my day, there was no such thing, just men marrying a dame so he could finally get her in the sack. They only pretended to be gentlemen."

The four of us cast furtive glances around the table, Jack's eyes wide as saucers and Eliza's ready with a laugh.

"You use the word dame, too, Auntie?" Jack asks her, adopting the family nickname for their great aunt. "Blokes back in the day were bored—they didn't have Netflix."

Aunt Myrtle shakes her head. "Netflix is the code word for sex."

"No, Netflix is the code word for 'I want to stay home and be lazy.'"

"Well we didn't have that when I was young. We didn't even have phones or computers. All I had was a Jack in the Crack."

Rome's dad laughs. "Don't you mean a Jack in the Box?"

"Had one of them, too." The old woman slaps at her knee, and I wish I felt as much gusto at the moment as she does. Instead, I'm *dreading* the night to come.

# CHAPTER 13
# ROMAN

There is no talking my mother out of having us stay; already she is a flurry of activity, bustling from room to room, making sure Eliza and Jack have enough warm blankets and pillows, toothbrushes and toothpaste, and towels for the guest bathroom.

It's as if the king and queen of England have arrived.

She is positively tickled we've been marooned.

Snowed in, as it were, a cliché if ever there was one.

We shouldn't be driving, obviously—the snow is coming down so heavily I can't see the street in front of the house, and in the distance, the telltale orange blinking lights from the salt truck and snowplow appear through the low visibility.

Another thing I cannot talk my mother out of? Rooming me with Lilly. Mom thinks we're in a relationship so naturally she'd pop us in my bedroom; I certainly can't tell her we broke up because:

1. That's a lie.

2. You can't break up with someone you're not dating, even if you are fake dating them.
3. Why the hell would I have brought her to Thanksgiving if we were broken up?

*"Oh by the way, Mom, she and I had sex and I came in three seconds and now I'm a laughingstock."*

Yeah, no.

Not happening.

Dining room table has been cleared. Dishes have been wiped clean, washed, and stored away—leftovers will be evenly distributed in the morning. We've chatted while the girls prepare the guest room, more blankets added to all the beds for adequate snuggling.

"No funny business under this roof," Dad intones after the rest of the evening is spent talking in front of the fire, in the living room. We're all yawning and tired—it's been a long day of *pretending.*

Pretending to be cordial to Lilly.

Ignoring her with her seated beside me, afraid to touch her or bump into her accidentally—which happened every ten seconds during dinner.

Sitting near her and smelling her shampoo and perfume only served to remind me of her naked body, her delicate moans, how quickly I came.

*Everything comes down to those last few seconds.*

"No funny business, sir," Jack tells him in that refined British accent the ladies all seem to love. "Wouldn't think of it."

He nudges me.

I nudge him back. "Knock it off, I'm nervous enough," I mumble.

"You're a corker, Romeo—you got this." He uses the

moniker my mother threw out tonight, and I cringe. I'm hardly anyone's idea of a romantic leading character, but I appreciate his confidence in me.

After Mom gives the girls each a set of her pajamas to wear for the night, I suddenly find myself alone with Lilly in my bedroom. I leave the door open longer than necessary, the lights and sounds from the interior of the house slowly fading into silence and darkness.

The stark white snow outside seems to brighten everything inside.

She is sitting cross-legged on the bed when I walk back through the bedroom door; I went to my brother's room to help him beat the next level of his video game, something I used to do all the time when I lived at home.

Alex is a little shit, but I love him to death.

"Everything alright?" I ask Lilly, slowly closing the door behind me, wishing I could leave it wide open. "Why aren't you under the covers?"

She shrugs her shoulders, clothed in my mother's blue and white satin button-down pajama top. It's a prim outfit, especially for bed. "I thought maybe you would...want me to sleep somewhere else?"

Where? The floor?

As if I'd make her do that.

I go to my desk and set my phone down. "Why would I want you to sleep somewhere else? Unless you're more comfortable in here alone? I can go to the living room, or sleep on the floor here?" I point to the beige carpet, already reaching for a pillow to throw down. "If anyone should take the rug, it should be me."

"Don't be ridiculous—this is your room." She goes to her knees but doesn't climb down off the bed. "If anyone should sleep on the floor, it's me."

"Why are we arguing about this? This is a queen-size bed—why should either of us sleep on the floor?" I mumble the next part under my breath; I can't stop the words from coming out. "*Why wouldn't you after the last time we were in bed together?*"

Too loud. Lilly hears me. "I'm sorry—what was that?"

My "*Nothing*" is such a feminine reply that her face pulls into a snicker.

"Because it sounded like you said '*Why wouldn't you after the last time we were in bed together?*' Did I get that right?"

There isn't much to deny.

I shrug.

Lilly plops back down on her ass, settling back into the cross-legged position. "You know I've been wanting to talk to you since we slept together. Why have you been avoiding me?" She continues before I can answer. "I mean, I know why you've been avoiding me, but I'd like to hear you say it."

She wants to hear me say it?

I snort. "Do you blame me? I embarrassed myself."

"How did you embarrass yourself?"

Is she being serious right now, or have I just entered a parallel dimension? "Don't make me say it."

"Did it ever occur to you that your avoidance of me had its own affect? Or were you just worried about yourself?"

I lift my head. What is she talking about? "What do you mean?"

She gestures to the foot of the bed and encourages me to have a seat.

I sit—mostly for lack of anything else to do, because who wants to stand around in blue plaid pajamas looking like a giant dork.

"I mean...we all have our baggage, Roman. Mine is feeling rejected because of my upbringing. And it certainly doesn't help that I choose guys who don't want to stick around when things get complicated. Like it did with us." She motions between our bodies with her hand. "It didn't go so great the first time we had sex, but so what? We're just getting to know each other. Were you expecting it to be perfect?"

"Kind of."

That makes her laugh. "Well fortunately for you, I wasn't. It never is with someone new." She shoots me a look. "That didn't come out right. What I meant was, people aren't perfect. No one gets it right one hundred percent of the time. Not even you."

I don't try to be perfect one hundred percent of the time."

"You don't?"

Okay fine—I do. "Not on purpose. It was drilled into me by my parents."

"Right. Exactly. But some things, by nature, aren't ever going to be. Like sex. It's..." She waves her hands around. "Messy and unpredictable. Sometimes it's too slow and sometimes it's too fast and sometimes it's just right—but who's to say when that will be?"

Why is she making absolute perfect sense? "You're not pissed I..." I swallow, unable to finish the sentence.

"That you...were so excited you came before I did?"

That's putting it gently. "I didn't just come before you did. I came like—after thirty seconds."

Why I feel the need to point this out is beyond me.

But oddly enough, I don't feel so self-conscious about it anymore now that I'm sitting here with her discussing it.

*Imagine that.*

Lilly laughs, a delighted little trill. "See! At least we can talk about it." She looks so pleased. "This is what I wanted—this is why I kept trying to get you to talk to me, for this." More motioning back and forth between our bodies with her hands.

She is animated tonight—so much more than at the dinner table earlier. I knew she wasn't sure how to behave in front of me and in front of my family considering the tension I've created.

Yeah—this was all my fault, but she's here giving me a chance to fix it.

I wring my hands nervously, in uncharted territory.

"So you're not upset that I came too quickly?" I cannot believe those words just left my mouth and I didn't choke on them.

Lilly takes a second to think about her answer, shifting her position from legs crossed to hugging her knees. She looks vulnerable but also comfortable in the space.

"I wouldn't say I'm not upset. I think more so than anything, I'm upset about the way you handled the situation and less upset about the actual act itself? If that makes any sense. I don't like how you reacted—it bothers me."

I mull this over in my brain. "I wasn't sure *how* to react—obviously I was embarrassed. Nothing like that has ever happened to me before, and if we're being completely transparent, I don't have much experience with sex. I wish I did, but I don't. Maybe that's what part of the issue was—I got inside my own head."

"What do you think I want from you? For you to be a sex god? I slept with you because I feel like we have an emotional attachment—or, a connection I mean. I really...like you, Roman. I like you a lot."

*Emotional attachment.*

*Emotional connection.*

*She likes me a lot.*

Like. Said in a weighty way that implies much more.

I add and subtract and multiply these sentiments over and over in my head, trying to come up with an equation that makes sense in my brain. Lilly is effervescent and beautiful and full of life, and she's choosing to be with someone like me to break her guy detox with. I am an intellectual who values science and engineering and logic over athletics and physical fitness. It's not that I don't believe I need to be physically fit, but I don't obsess over it, and occasionally? I have a dad bod.

Lilly isn't done pouring her heart out. "I like you a lot, Roman. I mean...with all my heart. You are my friend. You make me feel beautiful and smart and..." She fiddles with her fingers, twisting a gold ring she wears on the index of her left hand. "I don't know."

She glances up at me bashfully, beautiful in my mom's navy pajamas that are a bit too big on her, expression tugging at my heart.

It constricts, pumping.

I am not built for this; I still have lots of work to do on myself and confidence to gain before I'm completely comfortable confessing all my wants and desires to a pretty girl I have feelings for—but for Lilly, I will have to try.

I clear my throat, shifting closer to her on the mattress, leaning back so we're not far apart.

"I haven't had many relationships at all. The majority of them were based on curiosity." That sounded bad. "Based on friendship, mostly—I've never been..." *in love.*

Say the words, Roman.

Say anything—she's waiting. Staring at me, actually.

"Um."

No, not that.

"I've never had a romantic relationship is what I'm trying to say."

There.

Better.

Lilly nods in understanding. “I have, but they weren’t filled with...” She searches for the right adjective. “Respect.”

“What do you mean?”

“I mean...I always had respect for the guys I dated, but I don’t think any of them respected *me*. I don’t suppose many guys our age know what that looks like, know what I mean?”

Yeah, I know what she means.

Mutual respect is one of the hallmarks of a strong relationship, and let’s be real, when you’re dating dudes who smash their heads together as a full-time hobby, they’re not thinking about ways to bond with their girlfriend. They’re thinking about the next big game—the next win. The next championship.

Don’t blame them, but isn’t it a scientific fact that most men aren’t emotionally mature until they’re like, forty years old?

*That doesn’t bode well for you either, mate*—Jack’s voice pops into my head.

“We’re friends, aren’t we?” she asks quietly.

Friends. The kiss of death or the kiss of possibility?

“Yes, we’re friends.”

“Do you trust me, Roman?” Barely a whisper.

Do I?

I think I trust Lilly—I must. “Yes. Do you trust me?”

She nods. “I trust you more than I trust anyone. Is that weird?”

“No.” Sometimes you just...know. Sometimes you get a sense of who someone is without having known them at all. I want to have someone I can say anything to, share my day with and my frustrations. Tell my ideas to. Sit and talk cross-legged on the bed with them at night, in my parents’ house, after a holiday dinner.

Lilly is that someone.

"Do you remember what was going through your head the first night we met?" she asks, repositioning herself so she's lying back, head on the pillow.

"Sure. I remember thinking 'What's this pretty girl doing wasting her time talking to a nerd like me?'"

She sits up. "Roman Whitaker, don't talk like that."

I shrug. "You asked what I was thinking, and that's what was going through my head. That and watching the time. Essentially I was counting down the hours until I could leave."

"Yeah, same." She sighs, lying back down. "If you could live anywhere, where would it be?"

I hum. "I'm not sure I would live anywhere else, but I'm sure I'll settle somewhere farther away once I get job offers."

Lilly rolls her eyes. "Was that an actual answer?"

I laugh. "I don't know, was it?"

"Not really." She sighs again, patting the spot beside her. "I'd live in Arizona. I love the heat."

When I crawl up the bed and settle in next to her, her hand finds my head and begins absentmindedly playing with my hair.

"Do you want kids?" I blurt out the question. Kids? Honestly, Roman, you're asking her if she wants kids? She's twenty-one, for fuck's sake. Jesus, I wish I could facepalm myself without making it too obvious I feel like a freaking idiot.

"Yes—how 'bout you?"

"Sure. At least two, but who knows."

I pause as I think of another question.

"Favorite beverage?"

Lilly scrunches up her face. "Is it lame to say lemonade?"

"No, that's cute." I look over at her, and our eyes meet.

"You know," she says slowly, her fingers tracing the sensitive skin of my earlobe. "This feels like the first night we met, when we sat at the top of those stairs and asked each other questions because neither of us wanted to be at that party." She pauses. "I wondered what it would be like to kiss you. Your glasses were so cute."

Okay, that I don't believe—not for a second. "My glasses?"

"Yeah."

I sit up and roll off the bed, walking to my desk. Open the top drawer and root around for the only glasses I wear these days, my computer glasses. Fit them on my face and turn to face her again.

"These?"

Lilly bites down on her bottom lip dramatically. "Rawr."

I feel a blush cross my cheeks, warming my face. "Ah shucks."

"I'm serious. Get over here. And take off your shirt."

Take off my shirt? This is my mom's house—what if someone walks in?

*Stop being a prude, Whitaker. Take the damn shirt off—it's not like she's asking you to shed your knickers.*

I do as she asks and shed the shirt, tossing it to the ground.

Lilly grins and gets on all fours, tossing her long hair. It's messy—she had it in a tidy, low ponytail for dinner, classy and elegant. But now...?

She's a tigress on her knees crawling toward me, hands going around my waist.

"I've always wanted to kiss a guy wearing glasses."

"Is that a hard feat to accomplish?" I mean, how hard could a spectacle-wearing guy be to find?

"Stop asking questions and kiss me." Her lips pucker as she tilts her face in my direction so I can easily meet her mouth.

We roll toward each other, bodies now compelled to be together, lips pressed against lips. Hers are soft, warm—and can you miss a mouth?

This kiss is like the first one all over again; it feels new and different and exciting. I let my hands go to her backside, the silky fabric from the pajamas letting my hands glide smoothly across her derriere. Lilly's hands travel up my spine, to my neck, then to my hair—she drags her nails across my scalp like she's done in the past.

I never knew how much I loved having my head scratched until she does it now.

I feel myself getting hard; she apparently does too because she squirms, revolving her pelvis against my front side, teasing my cock.

"I love your dick," she murmurs into my mouth.

"You do?"

She pulls back so she can see my face. "Um, haven't you noticed that it's slightly bigger than average? Like, do you ever look at it and think, 'Phew, hey God, thanks for the little bit extra.'"

I chuckle, pulling her closer. "Ha ha, no."

"I would." She snuggles deeper against me. "Let's get under the covers, I'm cold."

We pull back the coverlet on my bed, the blanket, and the flannel sheets and climb underneath, yanking them back up around us, getting back into our snuggle position.

Kiss some more.

"You feel so good," I tell her shyly, the compliment a tad stilted. Still, I want to try to say the things that are on my mind. It's fair to her and good for me.

"So do you." Her hands travel up my stomach and pecs. "I love your chest."

Soon, those same hands are sliding into the backside of my sleep pants, the only thing I've got on having shed my boxer briefs when I put these pajamas on.

"Mmm," she hums happily. "I'm so glad we chatted." Lilly

kisses my collarbone, warm breath causing me to tingle. “Thank you for inviting me tonight.”

Technically it was my mother who invited her, but I’m glad for it. We wouldn’t be in this position right now if she hadn’t, or if Lilly hadn’t accepted the invite.

“Thank you for agreeing to come. You didn’t have to.”

“I’d rather be here with you.” More kisses. “I missed you these past few days. I felt very lonely.”

I’ve been lonely too, as much as I hate to admit it. I tried to lose myself in homework and studying and this project that is due at the end of the semester but failed miserably. It’s not easy concentrating when there’s someone on your mind, and I’ve never had anyone in my life to worry about other than my parents, aunt, and brother.

I’m still learning, but I’m coachable. And I know I’m going to fuck up again, but next time I’m not going to hide. I’m going to be an adult about it.

“I can’t wait to try having sex again,” Lilly whispers in the dark. I just shut off the light so we can attempt to sleep, although that’s laughable. I have a feeling we’re going to be up late into the night talking and fooling around.

“Oh my god, I would die if somebody heard us or walked in.”

“Everyone is asleep,” she whispers again, her fingers squeezing my ass cheek.

“I really don’t want to risk it.”

“Can I at least...” Her sentence trails off. “I don’t know—blow you?”

“You’re volunteering to give me a blow job?”

“You voluntarily went down on me—why wouldn’t I reciprocate?”

Because as far as I know, girls don’t love blowing dudes—

but I've been so wrong about so much shit before, so why wouldn't I be wrong about this, too?

"I don't want to make a mess," I choke out.

"That's okay, babe, I'll swallow. You just relax." Her fingers grip the waistband of my bottoms beneath the blanket and push it down around my hips, my dick springing free from my pants. "A little help here?"

"Shit. Right."

I kick the sleep pants off until they're lost in the dark depth of bedding and lie still, anticipation coursing through my veins. Every cell in my body sparks to life, a ripple effect of excitement that has my left leg wanting to bounce.

My body buzzes.

Lilly hums, kissing her way from the base of my neck down the center of my chest. Stomach. Belly button. She follows the happy trail until she reaches my cock, disappearing under the blankets. I can't see her, but I can feel her—can't see what she's doing, but I can imagine it.

Warm lips on my inner thigh.

Light fingertips tickling my balls, cupping them.

Shit that feels good.

This is...

Fun?

Is that right?

The unknown. The slight fear. The thought of getting caught a thrilling element, as much as I'd hate for it to happen.

Then my dick is in her mouth and she's sucking gently on the tip before taking me in, inch by inch. Wet and hot. Hands on my shaft, stroking up and down.

*Oh shit.*

I'm never going to last.

Holy hell her mouth is warm—like dipping my wick in,

fuck, I don't know—chocolate fondue sauce or something. *Goddamn what am I even saying?*

A moan escapes my throat; it's loud and unexpected. Another one comes out when Lilly fingers my taint, pressing on the spot between my balls and my anus as if trying to activate the launch sequence.

"Yes," I hear her say. "Make some noise."

Erm. Too much noise and the cavalry will arrive; my mother has the ears of a hawk or whatever.

But I seriously cannot stop the noises from coming, turning my head so they're muffled by a pillow. Lilly's hands and mouth sucking and tugging and stroking me into oblivion—the pleasure is so intoxicating my hips come off the mattress for a brief moment, thrusting.

*Do not fuck her mouth, you are not a porn star.*

I see stars, eyes closing and mouth gaping.

*Oh shit...*

Fuck.

Without thinking, my hands find her hair and I bury my fingers in the thick mass. I don't pull, but I'm tempted to, my brain functions not working. Short circuiting.

Malfunction.

Loss of power.

# CHAPTER 14
# LILLY

I lick, lapping up Roman's cock like a lollypop, just as my friends have taught me—okay, honestly it was my friends and *ex-boyfriends* and tutorials on the internet that taught me.

*It takes a village.*

If there's one thing I know how to do, it's get a guy off with my hands and mouth, the combination of the two a key component. Judging by the moaning and groaning coming from Roman's lips, I would say he's enjoying himself.

I know I am.

I feel powerful. Beautiful.

Sexy.

I can be in a stadium surrounded by people—men, leering and watching me instead of the football game in front of them—and it has nothing on this moment.

I feel in control, one hand firmly gripping the hard length of Roman's gorgeous dick, sucking on the end with my mouth. I use my lips and tongue to draw out another moan.

Feel the bead of pre-come and smile around his cock.

He's going to come soon—better for me since I'm under the blanket and it's not like I'm getting much fresh air.

It's too easy.

A few more strokes and his fingers tighten their grasp in my hair, gently jerking but not to the point where it hurts. Not that I mind having my hair pulled...

"Holy shit, I'm g-gonna come," he stutters adorably, panic in his voice. "Lilly, I'm...shit...oh god..."

Such sexy noises.

Mmm.

I know he thinks I'm going to take my head off his dick, but when he comes, it's in my mouth, deep in my throat.

He's warned me, but I don't care—I swallow it so there is no mess; he hasn't got any rags nearby, and the last thing I want to do is get out of bed and get semen off my hands and face and wherever it's going to unpredictably go.

This isn't my first rodeo.

I do, however, hop out of bed so I can gargle with mouthwash—but it's an easy task, taking no more than a few seconds—before climbing back in beside a limp Roman.

At first, we lie there cuddling, his arm around my shoulders as we lie on our backs, staring up at the ceiling in the dark, the only thing illuminating the room reflection from the bright snow outside.

Then he moves.

With a quick kiss to my mouth, Roman crawls down my body the same way I maneuvered down his, parting the bottom of the silky sleep shirt to kiss my belly button. His fingers pluck at the tie on the bottoms, undoing the bow and loosening the waist.

My heartbeat quickens, elated he's going down on me.

I want him to so bad. I want him to give me an orgasm; I've been craving it since we had sex.

Biting down on my lower lip, I gasp out an excited breath as soon as his mouth makes contact with my nether region, legs parting of their own accord. I'm a bit desperate, if I must admit—desperate for him and the contact and the connection. If I can't have his dick inside me tonight, I will sure as hell settle for his lips, teeth, and tongue.

He nips at the sensitive skin of my thigh, large hands caressing me, fingers seeking the warm heat of my pussy.

I cover my eyes by slinging an arm over my forehead, blocking out the light from the windows though it isn't much. I want every one of my senses for this moment; I've been waiting for it for a while, not really sure it would come.

*I think I love Roman.*

Actually, truly love him.

Which makes this all the better.

I mean, ideally we wouldn't be fooling around in his parents' house, but we're alone, everyone is in bed (allegedly), and it's not likely anyone will barge in (fingers crossed). Do younger brothers have a habit of busting in uninvited?

My ears strain for the sounds of footsteps down the hallway, and when I hear none, I refocus my energy on Roman down under.

For a guy who comes too soon during sex, he is truly gifted at oral. The right amount of pressure. The right amount of mouth and tongue. A bit of finger.

It. Is. So. GOOD.

"That right there," I encourage him. "Don't stop."

It seems he's not the only one who doesn't take long to climax, my lower half already doing that thing where it wants to have an orgasm...it only needs a little...more of...that... thing...he's...doing...

"Yeah, yeah, oh my god..."

I lift my ass up off the mattress, spreading my legs wider, which *doesn't help me come any quicker.*

I lower my ass.

Clench my pelvis.

Thank goodness the lights are off—I'm probably bright red, desperation blazing across my brow. There's definitely sweat on my upper lip; I want this so bad.

*Anything worth having is worth sweating for*, my coach always says—and she's right. This is worth it.

I tip my head back when the sensation hits and my knees start to quake and I'm unable to keep them apart, my body spasming in that wonderful way.

I make very little noise, only whimper, much quieter than Roman was when he orgasmed.

His mouth kisses my pelvis after I'm finally lying still.

"You sucked the life right out of me," I joke, running my fingers through his hair—my new favorite thing to do. He's so handsome, more so now that I can see his face.

"I could say the same about you."

"See," I tell him. "It's not just you who comes fast. How long did that take me, three minutes?"

"No one is timing it."

"Then you shouldn't worry about it either." Real talk, though—I don't want to always have to wonder if he's going to finish so soon before I do. Sometimes a girl just wants to ride a dick and come the old-fashioned way.

He rolls over and kisses me, arms around my waist, pulling me in. "Practice makes perfect."

But no one is perfect. We won't ever be, though we can try to be better.

# CHAPTER 15
# ROMAN

Lilly and I are going on a date.

Our first.

Odd that it's taken us this long to get to it, but I guess being in the friend zone derailed the concept of us dating. Plus I was too chickenshit to ask.

Tonight I have a few surprises up my sleeve, and I look out the window, grateful for the snowy surroundings. Couldn't be a more perfect backdrop for what's planned, and goddamn am I nervous.

I feel like this is the first time I've been out romantically with a young woman, and for all intents and purposes, it is. Odd how things work out, isn't it? Here I thought moving out of my parents' house wasn't going to change much about my life; I would still study hard, I would still be a homebody, I would still rather hang out with my family than party.

What I didn't think would happen is a relationship.

When I walked into that kitchen and saw Lilly sitting at the counter, I never in a million years would have guessed I'd be dressing to take her on a date weeks later.

Did not see this coming.

Standing in front of the mirror, I adjust the tie around my neck, wondering if the knot is too small. Or too big? Haven't tied one myself in years. Mom usually does it, which...makes me sound like a mama's boy, which I most certainly am not.

As I'm re-tying it for the third time, frustrated that I can't seem to perfect it, Eliza and Jack are bounding up the stairs, laughing and flirting, and I'm sure he just goosed her in the ass.

My timing seems to be impeccable, as I'm certain they're coming upstairs to have sex.

"Where you off to, mate?" Jack sticks his head in the open door, looking me up and down. Notices me struggling and enters the room, automatically coming over and smacking my hands away from the silk fabric between my fingers. "You do it like this. We'll do a Windsor knot, it's easiest."

Eliza plops down on the bed and crosses her legs.

Meanwhile, Jack is rambling on as he overlaps and tugs and tosses the tie around. "Here, perfecting the dimple takes practice, but I have faith in you, chap. All you've got to do is pinch the tie with your thumb and middle finger—like this. Then use your index finger to keep the dimple in place as you tighten."

Uh-huh. Yeah, *I'll probably never do that*, but okay.

"You are so sexy when you talk like that, babe," Eliza croons. "You're so fancy."

My roommate puffs out his chest as he takes a step back to survey his handiwork.

"We've all got our talents, babe. I'm shite at rugby, but I'm a masterful tie tier, which serves no actual purpose 'cept helping my flatmate." He slaps me on the bicep. "So where are you off to?"

I take another look at myself in the mirror and raise my

brows. Jack just did in twenty seconds what I couldn't do in twenty minutes.

"Actually, I have a date."

Eliza sits up straight, interested. "With who?"

"Lilly." Is that pride in my voice?

"Lilly! *Our* Lilly? Why didn't you say anything?! Where are you going? Oh my god, why didn't she tell me the two of you are going out? That little sneak." Eliza glances up at me expectantly. "Are the two of you dating? Like, *dating* dating?"

"Gonna give it the old college try."

Eliza rises, clapping her hands. "Oh I love this." She wraps me in a hug and squeezes. "You'll be so good for her—and she'll be good for you. I think opposites in a couple is a good thing."

"What are you doing on your date?" Jack asks, taking Eliza by the hand, the two of them walking back into the hallway, destination obviously their bedroom.

"I'll let her tell you after the date."

"You little brat! I want to know what the plan is!" Eliza pouts. "That's mean."

"Come on, love, let's leave him be. He looks like he's going to piss his trousers."

We all glance down at my navy dress pants. "Should I change into jeans?"

Eliza studies me. "Erm. If I knew where you were going it would be easier for me to answer that question. Fancy dinner?"

I shrug. "Nice but maybe not super fancy?"

She nods. "Then I would put jeans on. Love jeans and a button-down shirt with a tie—super on trend."

"I've never in my life been on trend."

Jack gives her a gentle nudge. "Have a fun night—give us the details when you get back."

"Unless you're not coming back alone." Eliza wiggles her

eyebrows. "Hang a sock on your doorknob if you want privacy."

Jack looks down at her. "When have we ever put a sock on our knob when we've shagged? Is that an American thing?"

She laughs. "I think it's something they do in movies, but might be fun for us to start."

He shakes his head vehemently. "Yeah—we're not putting a sock on our doorknob. I'd feel like a wanker."

"I should be going, so if I'm going to change my pants..." I give them both a pointed look, and they make their goodbyes before disappearing into their room and shutting the door behind them.

Off come my pressed pants.

On go a pair of jeans.

*Thanks, Mom, for turning me into a nerd.*

Lilly is waiting at the door when I fetch her from her house, smiling radiantly when she steps outside into the frigid cold. Kisses me on the cheek before threading her hand through my arm.

"Where are we going?" I haven't told her either.

"You'll see."

Her grin gets wider. "No one has ever surprised me with a date before—I'm so excited."

*Same, Lilly. Same.*

The butterflies in my stomach churn as we head out of town to the next one over, laughing and listening to the radio, my date in charge of finding a station.

When we arrive, Lilly gazes curiously out the window. "The ski hill? Why are we at a ski hill?"

She's wearing a dress and heels—and a dressy winter coat—but it's perfect for what we'll be doing.

"You'll see."

"Stop being so cryptic! You're giving me high blood pressure."

We unbuckle, but before she can open her door, I tell her to, "Wait here."

Quickly get to the passenger side and play the perfect gentleman by opening it for her.

"Aww, thank you."

Our shoes crunch on the ground covered in a thin layer of snow. In the near distance, the gondola moves in tandem with the chair lifts to the top of the small "mountain," the entire hill lit up by bright lights and moonlight.

"This is so cool, but...I still don't understand what's going on. Are we going to go skiing? I don't have any of my stuff."

"Nope."

Removing my phone from my jacket pocket, I tap it open. Hold it out as we step to the base of the gondola where a woman in a red snowsuit zaps the QR code.

She glances down at her handheld machine. "Two of you for seven o'clock?"

"Yup."

"Step this way please."

The gondola comes to a slow crawl, just slow enough for us to safely step inside, the door sliding closed behind us.

We sit just as it zooms to life and whisks us up the mountain.

"Roman, what is this?" Lilly looks around, marveling. "This is so amazing! I've never been on one of these before."

She's like a child on Christmas morning, and all I can think is *I did that—I put that smile on her face.*

It's intoxicating, this feeling, making her happy.

The city below comes into view the higher we climb, its street-lights twinkling, cars getting smaller and smaller and smaller.

"Wow," she says breathily. "Roman, I love this."

There is a restaurant at the top—it used to be a bar and grill, but it's been renovated into a chic steak and seafood date night destination. "*The most romantic restaurant in the Midwest*" according to the local newspaper. I trolled their social media for an entire day, watching video after video of the remodel online before choosing this as our first date.

Lilly is in awe.

The gondola comes to a gentle stop; when we step off, we're greeted by a winter wonderland of trees covered in Christmas lights and snow, a picturesque scene straight from a movie screen.

We both inhale an excited breath.

I take her hand, leading her in.

It's just crowded enough to give off good energy, and the table we're given overlooks the hill and beyond.

"This is so romantic," Lilly squeals. "I'm dying right now." She removes her phone to take a picture, flash going off when she pans toward the dining area. "These pictures don't do the view justice."

They never do.

Lilly fiddles around some more, as giddy as a little kid. Eventually she puts the phone down, quits taking pictures, and realizes I'm staring at her.

"Why are you being so quiet?"

*Because I want to shit my pants.*

"Because I'm too nervous to talk." I laugh anxiously, the small box in my jacket pocket burning a hole through the material. It doesn't have an engagement ring or anything, but it's the first gift I've given a woman, and it's so cheesy I'm not sure how she'll react to it.

I clumsily remove the box and set it on the tabletop after

yanking it out of my pocket, grateful the server has come and gone with our drink order.

The last thing I need is an audience.

Lilly's keen brown eyes flit to the cheerful red wrapping paper then up at my face; she doesn't ask what's in the box or who it's for.

I slide it across the table ever so awkwardly. "This is for you."

She bites down on her lower lip, excited. Gingerly plucks it off the table, pulling the ribbon that was painstakingly tied.

This tie around my neck feels like it's choking me, anticipation hammering away the only nerves I have left, palms sweaty.

I run them over the leg of my jeans as Lilly unwraps the present.

"I didn't get you anything."

"I wasn't expecting you to. Don't get your hopes up—it's not that exciting." I downplay it, a defense against rejection.

Watch as she carefully removes the square box top. Takes the object inside and lifts it by the silky ribbon so it dangles above the table between us.

"Our first Christmas?" she reads, glancing up. "Aww, this is so sweet, Roman. Thank you."

"I'm, uh—giving it to you for a reason."

She tilts her head to the side, waiting for further explanation.

"Obviously it would be to commemorate our first Christmas since that's coming up, but also I wanted..." I take a sip of water, needing to wet my suddenly dry throat. "I wanted to ask you..." *Shit.* It sounds like I'm trying to push out a proposal of marriage to her when what I really want to say is, "Will you be my girlfriend? I know this is our first date, but we've already done a few things out of order, and I already know I have feelings for you."

This is not at all the speech I prepared yesterday, rehearsing it in my bathroom mirror at least a dozen times.

"I know you weren't originally interested in dating due to your guy detox and you haven't been single long, but sometimes..." I clear my throat. "When you know, you know." At least, that's what my grandmother always used to tell me. Trust your gut; it never steers you wrong.

"You're right," she says at last, setting the ornament down on the linen tablecloth. "I wasn't interested in dating when I broke up with you know who, but that's because I thought all guys were going to treat me the way he and the guys before him treated me. Why? Because I always date the same kind of person. Not on purpose, but because that's who I'm surrounded by." She takes a piece of bread from the basket the server just brought over, cutting herself a small pat of butter to spread on it. "I see now how wrong I was."

"Wrong? About what?"

"My very short-lived hiatus from men. It was stupid—I don't need to give them up. I just needed to find the right one." The words are accompanied by a smile. "I wouldn't be here with you if I thought I wanted to be alone—I wouldn't do that to you. Lead you on, I mean." Lilly takes a dainty bite of bread and chews slowly. "This is so good."

She still hasn't answered my question.

To keep myself from asking again, I stuff some bread into my mouth, too. It goes down like cardboard, almost getting lodged in my throat.

"I think that...yes. I would like to try to be your girlfriend. We can label it, can't we? While we're just starting to date?" More chewing and swallowing. "Then we don't have the confusion later. Don't have to worry about having 'the talk.'"

She uses air quotes around the last phrase. “Yes. I want to be your girlfriend—I would be proud to date you.”

Proud to date me.

I sit up straighter in my seat as the server comes back to the table. “Are we celebrating anything special tonight?”

Lilly and I exchange a look.

“Um, yeah.” My words are less articulate than what I’m used to spouting, but I should probably get used to the fact that she strikes me dumb. “We’re celebrating our new relationship.”

# EPILOGUE

## ROMAN

"Honey, I have something I have to give you—take these and put them in your pocket."

Before I can ask what she's doing, my mother is pulling open the pocket of my jacket, and I catch a flash of bright red as she shoves something at me.

"I would give them to Lilly herself but don't want to embarrass her. Just put these in her bag before you leave and she'll be none the wiser."

"Uh—what are these?"

I go to pull them out but stop short when my mom says, "Lilly's panties—she must have left them after Thanksgiving, and I'm not going to ask what they were doing on the floor."

"Oh my g-god." I shove them back inside my pocket as far as I can shove them. "It's n-not...we didn't..."

I mean—yeah, we fooled around, but there was no penetration if you don't count tongues and fingers.

"I should hope not—not under my roof," Mom proclaims stiffly, nostrils flaring. "But I will say this: it's good to see you behaving like a normal twenty-two-year-old, and it's good to see you having fun. Dad and I were worried you took school too seriously to ever let yourself fall in love this young."

Fall in love?

Is that what this is? "Uh, thanks?"

"I'm serious!"

At that moment, Aunt Myrtle enters the kitchen, shuffling through in a muumuu, pink marabou slippers on her feet.

"If Roman's bedroom is rockin', don't come a-knockin'."

Mom goes slack-jawed. "Roman!"

"Mom—nothing happened in my bedroom, I swear!" Nothing except some oral and a hand job. Does that count as nothing?

She wouldn't understand that Lilly and I are on an edging quest so I won't come as fast when we have actual sex.

Aunt Myrtle hums softly as she putters around the kitchen, pretending to ignore us, tsking as she brews herself a Nespresso as if she were Gen Z.

"Jack said to see if you have Fritos," she randomly announces, turning toward me. "I knew I came in here for a reason."

Mom nods. "Yes, I bought him Fritos."

My friends—and girlfriend—are crowded in the living room of my parents' house, something that's become a habit for them since Thanksgiving. Jack loves hanging out here as much as my mother loves having him—I think it reminds him a little bit of home, and he is craving that. So almost every weekend, if none of the four of us has plans, we come here.

It's not my first choice in hangouts, but who am I to deny my new friend a family away from his family?

So much has happened since the last time we hung out here, too.

At the end of the football season, Lilly left the cheer team. Since then, she has been volunteering at a local dance academy and teaching classes to beginners. She loves it, is less stressed out, and finally gets to do what she loves best, but at no cost to her sanity.

Were her parents pissed off?

Absolutely.

Has Lilly stopped worrying about what they think? For the most part. Their opinion has been ingrained in her since she was born, so a part of her still worries when she does something they don't agree with, but she's been happier since she quit the cheerleading team.

We were all really proud of her.

Well, her roommate Kaylee wasn't, but honestly? We're both graduating at the end of the semester, and Lilly wants to get her master's degree; she feels her focus should be on that rather than a career in dancing that won't lead to anything further than more pulled muscles and sprained ankles.

It's not as if she's going to try out for the Dallas Cowboys Cheerleaders or a professional basketball dance team.

The time to leave was now.

She loves those little kids at the academy and wishes she would have done it sooner.

Mom goes to the pantry to fetch the Fritos while I watch my great aunt purse her hot pink lips at me from across the room.

"What?" I ask her, not sure why she's making faces at me. "Why are you giving me that look?"

"What look? I have a date tonight—does this expression make me look alluring?" Her lips do a trout pout.

"Alluring?" Um, no.

"Yes, alluring? Sexy. I want him to move in for a kiss. The old bastard hasn't made a move on me yet, and we've gone out twice."

"Aunt Myrtle, I'm sure he's trying to be a gentleman," Mom

says, walking back into the kitchen with a bag of chips and a few more snacks. She goes and grabs a few bowls, dumping the junk food into them and passing them off to me.

"I don't want him to be a gentleman—we've been over this four times. Either one of us could kick the bucket any day now, so what's he waiting for? An invitation?"

Mom laughs. "Possibly."

"Well he ain't gettin' one." Aunt Myrtle takes her tiny espresso cup with a huff, shuffling out of the room, marabou cascading behind her.

A pink feather flutters to the ground.

Mom sags against the counter. "I cannot with her. She thinks she's Bette Davis in a movie straight out of the forties."

"Whatever makes the old girl happy. She isn't wrong—they could kick the bucket any day now." I say it with a laugh as my mother gasps, shooing me out of the room by snapping a towel at my ass.

When I arrive back at the living room, I take in the scene from the doorway before entering; there is an emotion inside me swirling around at the sight of my friends laughing and joking that I've never felt before. Is this what being totally content feels like? I don't just love my girlfriend; I love my friends too. I love the place I'm in—and I'm not just talking about the house I live in with Jack and Eliza.

"Babe, come sit." Lilly pats the seat next to her, inviting me back to the couch to watch the movie we've all settled on; tomorrow night the four of us are going for dinner to celebrate Valentine's Day.

Another first for me.

Also a first? Someone calling me babe.

It felt strange at the beginning and took some getting used to, but I've recently started calling her babe, too. Other nicknames Lilly has taken a shine to for me?

1. Sugar bottom
2. Hot lips
3. Sweetie
4. Honey buns

I think she's made it her mission in life to use a new moniker each and every time she texts me, whereas I've stuck primarily to babe. I have enough going through my head; I don't need to be making up new variations of an endearment every single morning.

My girlfriend loves that I'm awkward and make mistakes. Loves that I don't seem to know what I'm doing but that I'm coachable and willing to try. She isn't shy about telling me what she wants and needs from the relationship, and I'm glad for it; I'm no mind reader, and neither is she.

It's something we both work on, though it hasn't come easy. Every day is a work in progress, but I'm proud of us.

I take my seat beside her, handing Jack the Fritos. He takes the bowl and immediately plows his hand through the chips, choosing three and sticking them into his open mouth.

"Easy there." Eliza laughs. "You're acting like no one has fed you."

"I'm always hungry. You know this."

"We know," the three of us chorus, because Jack is always hungry and has a history of eating all the food in the house, including leftovers that don't belong to him.

It's like we're the Four Musketeers now, spending hours of free time together, on double dates and doing whatever. On the rare occasion we'll even study in the library as a group. Not often, but sometimes.

"We don't have these in England. It's like Christmas every time I get a bag."

"The grocery store is literally full of them," Eliza deadpans, stealing a few chips. "If you want, I can start buying them for you."

Jack shakes his head. "They don't taste as good."

He's ridiculous.

Beside me, Lilly takes my arm and leans in, burrowing into me. "Am I spending the night tonight?" she whispers. "I have something for you."

I raise my brows. "Oh?"

Turns out that 'something' is a sexy nerd outfit, complete with black horn-rimmed glasses with a piece of tape in the middle. She climbs up the bed wearing a skimpy button-down shirt with a pocket protector (with a pencil inside), a loose tie, and white boy shorts.

Her hair is in braids.

My dick twitches.

Real talk: my dick has been twitching since the day we met and hasn't stopped tingling since, but there are worse things than a perpetual hard-on for one's girlfriend.

"How do you like my outfit? Do I look like a nerdy engineering student?"

Is that what this is supposed to be? "You look sexy, babe."

"And smart?"

"*So* smart."

She kisses my lips when she's done kissing her way up my body, fingers toying with the drawstring on my pajama bottoms.

"Why you bother with these, I do not know." She's playfully complaining as she pushes them off, down my hips, my heart already rapidly beating—it matches the heartbeat in my dick.

Ha!

"You don't like my flannel cock?" I tease without censoring, the first time I've actually used dirty talk in bed.

Lilly's eyes get wide. "Roman!" She laughs. "Listen to you, naughty boy."

"Did you like that?" My question is hesitant. Unsure.

"Obviously I liked it." She nuzzles my neck.

I exhale, hands running up and down her backside, palms cupping her ass.

She leans back, moving to straddle me, leaning down to look me in the eye. Her braids frame her face.

"Roman?"

My hands move back and forth. "Hmm?"

"I love you." The words are barely a whisper and shy, as if she's scared or worried I won't repeat them back to her.

They take me by surprise, but I'm ready for them. "I love you, too."

"You do?" Lilly is still whispering. "You don't think it's too soon?"

"No—we've been together over two months. I don't think it's too soon at all."

"Good, because I think I loved you the second time we met."

I pause. "That day in the kitchen when I dropped the box?"

She nods. "Yes."

"Really?" My hands never stop caressing her backside. "You know how much I love that award you made me."

"I didn't make it—I fixed it."

"You made it better." It reminds me of her, and I love looking at it there on my shelf. "I'm never getting rid of it."

She moves in closer, kissing me on the mouth. It's a tender kiss full of emotion.

"I'm never getting rid of you."

Good. "Say that again, you sexy little nerd."

"I'm never getting rid of you."

"And I'm never getting rid of *you*." Our tongues mingle.

"I love you, my romantic Romeo."

We're so mushy.

So gross.

But we're finally where we need to be.

With each other.

***THE END***

# ABOUT THE AUTHOR

Sara Ney is the USA Today Bestselling Author of the How to Date a Douchebag series and is best known for her sexy, laugh-out-loud New Adult romances.

Among her favorite vices, she includes: iced lattes, historical architecture, and well-placed sarcasm. She lives colorfully, collects vintage books, art, loves flea markets, and fancies herself British.

Sign up for Sara's Newsletter to find out about her book releases, and read real-life "Sara Dates A Douchebag" stories only found in her newsletter!

For more information about Sara Ney and her books, visit:
https://authorsaraney.com

# ALSO BY SARA NEY

***Accidentally in Love Series coming in 2022***

**The Player Hater coming February 15**

**The Mrs. Degree coming April 2022**

**Jock Hard Series**

Switch Hitter

Jock Row

Jock Rule

Switch Bidder

Jock Road

Jock Royal

Jock Reign

Jock Romeo

**Trophy Boyfriends Series**

Hard Pass

Hard Fall

Hard Love

Hard Luck

**The Bachelors Club Series**

Bachelor Society

Bachelor Boss

**How to Date a Douchebag Series**

The Studying Hours

The Failing Hours

The Learning Hours

The Coaching Hours

The Lying Hours

The Teaching Hours

**#ThreeLittleLies Series**

Things Liars Say

Things Liars Hide

Things Liars Fake

**The Kiss & Make Up Series**

Kissing in Cars

He Kissed Me First

A Kiss Like This

**The Bachelor Society Duet: The Bachelors Club**

**Jock Hard Box Set: Books 1-3**

Made in the USA
Monee, IL
18 July 2023